Praise for Deadly Cypher

Deadly Cypher has such ad exciting plot, and the pacing is just right. I didn't want to put it down! *Christy's Cozy Corners*

Another dark and decidedly complex mystery from amazing author Kate Parker. Based on actual historical events, this mystery draws the reader into a fascinating era.
Laura's Interests

Deadly Cypher fits the bill very well with intriguing characters and a congenial narrative voice. The mystery has several layers and readers will enjoy unpacking them with Olivia as the story progresses. *Reading is My SuperPower*

Deadly Cypher is a richly developed mystery filled with historical details, tough women, and good people giving up life as they know it in order to help their country no matter the cost.
Cozy Up With Kathy

Also from Kate Parker

The Deadly Series

Deadly Scandal

Deadly Wedding

Deadly Fashion

Deadly Deception

Deadly Travel

Deadly Darkness

Deadly Cypher

Deadly Broadcast

The Victorian Bookshop Mysteries

The Vanishing Thief

The Counterfeit Lady

The Royal Assassin

The Conspiring Woman

The Detecting Duchess

The Milliner Mysteries

The Killing at Kaldaire House

Murder at the Marlowe Club

The Mystery at Chadwick House

Deadly Broadcast

Kate Parker

JDP PRESS

Deadly Broadcast copyright © 2022 by Kate Parker

ISBN: 978-1-7332294-9-4 [print]
ISBN: 978-1-7332294-8-7 [e-book]

Published by JDPPress
Cover Design by Lyndsey Lewellen of Llewellen Designs

Dedication

For everyone taking a respite from the current trials in a
good book,
For my family,
For John, forever.

Late December, 1939

Chapter One

I opened the door to the Hallam Street block of flats that the Murrows lived in and walked inside. There was no doorman in the darkened lobby and little heat to fight the icy temperatures outside. I found my way over to the lift by following the illumination of recessed lamps, and rode upstairs unseen by anyone. Not a situation that Sutton, the doorman in my block of flats, would approve of.

Since the flat I was looking for was near the top of the building, I was glad I didn't have to walk up three flights of stairs. When I knocked on the door, a brown-haired woman of about thirty answered. Behind her, three Orthodox Jewish men debated in Yiddish near the front door. Beyond them, I could see the table with the telephone held Christmas ornaments and greenery.

"Mrs. Murrow?" I asked.

"Yes. Are you Mrs. Redmond from the *Daily Premier?*"

"Yes. Thank you for agreeing to be interviewed."

As I entered and stepped past them, the three men wished Mrs. Murrow, the resident, a good night in heavily accented English. She responded in English. I responded in Yiddish, which caused all three men to start talking at once, asking me where I had learned their language. I told them I only knew a little Yiddish and had learned it from friends here in London.

When they asked who, perhaps thinking we had acquaintances in common, I mentioned Esther Benton Powell's grandmother and aunts. They said in their language that they regretted they had never met these ladies. A moment later, they were gone.

I heard them begin speaking in Yiddish again as soon as they reached the stairs.

Mrs. Murrow showed me into the drawing room. I found the Murrows' large flat typical for this upscale section of London, with ample windows covered with blackout curtains and heavy, well-polished furniture.

"Friends of Ed's," she said, gesturing toward the front door with her chin. "He collects sources the way other men collect, oh, I don't know what. He was interviewing them before he left for the studio. You just missed him. You may have noticed that even as they donned their coats and scarves, they continued their discussion. And I have no idea what they were saying."

I had heard them talking as I walked in. "Something about whether Hitler was foretold in the Pentateuch."

"You are so clever, Mrs. Redmond." She sounded impressed. "Do you speak a lot of languages?"

"Not really, Mrs. Murrow. I'm fluent in German. I can almost get by in Yiddish because they are close. And I've had to understand it on occasion." Particularly when I was sent into Germany and Austria before war was declared to help rescue Jews.

"Please, if you're going to interview me, and over the Christmas holidays at that, you might as well call me Janet." She was about my age, average height, pretty, and with an upper-class American accent. I found her easier to understand than some Americans I had met. She also had beautiful taste in clothes that showed off her slim figure. She had the kind of presence that told me I'd remember her.

"Olivia Redmond. Everyone calls me Livvy." I wasn't so sure she'd remember me.

We seated ourselves on well-stuffed, comfortable furniture and after an offer of an American cocktail ("No, thank you, I'm working") and a cigarette ("No, thank you"), we began the late-night interview. "As I explained, my editor wants me to do a feature on influential American women who have stayed on in Britain despite the declaration of war."

"I hardly think I'm influential."

"Your husband is on the radio to the Americas most days. He's meeting all sorts of interesting people," this time I was the one who nodded toward the front door, "and sharing his experiences with America. And he's sharing them with you. That makes you a sort of bridge between our two cultures."

"As long as you don't have any expectations of my knowledge. Or what sort of a bridge I make." She gave me a smile.

"None at all," I told her. "Are you university educated?"

"Yes. Mount Holyoke College. That's in Massachusetts. I

studied economics and English. I met Ed at a National Student Federation of America conference." She smiled at the remembrance. "Are you? University educated, I mean," she added.

"Newnham College, Cambridge. Modern languages." Not nearly as exotic as Massachusetts, and I imagined a great deal gloomier with the British blackout regulations every night and students leaving for service to king and country.

We chatted for a while as I wrote notes in my little book, covering the differences between our two countries and what she found most surprising. She'd been in London nearly three years, so not too much about our country astonished her now. This was shaping up to be an excellent article.

I ignored the little inner voice that said, *I wonder who will rewrite my story?*

We talked about fashions, and I mentioned how English her wool dress looked. It was smart, in last year's longer length and this year's deep rust color.

She laughed and said, "It looks English because it's French."

Janet Murrow had been in England long enough to know how dependent English fashions were on French fashion houses.

The American woman and I had a lot in common, at least on the surface. My father was a baronet, very minor aristocracy, and her family was the American equivalent. We both enjoyed London's theaters and restaurants and French fashions. With my curly reddish hair, I didn't look as regal as she did, but she had an open, welcoming attitude that had us chatting as if we were old friends in no time.

I hadn't met many Americans, but those I had, such as Janet, were warm and friendly. Much less reserved than I was.

"I find it odd not to see many children about at Christmastime," she told me.

"I've seen more in the last week than I had all autumn, but there's still not as many as there were before the war," I said. "The authorities didn't want parents to bring their children home for Christmas from school or where they'd been sent to in the countryside, but it appears that some did."

"If I had children, I'd especially want them with me for Christmas. It's very much a children's holiday, isn't it?"

"Yes, it is. It's a family holiday. I'm on my own this Christmas," I told her. "My husband is in the army, and he didn't get leave. They let the men in his unit who have children take this holiday, since it would mean so much more to their families." I understood it, but I didn't like it.

"Oh, I'm sorry," Janet said in a sympathetic tone.

"It's fine. At least there's no shooting yet."

"Would you care to see Ed's studio while he's broadcasting?" Janet said as if she'd just thought of the idea. I suspected she had been given the decision to either bring me along to the studio or keep me away.

"Oh, yes, please." I leaned forward in my seat. "I've never seen a broadcast studio before."

"If we wait about ten minutes, we'll time it perfectly to get up to the fourth level of Broadcasting House just before the start of Ed's time on the air. They plan to move the news broadcasting studios to the sub-basement a few levels below ground in case of bombing, but they haven't finished the engineering work yet."

"I didn't realize your husband transmitted from BBC headquarters." I was taking more notes, fleshing out my article.

"Oh, yes. CBS doesn't have its own studios here."

"Why so late? Is it the only time they can get the studio?"

"No," she told me. "New York is five hours behind us. Ed wants to get on the air at least close to the prime listening evening hours. One a.m. is ideal, that's eight o'clock in New York and five in California, but tonight they've given him an earlier timeframe."

"Thank goodness. I'm not used to being up until two in the morning," I admitted with a laugh. "I left that behind along with my college days."

"With this blackout, I don't feel secure walking along the streets at any time after dark, even in a quiet part of town such as this one," Janet said. "You can barely see automobiles, so anyone lurking in the shadows is invisible."

"At least it's not far from here to Broadcasting House," I said, sounding braver than I felt. "This is a perfect location for a flat with your husband working just over there. And we'll have to walk quickly since it's too cold to linger outside."

We bundled up against the chilly air and went

downstairs to make the short walk to BBC headquarters. With the blackout, I couldn't see the greenery and the decorations still up along the streets on this Boxing Day, but I knew they were there. Normally, shop and flat windows would shine with dazzling lights during this season.

But not this year. Not during a war.

Even with a full moon, I could see very little with a wispy fog swirling around. Fog, a blackout, and a lack of children's excited voices made this one Christmas season I could do without.

Only an American, I decided, would have suggested holding an interview on Boxing Day Night during a blackout with cold and a fog worthy of an Agatha Christie tale. Maybe being so far from home made this holiday darker and colder for her than it was for me, and she wanted someone to talk to.

I needed to shake off my gloomy mood.

Once we turned from residential Hallam Street with its blocks of flats onto Cavendish and then the bustle of Portland Place, I could smell chestnuts roasting on curbside grills. Smells, at least, made their way through the blackout. I couldn't see people until they were quite near me, but that familiar roasted scent reached me and made my stomach growl.

I turned my head to apologize to Janet for my embarrassing internal noises when I tripped over something on the pavement. I stumbled a couple of steps, but once I regained my balance, I turned to see what I'd tripped over.

I couldn't see a thing. Not the pavement or anything blocking it. That section of the pavement was blanketed in deep shadow.

"Are you all right?" Janet asked, standing closer to the curb than I was.

"Fine, but there's a hazard here that should be moved. I'm glad it wasn't a brazier so I didn't get burned." Embarrassment always made me sound stuffy or annoyed.

I walked back, dragging my right foot, which was on the building side of the pavement. I quickly hit the object. I couldn't make it out in the darkness, the blackout to prevent German bombers from finding London being particularly effective on a cloudy, foggy night despite the full moon.

The blackout was equally effective on the ground, too, since it kept Londoners from seeing anything.

I bent down and shoved at the object. When it didn't move, I began to feel around gingerly, not certain what disgusting thing I would find.

It was a shoe, and a foot was inside it. And the foot was attached to a leg.

I breathed in hard from the shock.

"We need to hurry, Livvy, or we'll be late," came from behind me.

It took me a moment to make my brain think of a response and another to get my mouth to work. "You go ahead, Janet. I need to find a bobby."

Something in my tone must have warned her this wasn't an ordinary hazard. "What have you found?" She moved closer to me, peering over my shoulder.

"Someone injured or dead." Squatting by the building, I didn't have a good view down the road. "Do you see a bobby on Portland Place?"

Janet jumped a few steps away from me before she calmed down enough to try to get a good view up and down the busy thoroughfare. Headlights, even though partially covered, shone enough light on the pavement to illuminate the reflective parts of a bobby's uniform. "Yes, I think so. Yoo hoo," she shouted, waving her arms.

It was effective. She gained everyone's attention, not just the bobby's. Then she stepped toward me and said, "I don't know how you summon the police in England. I've never had to do it before. Not even in America."

"You managed it perfectly. Thank you," I told her, noticing a few passersby coming closer for a look, as if they could see anything in the dense darkness around this building.

The bobby joined us in a moment, shining his torch around in front of where Janet and I stood. The torchlight illuminated an angle between two buildings where they met, creating a sort of alcove where dust bins were kept and dried leaves and old newspapers collected. In this alcove a man sat slumped over slightly, his overcoat twisted around his body and his fedora pressed between his head and the wall.

He looked as if he'd been facing the street when he fell backward and landed in the position we found him. I thought possibly he had knocked himself out, but with the light from the torch shining on him, he looked pale. Cold. Dead.

The bobby felt for a pulse, but I could tell he had no luck. He straightened and blew long blasts on his whistle.

Janet, her hands over her ears, looked where the torch light shone on the man's face. In her quiet American accent, she said, "Good heavens, it's Frank Kennedy."

Holding his torch with one hand, the constable bent over and moved the man's coat with the other to reveal a knife handle protruding from the man's chest. Blood spilled down his beige sweater.

I shuddered and stepped away with a shiver. His blood didn't look as if it had completely dried. He couldn't have been dead long.

With a shudder, I realized that meant there was a killer lurking nearby in the darkness.

Chapter Two

"Frank Kennedy's one of the engineers at Broadcasting House. He frequently does the technical work to send Ed's broadcasts to New York," Janet told me when we'd moved a few steps back from the body. "It's all flipping switches, turning dials, and plugging in cables, but you have to know exactly what to do and in which order."

"Do you know this man?" the constable asked, overhearing her.

"Yes. He works at Broadcasting House, just down the street."

At that moment, two more bobbies arrived from different directions. We were questioned, gave our names and addresses, and then sent away as more staff of the Metropolitan Police arrived to cordon off the area, take photos, and look for clues.

We hurried toward Broadcasting House with Janet saying, "How awful," over and over.

We entered through the main, rather grand entrance to Broadcasting House. Since the war started, the bronze and glass doors had been taped against bomb damage and sandbags piled around the entrance.

I'd never been inside BBC headquarters before, so while

Janet went to the reception desk off to the left, I stared at everything around me. The large windows on either side of the wedge-shaped hall were taped and curtained. The walls and square pillars were a pinkish-gray granite with lighting at the top behind smoky glass and the floors were a bold mosaic. Directly in front of me, across the large lobby, were two lifts with embossed bronze doors. Next to them was a sculpture of a farmer from long ago. With the high ceiling and the leather sofas, this could have been the lobby of an opulent avant-garde hotel.

Janet walked up to the guard and said, "It's me, Mrs. Murrow, and I've brought a friend to see Ed broadcast."

"Yes, ma'am," the guard said, writing a note in his logbook.

"Was Mr. Kennedy here earlier?" I asked.

"You just missed him. He left maybe ten or twenty minutes ago." He glanced up at me, a suspicious expression on his face.

I glanced toward the door where a constable was walking in. "He'll explain it to you."

"This way, Livvy." Janet led the way to the lift and punched in the fourth floor. "Because we broadcast overseas, similar to the Empire Service, we use their news studio. It's sent, after all the technical stuff is done, to a whole field of towers out in the countryside. Then they send out the signal so it can reach the United States, Canada, all over Europe, most of Africa, and all the way to India."

We got off the lift and I said, "Where do they broadcast

the news we hear in London every night? Surely they don't need a group of antennas that size to reach Chelsea."

Janet pointed off to the right and said, "There are two more news studios over there for broadcasting to the British Isles. France and Ireland, too, for all I know. Much less distance, at any rate. I don't know how they send out their programs at that close a range."

I followed her down a long corridor away from where she had pointed until we stopped in front of a door marked 4C. She glanced at her watch before opening it. As soon as she had, she said, "Ed, we just found Frank Kennedy."

"And I bet he had plenty to say. I can't work with a man who can't or won't do his job properly. And you are?" he added when he glanced up, looking at me.

Janet introduced us and we shook hands. Ed Murrow was about the most handsome man I'd ever met. A dapper dresser, he was about my age, or possibly a little older, maybe as old as thirty-one or two. He was thin, with dark hair and eyes. Holding my gaze, he asked about the *Daily Premier,* the newspaper I wrote for.

"Ed, Frank is dead," Janet said, apparently determined to get his attention.

"What? He was just here. Got run over in this awful blackout? It's a wonder we all aren't. The traffic is dangerous."

"Knife in the chest," I said.

Ed Murrow opened and shut his mouth while making no sound, seemingly at a loss for words. I suspected that didn't happen often. I'd already guessed he was the type to take charge of any situation.

A young man with light brown hair stuck his head around the doorframe and said, "Two minutes to broadcast."

"Right," Ed said and moved to the seat in front of the microphone.

"Come on," Janet said to me. "We can sit in the listening room with the engineer." We hurried out of the broadcast booth and down the hall to a room that held a table crowded with wires and encased switches and gauges, and a few chairs on the far side of the space. We moved to that end of the room and sat.

"Do you sit in here for many of your husband's broadcasts?" I asked.

"Yes. That's how I got to know Frank. And Derek here. Derek Coward."

Derek, fiddling with his knobs and gauges, nodded a vague sort of greeting.

"Any relation to…?" I asked him.

"Noel? No."

"Why did Ed say Frank didn't do his job properly?" I'd just tripped over the man's body. I was curious.

"Yesterday, Christmas night, Frank came in late, smelling of booze, and didn't set up properly," Derek told me. "The first half of Murrow's broadcast was lost. Nothing was transmitted until the BBC received a telegram from CBS in New York and sent another engineer to the listening room to correct the mistake. Murrow called me in from holiday to do tonight's broadcast. When I arrived, he told Frank to leave, that he wouldn't work with him again."

"I imagine that—"

Derek held up a hand and spoke into the mouthpiece of what appeared to be a telephone operator's headset. "Broadcasting in five, four..."

He moved more knobs and switches and then with a nod, flipped one more switch. Ed Murrow's voice came out of a speaker against a wall. Derek flipped another switch, spoke to someone, and then changed the switch back. Only then did Derek take off his headset and listen to the broadcast with us.

Over the loudspeaker, I heard a deep male voice say, "This is Edward R. Murrow broadcasting to you from London on the CBS network. Tonight, Boxing Night in the United Kingdom..."

"This is how it is supposed to sound in New York. Storms and solar flares can make a mess out of the transmission before it reaches the far side of the Atlantic," Derek whispered as he sat down next to me.

"Could Murrow fire Kennedy without getting approval from the BBC?" I asked, keeping my voice low.

"Not from the BBC. But he could stop Frank from working on his programs. This is all BBC equipment and the engineers are BBC employees, including me. When my bosses hear I came in from my holiday, they won't be amused."

"That strict?" I whispered.

"Everything here is done by the regulations." He made a

face.

"Getting you ready for military service," I replied with a smile.

"Not me. Dodgy ticker."

I replied with a somber nod and we both listened to Murrow's word picture of life on Boxing Day in London with a war on and the fog creeping in. Somehow, he always brought it around to the war, which we were in and America was not.

Another young man, dressed in a knitted pullover vest no doubt made for his Christmas gift from a mother or aunt, came in, nodded to Derek, listened for a minute, and then left again without saying a word.

Derek rose and walked back to the table and put on his headset again. He talked to someone through the mouthpiece before changing a few dials. I heard a slight improvement in the sound, but nothing I would have picked up on if I hadn't been watching Derek.

Murrow spoke for a few more minutes and then silence. Derek flipped a few switches and said, "And we're off the air."

Ed walked into the room a minute later holding the papers I guessed were his script and asked his wife, "How did I do?"

"Brilliant as always."

"It was very good," I added. "It was clever how you worked the war into every story you told."

"America doesn't realize what's happening over here.

Trying to celebrate Christmas with blackouts and call-ups and shortages." He lit a cigarette and said, "How did it sound, Coward?"

"Near the end we had some interference, but I think New York received it all right," Derek told him.

"Thanks again for coming in. It was impossible to rely on Kennedy."

"It certainly will be now," I muttered.

"I'd appreciate it if you'd explain this to management. My coming in on my off day and everything," Derek said. "They'll yell at me. They treat you with respect."

"Sure," Murrow said. He appeared about to say more when a middle-aged man came into the room with a bobby.

The middle-aged man walked up to the newsman and put his face close to the other's. "Murrow, this bobby is here because your engineer was outside the building being murdered when he should have been broadcasting your show. How do you explain this?"

"Filbert, your boy Kennedy came in drunk last night and didn't broadcast my show. CBS needed to send a telegram and another engineer had to come in here and flip the right switches. New York only received the last part of the show for which the BBC has been paid for the entire session. I won't work with him ever again."

"You certainly won't since he's dead," Mr. Filbert said. "And what are you doing here, Coward?"

"Mr. Murrow called me in to take Frank's place tonight, sir."

Filbert's face was growing redder by the moment, making a nice, if unhealthy, contrast with his gray hair. "You don't get to make these decisions, Murrow. There are proper procedures to follow."

"I tried and got nowhere. By the time you followed all your procedures, we'd be in the New Year and I'd have had half a dozen broadcasts ruined." Murrow stubbed out his cigarette.

"We'll discuss this tomorrow. In the meantime, talk to this constable. While most people thought Kennedy was up here with you, you knew he was down on the street. I hope you have a good alibi." Mr. Filbert didn't slam the door on his way out, but he came very close.

"So, Mr. Murrow, you were aware that Mr. Kennedy had left the building, were you, sir?" the bobby said, readying his pencil over a new page in his notebook.

"No, I wasn't. All I knew was he wasn't here messing up my broadcast, and that was all I cared about."

"Where were you, sir, between a quarter to eleven and a quarter after eleven?"

"In the broadcast booth down the hall."

"Did anyone see you there?"

"Coward did."

Derek cleared his throat. "Derek Coward. Programming engineer. I saw Mr. Murrow when Frank left, and then I was in here until just before broadcast at eleven twenty-five when I went to tell Mr. Murrow it was almost air-time." He looked apologetic. "Sorry, sir."

"Don't be sorry. My wife and Mrs. Redmond saw me."

"After we found Frank's body," I said, truthfully but not helpfully, earning dark looks from both the Murrows.

"Anyone else, sir?"

"No. Everyone knows I prefer to be alone before a broadcast so I can figure out my wording. Finish writing my notes." Murrow looked at the constable and said, "I guess that puts me right in the center of your investigation."

"Not necessarily, sir. I just hand off my report. The inspector will figure out what's what. He may have the murder solved already." With a nod, the constable left, quietly shutting the door after him.

"I could do with a drink," Murrow said.

"I'll join you," Janet said. "Livvy, are you coming with us?"

"I'm heading home, if you don't mind. I have an early start tomorrow morning at the newspaper."

"Now that you've seen how our operation works, I hope I can get a tour of the *Daily Premier,*" Ed Murrow said.

"I'm certain something can be arranged. Since you're on the telephone exchange, I'll call you tomorrow. Is that all right, Janet?"

"Of course," she told me.

Ed led us down the hallway to the end where the lift was located, and we rode down to the lobby. We crossed the elegant marble lobby before the Murrows walked off to a local public house arm in arm, and I walked home alone through dark streets teeming with murderers, robbers, and scary monsters.

I wasn't usually this frightened while walking alone on darkened lanes, but I'd just tripped over a body. I'd seen the knife sticking out of his chest. I couldn't get the picture out of my mind, and I couldn't get over the feeling that the killer was out here somewhere following me.

A killer I couldn't see through the blackout and the fog.

Chapter Three

I was at work the next morning when Miss Westcott, now editor of the features section of both the *Daily* and the *Sunday Premier*, came over to tell me I had a phone call. Her expression looked as if she'd bitten into an impossible-to-find lemon.

The war had given both of us a promotion, thanks to the call-up of so many young male reporters. I'd worked for her for over two years and she still despaired of my writing anything correctly. I had brought in some good stories, but that hadn't improved her opinion of me or my reporting skills.

Women and society news was gone for the duration. Fortunately, Sir Henry Benton, the publisher of the newspapers, was a maverick from Newcastle and he moved us over to something he called the features desk. Basically, it was everything that wasn't news. He'd moved some of the women onto the news desk. I was thrilled for them, but I knew I would never be that skilled.

I walked over to Miss Westcott's desk and picked up the receiver. "Hello?"

"Hello, Livvy. This is Janet Murrow. I was wondering, since you were so helpful last night…"

Oh, dear. Here it came. Whatever *it* was.

"CBS wants someone from the organization here in London to pay a condolence call on Miss Kennedy, Frank's sister. She's the only family he has in the area, and his next of kin. Ed won't go, he's terrible about these things anyway, and I don't know what the police have told her about us finding the body or Ed throwing him out. I was wondering if you could…"

At least now I knew what she was asking. "What time were you planning to call on Miss Kennedy?"

"Two o'clock. Oh, thank you, Livvy. I'll be outside the *Daily Premier* building at one-thirty. See you then."

I was left holding the receiver of a telephone with a dead line. Turning to Miss Westcott, I said, "Apparently, I'm expected to pay a condolence call this afternoon. I'll take my meal break when it's time to leave."

"A family member?" she asked, sounding wary. I'd left on investigations before, and I was always backed up by the publisher, Sir Henry, because I brought him good stories, if not good writing. Miss Westcott would have preferred me to be present and doing my tasks with more regularity. She thought I might make a better reporter if I actually stayed around and did my job. She was probably right.

I thought I'd better be honest. "No, a murder victim I tripped over last night in the blackout."

"Why am I not surprised?" Miss Westcott murmured, shaking her head.

I suspected I'd better let Sir Henry know what I might end

up working on before I left that afternoon. I went back to writing up the feature article on Mrs. Murrow that I'd been assigned, without a doubt in my mind that Miss Westcott or a colleague with more ability would rewrite it.

I would never get a byline.

When Miss Westcott went to lunch, I used her telephone to call upstairs to the top floor to Sir Henry. His first words, once he learned it was me on the other end of the line, were "I heard you found a murder victim last night."

No sense in asking how he'd found out. Sir Henry had the best sources in London. "I did. And I'm paying a condolence call on his sister this afternoon, if you don't mind my taking the time off."

"When did I ever mind that? Just keep good notes for the newsroom."

"I will," I promised. "By the way, Edward R. Murrow with CBS Broadcasting, they're American, would appreciate a tour of our newspaper."

"I'll have my secretary set one up. Now, see if you can find an angle for a story about this murder."

Thinking I was covered for however long this took me, I went back to my heavy, dark-stained wooden desk and clattered away on the typewriter.

Fortunately, I had worn a gray woolen suit with a green blouse to work that day. Drab enough to pass for a condolence call. I had plain calling cards with me in my bag. My coat was tan, too light a color to be appropriate, but that couldn't be helped.

Janet was waiting in the lobby when I reached it, dressed more appropriately in a funereal black skirt and coat, with a black hat and a gray blouse. Beside her, I looked gaudy.

"I hope I'm not doing the wrong thing, making a condolence call on someone I've never met," Janet said.

"You said someone from CBS needed to, and I'm sure you'd be more tactful than a man would be, particularly calling on a woman. Is she Miss or Mrs.?"

"Miss. Miss Kennedy."

We took the Tube to Wimbledon and walked through a neat middle-class section to the Kennedy house. The same as its neighbors, the paint was in good shape, the front garden had been raked and tended for the winter, and there was a good view of a golf course beyond the end of the street.

We walked up the front steps and Janet rang the bell.

A middle-aged woman in a maid's gray dress and apron answered the door. We gave her our cards and asked to give our condolences to Miss Kennedy in person. She nodded and allowed us to wait inside the front door while she walked into a room to the right of the hall.

I was glad to be out of the wind. Janet looked all around as if she'd never been in a brick semidetached before. Not growing up here, maybe she hadn't.

I noted the well-scrubbed floors, the umbrella stand, the table with the silver tray for calling cards, the large roses on the faded wallpaper. I suspected nothing had changed in this house since the beginning of the Great War.

She was back in a moment. "This way, ladies," came out

in a heavy Irish accent.

We followed her into a drawing room of creams and blues with heavy, dark Victorian furniture. A woman stood by the fireplace where a wrought-iron stove had been inserted, a coal fire inside making the room warm. Still, she pulled a cardigan tighter around herself as if she were cold.

Under normal circumstances, she would have been pretty in a faded sort of way, but grief pinched her features and blanched her skin.

She stared at us for a minute before she said, "Thank you, Mary."

The maid departed and shut the door.

The woman appeared to be in her late thirties. She gestured for us to sit and said, "I'm Christa Kennedy," as she took the chair closest to the fire.

After we introduced ourselves, Janet said, "CBS wants you to know how sorry we are about your brother's death. The BBC assigned him to do some of the engineering work for the CBS broadcasts, so we were able to get to know Frank a little. You must miss him terribly."

What did she need me for, I wondered. She was doing brilliantly on her own.

"Frank was my younger brother. I kept house for him. I don't know what I'll do now," she told us.

"Take your time. Look around. You'll find something you'll want to spend your time on," I told her before I thought about how my advice might be taken.

"And how do you know this?" she asked me in a stiff

voice.

"I was widowed at twenty-six. The numbness took weeks to subside before I could form a coherent sentence again."

Christa took a deep breath. "Frank was murdered," came out in a sob.

"So was Reggie. The suddenness and the cruelty of his killing was a shock. And the pain..." I shook my head. When she settled a little in her chair, studying me carefully, I continued. "The point is, I understand. Even though it doesn't seem that way now, you will get through this. Do you own the house?"

"Our parents did. Then Frank. Now our cousin Patrick does, he tells me." There was no mistaking the bitterness in her tone.

"You haven't seen your brother's will?" Janet asked, sounding somewhere between amazed and horrified. I hadn't much experience with American women, but they seemed to be more forceful in protecting their rights than most Englishwomen I knew.

"No." Christa sounded startled. "It would never occur to me..."

"Perhaps you should visit your brother's solicitor and find out exactly what your position is. What provisions have been made for you," I suggested.

"It would be better than not knowing," Christa admitted. "I don't want to have to enter a convent the same way that many single Irishwomen do." Then she looked from one of us to the other. "Who killed my brother? Who would do such a thing?"

Both Janet and I shook our heads in mute grief.

I didn't want Christa to start sobbing on my shoulder. "Does your cousin Patrick live close by?"

Christa gave a scoffing laugh. "He lives on one floor of a house in Kilburn among the Irish riffraff. He and his large family are all squeezed in there. The only thing Patrick is good at is producing children. Heaven knows what the neighbors would think if *they* moved in here, but he'd kill to get this place."

She saw the shocked looks on our faces and added, "Just a figure of speech. But you can be certain there won't be any room for me here once he and his brood move in." She sounded bitter.

"All the more reason to see the solicitor as soon as possible. So you know your position," I told her. "Do you have any other relatives?"

"Not in this country. Our parents came over when we were small. Frank said he'd never go back. He didn't want to be a professional Irishman, was how he put it." She dabbed at her eyes with one jerky movement of her handkerchief. "How I'll break the news to Dermot, I'll never know."

"Dermot?" Janet asked. She looked as if she were out of her depth with these revelations.

"Our younger brother. He went back to Ireland a year or so ago, making Frank very angry."

"Do you have his address?" I asked. I suspected Christa Kennedy needed to express all the hurt and confusion she was feeling, and we'd been the first people to come into her isolated life. And as strangers, never to be seen again, we were safe to tell these things to.

"No. I think Frank did, because he said he didn't want me contacting him. He said it wouldn't do me any good."

Frank Kennedy was sounding more like a selfish prig by the moment. Keeping that thought to myself, I suggested, "You might search your brother's room for an address book. It should make notifying friends and relatives easier."

"But Frank wouldn't want me to do that."

Janet's eyes widened.

"Oh, I know Frank is dead. The police told me. But he wouldn't like it." Christa sighed and then squared her shoulders. "I suppose I'll have to do it, whether he'd approve of it or not."

"Do you have any women friends who can sit with you until you feel stronger?" Janet asked. "Someone who could help you look for the address book?"

I was impressed at how genuinely nice Janet was. And how practical. Probably because I was the type to just march in and look for his address book, a copy of his will, anything I'd find useful if I were in Miss Kennedy's position.

"Not really. Frank didn't want me to go out visiting. He felt I should stay at home where I'd be safer with the war on. Especially since, as an engineer, he worked all sorts of strange hours and wouldn't be here to protect me. And he wanted his meals at odd times."

Whose comfort was he really interested in? I wondered.

Her voice faded away as she faced the doorway. We could hear an argument in the hallway before the maid came in, trying in vain to block the door before a young, dark-haired man could gain entrance to the room.

He burst into the room and strode toward Christa, who leaped from her chair. "Dermot."

As she practically jumped into the young man's arms, I asked, "Are you the younger brother living in Ireland?" He was tall and thin, with a thick head of dark hair that was in need of a trim.

"Yes. What's going on?" He glanced at us as he dropped his pack on the rug and held his sister.

"Oh, Dermot. Frank's dead," Christa sobbed, pressing her head into his shoulder.

"You didn't know?" I asked.

He shook his head, looking bewildered.

"You mean your arrival here is fortuitous?" Janet asked.

"I got a bit of Christmas leave, starting Boxing Day. I got the night train over from Ireland and just arrived to see if Frank would let me stay here during my visit."

If this was true, then Dermot couldn't be his brother's killer. Sorting that out, I was glad, was a task for the police.

Chapter Four

"Oh, Dermot. Patrick's already been here to tell me he gets the house," Christa said, looking up into her brother's face.

"What?" His voice echoed around the drawing room. It was not a happy sound.

Janet and I looked at each other, ready to leave as quickly as possible.

"And who are you?" stopped us before we could escape this conversation.

"Mrs. Murrow and Mrs. Redmond representing CBS network, that Mr. Kennedy worked for while he was at Broadcasting House. We came to tell your sister how very sorry we were to hear this distressing news," I said.

"How did he die?" Dermot still sounded baffled.

"You'll have to ask the police," I said, "but we were told it was murder." Janet glanced at me when I told this fabrication, but she didn't make a sound.

"Why would someone kill Frank? He was a toothache, but that hardly seems to be a reason to kill him," Dermot said. Then he turned to his sister. "Does Mimi know?"

"Well, I certainly haven't told the floozy," Christa replied with a sniff, folding her arms across her chest.

"Who's Mimi?" I asked.

"Frank's fiancée," Dermot said.

"Former fiancée," Christa said. "Frank called it off about two weeks ago. There was an unholy row. She had the nerve to throw that blue vase that our mother set such store by. Just missed Frank's head and hit the wall behind him. Destroyed the vase. Shattered in a million pieces. Frank and I joined forces to throw her out."

A silence fell then. After a moment, I said, "We should leave you two alone with your grief, but if I may suggest, I would take your sister to the solicitor and find out the details of your brother's will."

"Leaving the house to Patrick sounds the type of thing Frank would do," Dermot said as we shook hands and I murmured sympathetic noises.

"At least you know you're welcome here now," Christa said, once more clinging to her younger brother. She appeared to have forgotten our presence.

Janet was clearly a master of condolence calls. She said all the right things and left making the family feel as if Frank Kennedy had been well liked at work, which I already suspected wasn't true.

Once we were outside and down the street, I shouted against the wind, "You didn't need me along at all."

"Oh, but I did." Janet gave me a smile. "I had no idea how to handle that. And you were the perfect person to talk to her, since your husband was murdered. You assured her having a murder victim in the family is acceptable in polite society."

"I'm sure Christa Kennedy is not to blame for her brother's death. She seemed under his thumb."

"I hope she'll be all right," Janet said.

"Dermot seems to be a nice kid. He'll look out for her," I replied. I hoped he really had been on the night train ferry the previous night.

* * *

I arrived back at my desk in midafternoon to be told by a colleague in a hushed voice that Sir Henry Benton, our publisher, was looking for me. Miss Westcott looked up from her desk and glared. I finished putting away my outerwear and then took the lift up to the top floor.

Sir Henry's secretary nodded for me to go in. I knocked on the door and walked into the spacious office with the huge raised desk and extra chairs for editorial discussions that were uncomfortable enough to make sure they weren't long discussions.

Sir Henry was seated behind several yards of polished wood in a chair that raised him up above those before him. His thin hair was all gray now, but he hadn't lost any of his stockiness. He greeted me with twinkling eyes. "You certainly have a talent for tripping over bodies."

"A gift I'd rather not have."

"Have you learned anything we can use in the newspaper?"

"He shared the family home with his sister. A younger brother has now shown up, and there's a cousin and his family in Kilburn. Hardly earth-shattering," I told him.

"That's more than we'll learn once you talk to Sir Malcolm."

"Why would I talk to Sir Malcolm?" Britain's counterintelligence spymaster and my sometime employer wouldn't have anything to do with the murder of a BBC engineer on a London street, would he? I certainly hoped not.

"He called me while you were gone, saying he wanted you to go to his office and talk to him about the body you found last night." Sir Henry stared at me with raised eyebrows.

I took a deep breath. "When?"

"Now."

"Why?" Oh, why? I didn't want to go.

"We're talking about Sir Malcolm. How would I know?" Sir Henry said, his eyebrows still raised.

"Are you going to square this with Miss Westcott?"

He smiled. "Don't I always? I am in charge." Though to hear the two of them argue, you'd think Miss Westcott was Sir Henry's superior.

Within ten minutes, I was out of the *Daily Premier* building and heading toward Sir Malcolm's office on the fourth floor of a former residential hotel. It had been completely taken over by the government now that we were at war. As I reached the area around Whitehall, I noticed every time I approached Sir Malcolm's building that more and more people passing on the pavement were wearing military uniforms.

The times we were in might be called a phony war, and it had been called that, but in many ways, it now felt as if we were in a war and everyone should get on with their work.

Once again, I was escorted upstairs to the office by a soldier carrying a sidearm in a holster on his belt. In response to Sir Malcolm's "Come," I opened the door and walked in. The soldier turned smartly and left.

Sir Malcolm was on the telephone. He pointed to the chair in front of his desk without looking directly at me and continued to listen to the voice coming from the receiver. He made a few grunts, said "No," and hung up.

"Tell me about this body you found last night." I wasn't certain if he was staring at me or through me with his dark eyes.

I told him everything I'd learned about Frank Kennedy, his murder, and his family. It didn't amount to much. When I finished, I asked, "What difference does it make to you?"

"You are aware the Irish Republican Army has stepped up their attacks in England as well as whatever trouble they are causing in Ireland?"

I thought for a moment. "It's been in the newspapers. Damage to rail lines, shipping, bombs on high streets. And now five people have been tried for murder and two will hang over the deaths in one bombing," I added, referring to the only deadly attack by the IRA in their yearlong campaign.

"The IRA has made clear they want to aid the Nazis any way they can. They want to hurt Britain. That's why Frank Kennedy was infiltrating the IRA for us here in London, particularly around the docks."

"Was he getting you good intelligence?"

Sir Malcolm swung his large head from side to side. "Some lower-level contacts. Thugs, mostly. He said he was getting approached by the upper levels of the organization, but nothing helpful so far."

"Why was he willing to assist you? He wasn't a kind or altruistic person from what I've heard. Quite the opposite." Actually, he sounded as if he were a prat.

"He came to us. Said he'd been approached. He was willing to inform on his brethren for money. Lots of money."

"That sounds quite similar to the man I've heard about." Definitely a twerp.

"Would you trust him?"

An odd question for Sir Malcolm to ask me, since I'd never met the man when he was alive. "I saw the way he treated his sister. I wouldn't trust him, but I'm a woman. Did you trust him?"

Sir Malcolm smiled slightly. "No, but I'm a permanent skeptic." Then the smile left his face. "We have trouble finding any Irishmen willing to inform on the IRA. Not only is it dangerous, most of them are loyal to Ireland and hope we lose the war."

None of this told me what I wanted to know. "Why am I here?"

"I want you to find out who killed Frank Kennedy. More than that, I want to know why. Was it the IRA because he was a traitor, or was it more personal?"

"You know I can't infiltrate the IRA. Wrong nationality." Despite my reddish hair.

"Do you really think I'm that foolish?" Sir Malcolm grumbled at me fiercely enough that I wanted to cringe. "I want you to attack this from another direction. Broadcasting House and his family."

"There are enough people who didn't like him, but to kill him? That's desperate."

"Find out which one it was. Make friends with that broadcaster's wife who was with you when you found the body."

I didn't think that would help. "Kennedy worked for the BBC. Can you get me an interview with the personnel office at Broadcasting House?" I'd need to find out what they thought.

"I can set that up for tomorrow morning."

"Are you going to clear my absence with Sir Henry at the *Daily Premier*? And get me paid?"

Sir Malcolm's expression matched the cat that cornered the mouse. "Don't I always?"

Trapped, I surrendered.

I thought the best place to begin was with Gerald Fitzroy. I had reviewed a few live concerts, but I had never worked directly with the chief theater and music critic for the *Daily Premier*. I wanted to find out how much Fitzroy, an outsider, knew about the personnel at the BBC and Frank Kennedy and who, exactly, the murdered man had angered and offended.

I'd heard Fitzroy was an eccentric who worked mainly

from home. He came into the *Daily Premier* building twice a week with his copy all neatly typed. Otherwise, you'd find him in the cinemas, the concert halls, the theaters, and Broadcasting House.

My first stop was the *Daily Premier* building, but Fitzroy was not in his office. With the realignments due to the war, Miss Westcott was now his editor. With a great deal of trepidation, I walked across the building to our enlarged features office.

When she saw me enter our area, Miss Westcott stared at me. It was not a friendly stare. Sir Henry must have spoken to her already.

I walked up to her desk and smiled. "Do you know where I can find Gerald Fitzroy?"

"What do you want with him? No, don't tell me. It must have something to do with your latest investigation." She made "investigation" sound as if it were a description of an obscene sex act.

"Do you know where he is?"

"No. Stop wasting my time. And his." She looked back down at the copy in front of her and picked up her pencil.

"What's his home address?"

She glanced back up at me. "Olivia. Really."

"Would you rather I asked Sir Henry?"

She gave a muffled shriek, which made a few of my colleagues look up in surprise before she pulled out a list and jotted down an address.

I thanked her and left. Quickly, before my presence

made her even more angry.

I expected to find that Gerald Fitzroy lived in a modern flat. Instead, he lived in a small Victorian terrace house in South Kensington. A thin, middle-aged man in a black suit answered my ring.

"Mr. Fitzroy is working. He is not to be disturbed," he said when I asked to see him.

"When will he finish?"

"I really couldn't say."

"I'm here with the blessing of Sir Henry Benton. The man who signs our pay slips. I need Mr. Fitzroy's help."

Unfortunately, the butler was resistant to my request. It took twenty minutes for me to meet Mr. Fitzroy, and that was only because I waited to meet him as he was heading out of the house.

He was an inch or two shorter than me, with a thin build, gray hair, and pale eyes. He reminded me of the hare in the tortoise story, fast out of the gate.

I quickly told him what I wanted.

"I'm on my way to a concert at the Royal Albert Hall. Walk with me, and I'll tell you what I know." He took his gas mask case from his butler and walked out the front door with a pronounced limp.

When we reached the bottom of his steps, I said, "If I knew the BBC productions Frank Kennedy was involved with in the month of December, which ones would I find had strife because of him?"

"All of them." A smirk crossed his face.

I tried again. "Which were the worst?"

He stopped on the pavement and considered for a moment. "The radio plays on Monday and Saturday evenings, the chamber music concerts on Tuesday and Friday evenings, and once in a while the five o'clock national news. Of course, it wasn't everyone on these programs who had trouble with him." He smiled then, reminding me of a reptile. "Tell me, what is your interest in Frank Kennedy?"

"You know he was murdered."

He again started his quick walk toward the nearby Royal Albert Hall. "Hardly surprising. What is your interest?"

"I'm part of the investigation into his death."

"Which part?" He resumed smirking.

"The part of the government that is calling most of the shots right now."

"Ooh, a lady spy." He pursed his lips at me. "I can't say I'm surprised Kennedy was a German agent. They probably pay well."

"You know for a fact he was after any money to be had?" I wondered if he knew anything useful.

"I know he was blackmailing three people involved in those broadcasts. Not large amounts, but it's the thought."

Wow, but Fitzroy was a smarmy twit. His phony-friendly tone of voice was making me hope he was the next victim. "Who?"

"I'm not going to make your life easier, Miss Intelligence."

"Were they male or female?"

"Both."

"Were you one of them?"

He laughed. "I wouldn't tell you if I were."

I bet he'd tell me if he wasn't. "So, you were one of his victims," I concluded. "And therefore, a possible killer." I gave him an angry glare. It had grown dark and it wasn't likely he could see my displeasure. "Should I put you on the suspect list, Mr. Fitzroy?"

Chapter Five

Even with the darkness of the blackout, I could clearly see Gerald Fitzroy return my glare in the dim light of shaded automobile headlights. "I wasn't one of his victims. There were two female, one male. Mind you, those are only the ones I noticed. And of course, there were several other women who would have killed him for the pleasure of never having his paws grabbing at them again."

"Names?"

"I'll let you figure it out. It's not difficult."

Great. He seemed to enjoy not being helpful. "What did his fiancée think of all this?"

"Not much. That may be why she was his ex-fiancée by the time of his death." When I kept watching him, waiting for more information, he sighed and added, "Mimi Randall is one of the actresses in the radio plays. That's where they met."

"When do they rehearse the radio plays?"

He rolled his eyes. "Do I have to do all your work for you? The plays are rehearsed Tuesday, Wednesday, and Thursday evenings, while the chamber music concerts are rehearsed on Monday and Thursday afternoons."

"So, both groups would have been at Broadcasting House Tuesday evening when Kennedy was killed," I said aloud. "The chamber music orchestra would be giving a live performance, and the radio players would be rehearsing."

I wished I hadn't said anything when I saw Fitzroy's smile. "Now you're catching on. And here I am. I wish you luck." The rounded top of the Royal Albert Hall cut into the lighter shade of the sky. Fitzroy ducked into an entrance of the hall and I walked away.

I needed to get back to Broadcasting House to find out the times and locations that this week's play and concert rehearsals would take place.

It wasn't any great distance, but the blackout slowed everything down. When I arrived, blinking in the bright light of the lobby, I asked the guard at the main desk where I might find a list of rehearsal times and locations. She directed me to the artists' foyer off the lobby, where I found a large board with that day's rehearsals listed and all the information I needed. The BBC players would begin rehearsals at six.

Being on my own meant I could get a late dinner and stay around now to speak to people before the rehearsal began.

I went back to the lobby, signed in for rehearsal room 6C by the bored-looking guard, and took the lift up. I popped my head through the doorway to take a look, and heard, "What do you think you're doing?"

"Looking for Mimi," I answered. I came back out into the hall to find I'd been challenged by a man in his late thirties or early forties, healthy looking, but safe from conscription so far due to his age. He had dark hair, rumpled clothes, and a permanently worried expression.

"She won't be here until near six on the dot. Who are you?"

"Olivia Redmond. Who are you?"

"Keith Bates. Director of this sinking ship."

"Why sinking?"

"With actors, the ship is always sinking. They can get more dramatic mileage out of those scenes. And they don't have to be played on the stage."

I smiled at what I thought was an exaggeration, and he grinned in return.

"I take it you're not an actor?" he asked.

"I'm supposed to find out who killed Frank Kennedy. So far, I get the impression the killer will get a medal and a standing ovation."

"Ah, you knew Kennedy."

"Never met him. However, he seems to have been universally disliked." I gave Bates a smile, hoping he'd think me harmless to talk to.

"I tried a few times to have him ejected from our rehearsals. The powers that be told him to leave if he didn't have any reason to be here, but they never enforced their rules. Being challenged just made him more obnoxious."

"Who did he annoy the most?"

"Clarissa Northfield, our ingenue. She's very talented. She's also young, shy, and soft-spoken when she's not on stage. He'd put his hands where they didn't belong and make her cry. We tried to get her to report him, but she wouldn't. And when I tried to report him, I was told it didn't involve me.

I'm the director! How could it not involve me?"

"Who was angriest with Kennedy? Obviously not Clarissa."

"Paul White. A versatile young actor. Wouldn't ordinarily stand a chance of still being here with all these call-ups. However, he gets around on crutches from having had polio as a child."

"I imagine Kennedy gave White a hard time even without mixing up Clarissa in this." I was getting a good idea of just how awful Frank Kennedy could be.

"Called him 'Crip.' Made fun of him. And when Paul tried to defend Clarissa, Kennedy told him to stand aside and let a man show Clarissa how it's done."

Two possible killers, but none for blackmail that I could see.

Bates smiled. "Paul got his revenge when Kennedy tripped over one of his crutches and landed on the floor. Two of the other actors and I had to hold Kennedy back to keep him from hitting Paul."

"When was this?"

"Two weeks ago, more or less."

Recently enough that Kennedy might have started a fight with either Clarissa or Paul in front of Broadcasting House and been stabbed by one or the other in self-defense. But then why not report the attack?

"What time did you finish rehearsing last night?"

Bates frowned as he thought. "Ten-fifteen? Ten-twenty?"

Giving anyone involved a chance to meet Kennedy leaving the building and kill him.

The actors began to arrive in the studio. Paul White was easy to pick out, and I guessed Clarissa Northfield was the delicate-looking young blonde. A few older actors, male and female, arrived, and then at a few seconds before six, a platinum blonde with bright red lipstick, a tight sweater, and a long, slim skirt rushed in.

"So glad you could make it, Mimi," Bates said in a dry voice. "Places, everyone. We don't have a long time to rehearse this, so let's make it worthwhile."

I took a seat behind Bates, who sat facing the actors. They formed a semi-circle around two tables, and at his signal, one of the middle-aged women, dowdy looking, wearing a brown tweed suit, began a scripted conversation with a gray-haired man in a rumpled two-piece gray suit and a stain on his tie. Their voices didn't match their appearance at all.

I closed my eyes, and it was easy to imagine an elegant couple in expensive finery speaking these lines in a Mayfair drawing room. I opened my eyes, and the reality I saw around me didn't look anything at all similar to the fantasy everyone would hear over the radio.

The play was good, with a few well-placed jokes. Bates stopped and started the actors as he noted things in his script and the actors affected by the changes made notes in their copies as well.

They worked hard for nearly an hour before one of the

middle-aged women asked leave to go to the loo. Bates said, "Let's take ten, better make it fifteen, and then we'll work through to the finish of this play."

Mimi strolled over to the far side of the room and lit a cigarette. I walked over to her and said, "Mimi? Mimi Randall?"

"Yes."

"I'd hoped to talk to you about Frank Kennedy."

"I don't want to talk to you about him." She swung around on her heel and faced away from me. "I don't want to talk to anyone about that heel."

"Why wouldn't you want to talk to me about Kennedy? He's dead. He can't hurt you now." It was a shot in the dark. I hoped it would work.

"He played me for a fool. I don't want to be reminded of my less than stellar judgment of men." Then Mimi turned and glared at me. "Did his simpleton sister send you?"

"No."

"Then who did?" The scowl was still there.

"The government." I decided to tell her, "Frank's been a bad boy."

"Not too surprising, since he got himself killed." The smile she gave me was definitely conspiratorial.

"So, tell me about him."

"Are you going to find out who killed him?"

"Possibly." I hoped sounding enigmatic might work on her.

"I'd look closely at his sister for his killer."

"Why?"

"It stands to reason, doesn't it? She hated him, the way she had to wait on him hand and foot. She was little more than a slave. And he'd never get married, not when he had her to do his darning and cook his meals." She sounded bitter when she said this last.

"How did she feel about Frank having a fiancée? Was she afraid you'd supplant her?"

"She was afraid we'd get married and I'd move in. Then she'd be no more than a slave to the both of us."

"What caused the argument two weeks ago? The one where you threw the vase." It must have been impressive for things to be thrown.

"It was much ado about nothing." Mimi gave one graceful gesture with her hand. "I'm an actress. I'm volatile. I throw things when the mood strikes. It comes from working on the music hall stage. Everything larger than life."

She shook her head. "But that silly cow was attached to that stupid vase and she started screaming. She wouldn't stop. Frank asked me to leave since she wasn't going to quiet down while I was there." Apparently, Mimi thought nothing of destroying other people's possessions.

"His sister said he ended your engagement."

"He just told her that to keep her happy, I imagine."

"Then you were still engaged?"

She appeared as if she'd agree, but then she shook her head. "I caught him in the little stairwell off this hall with some tart from the orchestra. Had her pressed up against the wall. When I shouted at him, she ran off in tears, embarrassed I guess, and he turned on me. Said I shouldn't be so naïve as to think I was the only one for him."

I'm sure my wince was visible.

"Yeah. I called off the engagement that instant." She gave a shrug. "I'm done with any man who has that kind of attitude."

"When did that happen?"

"A few days after the vase was shattered."

"I'm surprised he didn't chase Clarissa."

"He did, but Paul fought him off." She ground out what little was left of her cigarette. "Got to admire Paul. He won't back down from anybody."

"Didn't that bother you, that he'd make a move on another woman in the studio where you work?" I thought it showed just how unreliable Frank Kennedy was.

"Oh, he tries—tried it on with everyone. Clarissa wasn't interested, and he'd have soon stopped if Paul hadn't challenged him. Frank didn't like anyone to challenge him."

"What did he do if someone warned him off?"

Bates called the actors back to work.

"He'd find a way to get even. The sneakier, the better."

"Blackmail?" I asked quietly as Mimi walked past me.

"If he could. Revenge and profit."

* * *

I'd had the skirts to two of my older suits shortened into the latest style, making them look newish again. It was our patriotic duty to use less fabric for our dresses and coats, fabric that could be put to use for the war effort. The dressmaker had given me the leftover fabric, which I'd put away in our basement box room since I didn't currently see any use for it.

The next day, I wore the redone navy-blue suit to my ten o'clock appointment with the personnel office at Broadcasting House. With the addition of a white blouse, I had the bespoke tailoring of a cabinet minister and the style of a private secretary. Perfect for my mission.

The first thing I noticed was that their offices were nearly empty of young men, similar to the newsrooms of the *Daily Premier*. As I stood there looking lost, the young woman at the closest desk said, "Are you looking for Mr. Gray? That's his office through there."

I thanked her and walked across the larger office to the accompaniment of typewriters clattering and pens scratching at heavy, dark wood desks occupied by women of every age and description. I reached a door at the end, where I was stopped by an older woman whose desk, while in the main office, served as a gate to enter the chief's lair. "I have a ten a.m. appointment with Mr. Gray. I'm Mrs. Redmond."

She looked me over, didn't see anything that would bar me from the premises, and rose to take me into the private office.

Mr. Gray was not in any danger of being called up to serve his country. He was nearly bald, overweight, and he appeared to sag under the cares of his duties. He rose as I walked in behind his secretary and held out his hand.

I shook it as he thanked his secretary and she shut the door as she left. Then he sat, the chair creaking as he settled in, and asked, "What does the government want to know about Frank Kennedy?"

I had wondered why Sir Malcolm had been willing to set up this appointment. Now I understood. The BBC worked closely with the government, especially now that we were officially at war. I was just Sir Malcolm's errand girl.

"What kind of employee was he?"

He glanced at the file as he made a face as if the milk had soured. "Satisfactory."

"That sounds as if it were a negative assessment."

"It wasn't meant to—"

"We need your complete honesty. In return, we will protect your anonymity and that of the BBC." I tried to convey the power and dignity of the government.

It turned out it was worth a good deal more than the chummier tone I had to use as a reporter for a newspaper. He folded immediately. "He did his job well enough. He understood the technical aspects of his work better than most."

"But?" There had to be more to that file.

"But?" he repeated.

"He sounds as if he were less than an exemplary employee, even if you were happy with his technical abilities."

Mr. Gray sank into his chair a little more. "He had difficulty getting along with his colleagues."

I was already expecting this. "In what way?"

"Where shall I start?"

Chapter Six

Mr. Gray opened the file on his desk. "Over the past few years, several of our broadcasters have refused to work with him again. He called people ugly names. It was difficult to convince him to cooperate. He was perhaps overfamiliar with young ladies in the actor groups and the orchestras. And if he didn't approve of what someone was saying, once or twice he lowered the quality of the transmission. He blamed it on sunspots, but we suspected differently."

"So, his not transmitting the Christmas night broadcast for CBS until someone came into where he was working and flipped the switch was part of a pattern?"

"Oh, dear me. I hadn't heard about that."

"That's why CBS was refusing to use Mr. Kennedy anymore." I stared at Mr. Gray, who stared back. When he didn't say anything else, I said, "How many incidents have you recorded in the past year?"

"I couldn't really…"

"Yes. You can. And must." I could sound officious when I tried. It was a skill I was still developing.

"Three."

I blinked. "Only three?"

"We heard rumors of others, but they were not reported

to us. Officially, you understand."

"Why?" Why report them unofficially?

"Kennedy could be an overbearing man—"

"Threatening?"

He ignored my interruption. "Many people just avoided him when possible and ignored the insults when they couldn't." He steepled his fingers and continued. "Most of our programs are an hour in length. Add to that setup and rehearsal, but still. Only a couple of hours to work with him, and then they could leave—"

"Escape?"

He gave me a puzzled gaze. "You never had to deal with him, I understand."

"Not until he was dead. Just outside this building." I spoke deliberately so he'd be clear why I was going after what had happened with Kennedy's work colleagues.

Mr. Gray straightened up and put on an officious tone of his own. "Yes. Well. The BBC doesn't approve of intimidation and harassment, but it also doesn't condone murder. Kennedy was unlikable, but no one had to deal with him for long."

"Someone thought it was too long," I told him. "I want a list of all the broadcasts he's worked on in the past month."

"I'm sure you can understand why I can't do that, Mrs. Redmond," Mr. Gray said in his stuffiest tone.

He still hadn't made up his mind how much he would cooperate, and I was getting tired of him. "You don't want to disappoint Sir Frederick Ogilvie, who has already pledged the full cooperation of the BBC to the government." I was relieved, and surprised, to see Mr. Gray fold immediately. Sir Frederick was the Director-General of the BBC.

He pulled out a program list for the month of December 1939 and then ticked off the programs Kennedy had been an engineer for. "I hope this will satisfy your requirements," he said as he handed it over.

"For the time being." My words brought a look of panic to his eyes before I thanked him and left the office.

* * *

I went upstairs to the chamber concert studio before the rehearsal. I thought of speaking to the conductor, but he looked right through me and every other person in the room. I walked over to a group of female string players and said, "I've been sent to investigate Frank Kennedy."

"Haven't you heard?" one of the women asked. "He's dead. Murdered."

"I've heard."

"Then why investigate him?"

"You think death should give him a pass for his dreadful behavior?" What it lacked in logic I made up for in a challenge.

"No," a short brunette said. "He was horrible. Brutal. Hands everywhere. And not gentle."

Two other women, who appeared to be the youngest of the group, nodded.

"Did you report him?"

All three shook their heads.

"Why not?"

One of the youngest, a blonde, said, "We were going together to the personnel office when Markowitz told us not to be silly. He doesn't want women in his orchestra, and he said this just proved why."

"Why?" I was confused.

"He's the maestro," one of the middle-aged women, holding a cello, said. "He has the final say on everything. When Frank made a nuisance of himself, Markowitz threw him out. He felt that should be the end of the problem and we should all get back to work."

I glanced at the conductor. "He threw Kennedy out? All by himself?"

"No. He sent a French horn to the control room to find the foreman and bring him down here. Then the maestro ordered the foreman to keep Frank Kennedy out or he would go directly to Sir Frederick Ogilvie. Markowitz and Ogilvie are good friends. Kennedy wasn't seen around here again." The cellist shrugged.

"But it didn't solve the problem," the short, dark-haired girl said. "Anywhere else, in or out of the building, was fair game."

The conductor walked toward the podium holding a stack of sheet music. The women scattered to their seats as they took up their instruments and I slipped out into the corridor, planning to talk to them after rehearsal.

As long as I had a long time to wait, I decided to find the control room for the building. I asked a janitor and followed his directions up to the eighth floor. The room was well lit with large windows slanted at the same angle as the roof. Large boards that had been painted black waited to be hauled into place for the start of the night's blackout.

A half-dozen men moved purposefully around or listened with their headsets plugged into consoles while I watched. Their desks were all a sleek, modern art deco design. I stopped one of the men and asked for the foreman. He gestured to a stocky, red-haired man sitting at a desk looking over papers. I walked over, and when he looked up, told him I was investigating Frank Kennedy's death.

"I hope you don't mind if I don't care whether you find his killer or not," the man said in a Scottish accent.

"There seems to be a lot of that around this building." I gave him a smile.

The man returned my smile and held out his hand. "Donald Mayhew."

I shook his hand. "Olivia Redmond."

"How can I help?"

"How did he get along with his fellow engineers? I assume they're all male."

"All male and refused to put up with his guff. He didn't cause us any difficulties."

"I was told the orchestra conductor spoke to one of the foremen about banning Frank Kennedy from the concert studio. Said that if he appeared there one more time, he'd complain to Sir Frederick Ogilvie. What about him?"

He made a face. "That was me. Old Markowitz would do

it, too. I told Kennedy I wouldn't protect him. If he was fool enough to go back there, he was on his own and could whistle for his place in our shop."

"What was he doing there?"

"What was he always doing? Chasing some skirt. The girls around here seem to have more sense. They didn't want anything to do with him. Constantly getting his face slapped or his toes stepped on."

"But he kept trying." That seemed strange to me.

"Hope springs eternal." Mayhew shrugged.

"I've heard he was a blackmailer."

He grinned at me. "I've heard that, too, but I don't know who he could blackmail."

"If you were to take a guess, who do you think was angriest with Frank Kennedy?"

"The other engineers paid little notice of him. We were all hoping management would send him off to the countryside where so many of our productions are being performed every day."

"So not all of what we hear on the BBC comes from here?" I was surprised.

"Never was, but once war was declared, all sorts of shows were moved to various parts of England. Frank would have had just as good choices to harass from among the performers sent to any of these towns as he had here, but he didn't want to leave London."

"Why not?"

"I don't know. And I sure wasn't going to spend time with

him to ask him." He made a face of disgust.

"But you are still broadcasting concerts and plays and talks from here?" I wanted to be certain that the people Frank Kennedy was harassing were all here at Broadcasting House.

"Yes, but not nearly as many as before. And the performers who are still working here in London are glad. They can not only work here, but they can also get work in the London theaters and dance halls. That's not as available to the artists working for the BBC in smaller towns."

I wanted to be clear on who Kennedy was aggravating at the BBC. "Who was he bothering in this smaller group of colleagues?"

Mayhew tapped his pencil. "The office girls were pretty safe from him. My guess is it would be some of the performers, the female performers, that he bothered."

"Why were the office girls safe from Kennedy's attentions?"

Mayhew's grin broadened and his accent thickened. "A few months ago, he started to follow one of the girls in booking. She was young and naïve and tried to brush him off with no luck. She had a cousin in payroll. After this went on for a while, at the end of one week, Kennedy didn't get paid."

"Wouldn't he have just bullied his way to his paycheck?"

"He tried. It didn't work. It was booked that his pay was docked for not being present for his shifts. That's a serious offense around here. Took him five days of dealing with one manager after another to get it straightened out."

"And there was no one to blame it on?"

He laughed. "That was the really good bit. Not knowing who to blame, he left all the girls in the offices alone."

"So, none of them would have had a reason to kill him."

"No, nor would any of us. Regular employees of the BBC were safer from his tricks than the performers. They're hired or let go depending on what is needed in the next week or two. It's a good gig and they want to hang onto employment here. That means no complaints, no rocking the boat. And Frank used that to his advantage."

"He sounds as if he were a reprehensible man." I really hoped his killer was a member of the IRA.

"He was." Mayhew thought for a moment and then said, "But if he was blackmailing someone, it may be why his locker was searched."

"Searched? By whom?" This was a new piece of information, and I was keen to hear about it.

"I have no idea. Our lockers are in a small room off the hall," he said, gesturing to his right, "and the hall isn't used much. It's a dead end, except for a cupboard for our lockers and a couple of storerooms."

"Was anything taken?"

"I don't know. Kennedy was dead, so he couldn't tell us—"

"He was already dead when this happened?" It had to have something to do with his murder. But what?

"Oh." Mayhew thought. "It must have been yesterday sometime. Wednesday morning. About the time we were all learning of his murder."

"Was his locker locked?"

"No. The lock was on the floor." He held up a hand. "And before you ask, he didn't keep it locked all the time."

"And you have no idea what was missing?"

"No. Now, if you don't mind..." He gestured to his paperwork.

"Not at all. Thank you for speaking to me." I left the control room and went back downstairs to the concert hall where the orchestra was rehearsing. I waited in the hallway, listening to the beautiful melody, when they came to a clattering halt. Then a male voice snapped out orders to various instruments, followed by the music beginning again.

This happened a few more times before they came to a stopping point, final instructions were issued for the next day by the loud male voice, and then musicians fled the room.

I walked in and quickly found the young blonde packing up her violin. "I wanted to talk to you some more. Can I buy you a cup of tea?"

"I walk back to the rooming house with Celeste," she said in a hesitant voice.

"I'll be glad to buy her a cup of tea also and hear what she has to say."

"I don't want to get anyone into trouble...."

"He's dead. There's no one to get into trouble."

"I'll take that cup of tea," the short, dark-haired girl said. "I'm Celeste Young."

I introduced myself, and then the blonde half-whispered

that her name was Roxanne Scott.

Celeste told me there was a restaurant in the basement where we could get a good cup of coffee or tea and led the way to the ladies' dressing room. There were lockers in the room where they could store their outerwear and their instrument carrying cases with their instruments tucked safely inside. Then we took the stairs down. As it turned out, we each got tea, and I paid the bill.

We sat at one of the shiny metal tables in a utilitarian modern style with metal tube chairs with seats and backs of a canvas material attached. Once we had our cups fixed to our satisfaction, I said, "Who had Frank Kennedy been annoying the most recently? I take it he shared his unwanted attentions with every female within sight?"

"He spent a lot of time bothering me, but I wasn't the only one," Roxanne said.

"How long have you been in the orchestra?" I asked.

"Six months."

"And he started flirting with you as soon as you arrived?"

"It was worse than flirting," Celeste said. "He put his fat fingers all over our blouses."

"How long have you been performing here?" I asked Celeste.

"Over a year. He tried it on with me at first, but I elbowed him in the gut one day, really hard, and he didn't bother me after that." She lowered her voice so I had to lean forward to hear her over the clatter of talk in the café.

"So, if you used force on him, he'd move on to someone

else?" He sounded appallingly rude.

"Sometimes," Roxanne admitted.

"You just weren't vicious enough with him, Roxie," Celeste said. "Drawing blood would have worked wonders with that man."

"It bothers me to do things that are so brutal." Roxanne squeezed up her face and cringed.

My opinion of Frank Kennedy dropped even more.

Celeste looked at me and shook her head. "She's too nice. What he really needed was someone tall enough to give him a knee in his..."

I nodded, understanding what she meant. "Who else from the orchestra was he annoying lately?"

"Beside Roxie?"

I nodded.

"The most recent one was Harriet Berg. And he wasn't just annoying her, he was tormenting her on account of her being German and Jewish."

"Is she a recent refugee?" I wasn't certain it made any difference.

"Not really, she's been here four or five years. Her brother was in the orchestra too, but he was called up. He flunked his physical, he has weak eyes, but since his German is excellent, they put him to work in some office in Horse Guards."

"He's still in London?"

Celeste nodded. "Whenever he can, he walks his sister to Broadcasting House and home afterward. There she is now. Harriet, come join us."

A dark-eyed young woman in a faded brown dress was walking by with her teacup. "You don't mind?"

"Of course not. We were just talking about how horrible Frank Kennedy was, and we said he'd chosen you to be rude to lately," Celeste said in a friendly tone. "Sit with us."

Harriet sat in the empty chair on my left.

"I heard he resembled nothing so much as a schoolyard bully," I said. "I'm Livvy Redmond."

"Hello. Harriet Berg. He was worse than that. He was— filthy." Her German accent had faded, but it was still noticeable.

"Filthy how?" I asked.

"He not only ran his dirty hands all over me, he called me terrible names while he did it. He said Hitler was right, we should all be thrown into the sea. Things such as that. But he made a mistake."

"Did he?" I asked and smiled as I watched her dark eyes gleam with remembered amusement.

"He taunted me in front of the conductor and some of the male orchestra members. All Jews. He was ordered out of our studio and whenever he was spotted near me outside of our theater, the men would block his way until I could get away."

"That sounds fortunate."

"It was. I'm sorry, Roxanne, that he had come back to bothering you again. We are fortunate he is dead. We are all fortunate," Harriet said.

Roxanne nodded, still looking miserable as she finished her tea.

The building seemed to be full of possibilities. All nice people bullied by Frank Kennedy. How I hoped the IRA had killed that rotten man.

Chapter Seven

I looked at Roxanne, who'd been listening to us. "Do you have anyone who tried to protect you from Kennedy?"

"My family and friends are in Yorkshire. Celeste and some of the others have been kind and tried to chase Frank away, but he always came back." She finished her drink. "I don't want to talk about him. Are you ready to go, Celeste?"

Celeste had given her a moment's puzzled look. Then she nodded and quickly finished. "Thank you for the tea," she said.

"Thank you for speaking to me. One more thing. What time did your performance end on Tuesday?"

"It finished at ten, and then we were privileged to hear a fifteen-minute lecture on everything we did wrong," Celeste said.

"The maestro was not happy," Harriet added in a serious tone.

Anyone in the chamber music orchestra could have met Kennedy on the street afterward as easily as the radio players.

I finished my tea, knowing I had just enough time to reach the radio players' studio to attempt to speak to more of the performers in the theater group before they began.

We went upstairs together and while Roxanne, Celeste, and Harriet continued up the stairs, I took the lift from the lobby up to the sixth floor. When I arrived, I found Clarissa Northfield in a corner talking to Paul White. I nodded to Mr. Bates, the director, and joined them.

"We heard you talking to Mimi yesterday. I don't want to talk about Frank Kennedy," Paul said. "He's dead and gone."

"Why not talk about him? A good gossip could clear the air and banish his specter," I said. I knew of no reason why either of them would have killed the dead man. At least not with premeditation.

"I couldn't stand him," Clarissa said. Her voice was sweet and soft, good for radio but not for the theater, where the audience in the back needed to hear the actors. She reminded me of young ladies I had gone to university with. She couldn't have been more than twenty, and probably less.

"Neither could a great number of people." I watched them both as I added, "He had made enemies in Irish politics, he was bothering women in the chamber orchestra as well as here, and," I paused, "he was a blackmailer."

Clarissa went so pale I thought she would faint.

"Well, I'm glad he's dead," Paul White said firmly. His voice would be good on radio as well as in the theater, I decided. Balanced against the wall instead of leaning on his crutches, he appeared taller, but still only medium height. He'd have been good-looking if pain hadn't been etching his features. It was hard to tell because of the lines in his face, but I thought he was only in his early twenties.

"Do you know where he was keeping whatever he was blackmailing you with?" I asked the ingenue.

She shook her head.

Paul stared at her. "What is this, Clarissa?"

Clarissa Northfield burst into tears. I couldn't tell if they were stage tears or if she was really frightened and embarrassed.

"You have no right to upset her," Paul snapped at me.

"If she has some idea where he kept whatever it is, I might be able to get it back for her." I turned to her. "You want it back, don't you?"

She nodded, tears still leaking from her eyes.

"Do you have any idea where he kept it?"

She shook her head, keeping her eyes on me.

"Is it paper of some sort?"

Another nod of her innocent-looking face.

Paul kept silent, for which I was grateful.

"Letters?"

She nodded, with another burst of noisy tears.

"Think you can get them back?" Paul asked me.

"I can think of one place they might be that would be easy for me to get them back. Beyond that, I was hoping Clarissa might have an idea."

"Will you try the place you think they might be? I'll see if I can get Clarissa calmed down for our rehearsal and later, I'll see if she has any idea where else that swine might have kept her letters." Paul patted Clarissa on the back.

I began to suspect her tears were more for Paul's benefit than anything else. Nodding to him, I said, "I'll see you before rehearsal tomorrow."

"There's no rehearsal on Friday nights. Can we meet you somewhere after our performance? We're in a pantomime at two out in the suburbs."

"Let's plan on meeting before the next rehearsal. I don't know how long it will take me to get access to where I think the letters might be."

Paul nodded. At that moment, Mimi ran in as Keith Bates was looking at the clock over the door and I knew they were about to start. "Good luck," I said and headed toward the door.

"Happy hunting," Paul said in a sarcastic tone.

* * *

The next morning, I arrived on Frank Kennedy's street about eleven o'clock. When I rang the bell at the front door, the maid again answered it. "May I speak to Miss Kennedy, please?"

"She doesn't want to see any more of your lot." The woman began to shut the door in my face.

I stuck my foot in the way and nearly had it crushed. "My 'lot'? Miss Kennedy was very cordial when I spoke to her earlier this week. We were paying a condolence call."

"Who is it, Mary?" a man's voice said.

"Is that Dermot?" I asked.

The pressure was eased on my foot as the maid turned to look behind her. "Do you want to speak to her? She was here Wednesday."

"Who?" he said as he came closer.

"Olivia Redmond. I was here with Janet Murrow. From CBS," I called out. "We met Wednesday."

Christa's younger brother opened the door wider. "I'm afraid my sister doesn't want to see anyone until after the funeral tomorrow."

"You can help me just as well," I told him. "Can we speak inside?"

"Of course." He led me down the hall, the floorboards scrubbed nearly white, to the elegantly old-fashioned drawing room I'd been in before, but he didn't sit down nor did he invite me to. The coal fire still burned in the hearth.

"There is no polite way to tell you this," I began.

He slowly shook his head. "It can't be worse than all the other things I've heard lately."

"It is alleged that your brother came into possession of some letters written by an actress who works at Broadcasting House. He's been blackmailing her with them. She wants them back."

"Good heavens." Dermot sank into a chair and looked up at me. "Frank was a blackmailer?"

"I've heard there are a few more people he was blackmailing besides the woman I spoke to. Did he hide his 'treasures' here in this house?"

"If he did, they'd be in his room." Dermot looked at the ceiling with a thoughtful expression. "Does my sister need to know about this?"

I shook my head. "I don't know. If we find his evidence and get it back to his victims, it may be that nothing needs to be said."

"What about the police?"

"They aren't looking this way. As shorthanded as they are, they aren't able to look too deeply into his murder. No witnesses. No suspects. If they stumble across the blackmail, I will tell them who was targeted. I won't tell them why."

"I guess the evidence would have to be up in Frank's room. I'll have a look."

"I'll come with you," I told him.

"I don't think—"

"You don't know what you're looking for."

He thought a moment and nodded before we left the drawing room and climbed the dark wooden stairs. Frank had what I guessed was the largest bedroom, decorated in blues and grays, with heavy patterned brocade draperies covering the windows that faced the front of the house.

With Dermot looking over my shoulder, I started on the wardrobe. After I looked in it, I looked on top of it and then lay on the floor to try to look under it. I couldn't see a thing. "How hard is it to move this?"

"Difficult. It's a heavy piece of furniture."

"We need to look under it. Just to be certain." I didn't want to leave without either finding those letters or checking every possible spot.

"How would Frank have moved it? Especially by himself?"

"Nevertheless."

We worked together, but found we couldn't move it. Then I knelt in front of the wardrobe and removed Frank's shoes and a couple of empty liquor bottles. Borrowing Dermot's knife, I eventually lifted the floor of the wardrobe, praying there were no mousetraps under there. There wasn't, only dust on the floor at the back, and a stack of paper in the front beneath the now-lifted bottom.

Balancing the solid bottom of the wardrobe on one shoulder with my top half inside, I couldn't get a good grip on the thick, messy bundle, and the papers spread out in all directions. "There's quite a bit here, but I can't lift it all at once. Give me a little more room."

Dermot walked over to the window, removing his large feet from the rug beside me, and looked out. I changed position and pulled out one large stack. "There's more under there."

I lay the first stack to the side on the thick patterned carpet and leaned forward with my head against the back wall of the wardrobe to get a better hold on the rest of the papers. Once they were out on top of the first stack, I felt around one more time. There was nothing else.

I sat on the rug, placing all the papers on my lap. One of the top ones appeared to be Frank Kennedy's will. I handed it to Dermot. "I think you'll be in need of this."

He took it and sat down on the bed while I flipped through the envelopes on my lap. There were five different letter writers represented by this pile of mail.

There were three letters by Clarissa Northfield and two by Roxanne Scott. Two were by a priest with an Irish name, Father Peter O'Malley. The other two writers were men I'd talked to, one of whom denied he'd been blackmailed.

I never would have suspected Keith Bates, the director, was a victim of blackmail. And Gerald Fitzroy, chief reviewer for the *Daily Premier*, had lied to me when he said he wasn't being blackmailed by Frank Kennedy.

After I replaced the bottom of the wardrobe and put Kennedy's shoes and empty bottles back, I climbed up from the floor. I dusted myself off and then began to pick up all the letters as the door to the room opened. Christa Kennedy saw me before she saw her brother as she stared in anger at me. "What are you doing?"

"Christa, look." Dermot held up the legal document.

She didn't spare him a glance. "What are you doing?" she demanded, staring at me. "This is a private home. Give those to me."

"I am aware this is private property. I asked Dermot's perm—"

She cut me off. "This is not Dermot's house. It's Frank's, and you're in his bedroom."

"He's not in a position to complain, Christa," Dermot said softly.

She fired back at him, "All the more reason to protect his privacy."

"These didn't belong to him," I said and stared at her, holding the letters close to my chest.

"Of course they do. They're in Frank's room. Hand them over."

I looked at Dermot and raised my eyebrows.

He blew out all the air in his lungs. "Christa, you're not going to be happy about this."

"What?" she snapped, still not sparing him a glance.

"These letters weren't to or from your brother. He stole them from other people and then—used them," I said.

"Of course they were his."

"His name wasn't Roxanne Scott or Mary Lee, was it?" I asked, waving a letter in its envelope addressed by Miss Scott to Miss Lee.

"That must have been a mistake. He would have returned it if he'd known where to find the writer."

"Oh, he knew Roxanne, all right. He tormented her at Broadcasting House daily over these letters." I was glaring at Christa Kennedy now. "He tormented these other people, too."

"How do you know?" There was a hesitancy about her defiance now, as if she half expected her brother to turn out to have been a bad guy.

"I've spoken to them. They told me about their missing property and how your brother said he had it and he wouldn't return it."

"Oh, that doesn't sound like Frank..." Then she looked around the room. "Although it might explain..."

"Explain what?" This family was full of surprises.

Christa looked at Dermot, who answered. "While we

were out yesterday, someone broke into the house. They didn't take anything, which seemed strange. I reported it at the local police station, but they're so overwhelmed..."

"Did whoever it was search in here?"

"All over the house, I think. It seemed odd."

I nodded. Everything about this case seemed odd.

Dermot said to his sister, "Look what else was down there."

Christa turned to look at him, chewing on her lower lip.

"We found Frank's will. And look what it says. I get the house." He smiled at her. "We're going to be all right, Christa."

"What's the date on it?"

He grinned at her. "After the one giving the house to Patrick."

She smiled until she remembered my presence and then promptly scowled. "You shouldn't have been up here, moving Frank's possessions around, digging into our affairs."

"I didn't read the will. Your brother did. All I want is to return these letters to their owners."

"How do I know you're going to do that? Blackmail is disgusting. How do I know you're not a blackmailer?" She looked just as fierce as before she learned she wouldn't be homeless.

"I'm not. If you want, you can face these people and they can tell you how awful your brother was. How he was draining them of all the money he could squeeze out of them."

"Well, they shouldn't have written those terrible letters."

I faced her, unwilling to give an inch on this. "How do you know they were terrible? Did you read them? Did Frank share his blackmail material with you?"

"No." She looked horrified. "He wouldn't do that. Those are his."

"No, they're not. These were neither addressed to nor signed by him. And they were hidden where even your maid wouldn't find them."

"I can't explain it, but I'm certain you're wrong."

"Whatever you want to believe, there are people who will be grateful to get these back."

"The police should get them."

"So they can spread their secrets in the newspapers and all over the city?" I took a step toward her, the envelopes in my hands. "Do you want your secrets known to everyone in London?"

"You wouldn't," she whispered, her face chalky.

I took my loot and walked past her out of the room and down the stairs. For a moment, I wondered what she feared I would reveal.

At least, Christa didn't seem to be a victim of blackmail by Frank. She didn't have any money to give to her brother. Unlike his other victims.

Chapter Eight

The first thing I did was go home and copy all the correspondence. I tucked the copies away in an old trunk full of books that had belonged to Reggie, my late first husband, that was now kept in our storage unit in the basement of our building. I only partially understood why no one wanted these letters to see the light of day. Then I sat at the dining room table and read through the letters again.

Peter O'Malley's letters weren't incriminating in and of themselves. They were written to "My lady Althea," quoted various books of the Bible, and signed "Father Peter O'Malley." I was pretty sure the flowery nonsense contained a code. If it didn't, there was no reason to fear exposure.

Did O'Malley's Irish name proclaim his allegiance to the IRA? The IRA was blowing things up and hurting our war effort, so helping them was probably illegal.

So was prostitution, as I felt certain Roxanne Scott knew. So was homosexuality, as Gerald Fitzroy must have been aware. Even if it wasn't illegal, the courts would still take a dim view of adultery if Keith Bates's wife used these letters in divorce proceedings.

The puzzling letters were Clarissa's. They read as if she'd

taken part in a murder. Her aunt's murder. I reread them, wondering what I should do. Really, what I should do about any of them.

I decided to tell them not to worry about being blackmailed, that the letters Frank Kennedy had were destroyed. If they had nothing to do with his murder, those letters would be destroyed along with the copy.

If the police would need the letters to present in court to convict a murderer, they would be available for them. I hid them among the books that filled the shelves in the drawing room, thinking I could find a better place to stash them later.

I knew I couldn't reach the actors or director that night at Broadcasting House since the radio players never performed or rehearsed on Friday nights, but I might be able to find Gerald Fitzroy. It was a Friday night, and while there wasn't anything noteworthy happening at Broadcasting House, according to the morning *Daily Premier,* the Royal Albert Hall was having an orchestral gala.

Not something Gerald Fitzroy would miss.

I went to his house, thinking he would be putting on evening dress for the big occasion.

His butler or footman or valet or possibly all three made me wait out in the cold on the front steps until Mr. Fitzroy was ready to go out. When he did appear, others were walking along the pavement, which meant his tiny front garden was not a place to discuss blackmail. "You might want to carry on a conversation about your correspondence in a more private location."

"Very well." His voice was sardonic, but he'd paled when I said he'd want to speak to me privately. He had an idea what the subject would be.

We stepped back onto his front step and then inside the alcove between the outer and inner front doors. I said, "Frank Kennedy had some letters of yours. Letters his brother and I found and destroyed. You're not in danger of anyone blackmailing you again."

He said, "I don't know what you mean," in a feeble tone.

"Oh, please. We read them before we destroyed them, in case they were not meant to be blackmail, but were deeds or something."

"Are you sure they were destroyed?" Fitzroy was whispering now.

"Burnt to a crisp."

"You saw them turned to ashes?"

"Yes."

His expression turned hard. "You should have let me do that."

"Well, we didn't. You're safe, and that's all that's important."

"I won't go to jail," he told me, trying to look fearsome. He was short and thin and definitely out of shape, ruining any threat he might be attempting to convey.

"I don't want you to go to jail. Besides, it's such a waste of time and manpower when we can use every Englishman to help repel the invasion we all face." I wasn't going to explain that after knowing Reggie so well and dealing with spies, I found there were more important crimes to incarcerate people for.

"If we win, the government wants to put me in jail. If we lose, the Germans want me in a concentration camp. Either way, I can't risk anyone knowing. Anyone talking."

"Nobody's going to bother. Nobody really cares," I nearly shouted at him before I thought about where I was. "Your secret is safe. Just don't write any more to your lovers. Especially the male ones. You put yourself in danger that way."

"How do I know you burned them all?" He still tried to sound threatening, and failed miserably.

"We burned three letters signed by you."

He thought for a moment. "There might have been more."

"I don't think so." He sounded paranoid to me. "Just wait. If you don't hear from anyone else, you'll know you're safe."

"What about Kennedy's brother?"

"He didn't read the letters. He helped me find them, but he didn't know anyone involved and he wanted to keep it that way."

"That doesn't sound as if he were a relative of Frank Kennedy."

I shook my head. "His siblings don't seem to have much in common with Frank. When I suggested we burn the letters, he agreed. He didn't want to touch them."

"You were the one who burned them?" He was flexing

his fists, crowding me.

"Yes." Fitzroy was beginning to make me nervous. I could picture him running a knife into someone when he was worked up the way he was at that moment.

He took an additional step forward, clipping my shoe in the small space. "If I get another blackmail threat, I'm coming after you."

I was looking down a little on him, which should have made his actions meaningless. Somehow, he still managed to scare me. "You won't get any from me about those letters. I don't know who else you wrote to, but you can be certain the incriminating letters we found in Frank's possession have been destroyed."

"Then stay away from me." Fitzroy brushed past me and strode, despite his limp, out the door, down the stairs with the wrought iron railings, and along the pavement toward the Royal Albert Hall.

It had been dark out for quite a while when I finally reached Broadcasting House at nearly seven and went to the chamber music room. The area was dark and empty.

I wandered around the floor and finally found an engineer, who told me they'd finished at six-thirty and all the musicians had left immediately afterward.

I'd have to wait until Monday afternoon to speak to Roxanne.

I went back to the flat to dress for dinner at Sir Henry's but walked in to a surprise. Adam was home!

When we came up for air, he said, "I have until Tuesday

morning. The men with kiddies got Christmas, and those of us without get New Year's."

"I was supposed to have dinner at Sir Henry's. Shall I cancel, or shall I ask if you can come along?"

"A dinner cooked by a real chef and not an army cook? See if you can get me an invite." He let me go so I could reach the telephone in the hallway.

When I reached Sir Henry and explained my dilemma, his hearty voice boomed through the phone. "Excellent. This will even up the numbers. Bring him along, please. How is our Captain Redmond?"

"Delightful as always." I smiled at my husband and he winked back.

We dressed for dinner, something I found I was getting out of the habit of doing. Either I brought in fish and chips or a piece of cheese and an apple, or I wore the suit I dressed in for work to eat in a local restaurant. I only dressed for dinner at someone's dinner party or on Sundays when I ate out with my father at a hotel restaurant.

Adam was equally out of the habit of wearing civilian dress, but he appeared thrilled to be wearing something other than his uniform.

We took a cab to Sir Henry's large home, both of us cringing at the cost now that the government needed most of the available fuel. Once the maid let us in, we handed off our coats and hats and went in to get a hug from Esther. She looked as slim and elegant in a silvery evening gown as her father looked round and rumpled despite his evening attire.

"Livvy," Esther said, "I didn't think I'd ever get to see you this holiday season. And Adam. I'm so glad they let you off for a little while. James has had the whole week off."

After I greeted James, he and Adam shook hands and complimented each other on escaping their uniforms for a few hours. As much as I wanted peace, soldiers must want it so much more. The lack of fighting in this phony war probably preyed on their nerves more than mine. I was just glad there wasn't any danger at the moment.

Besides the four of us and Sir Henry, there was the elderly widow of a conductor and Ed and Janet Murrow. "I didn't know you knew Sir Henry," I said after I got over my initial shock.

"We only met yesterday, but when I said I wanted to discuss London and the war, Sir Henry was kind enough to invite us tonight," Ed Murrow told us.

If I thought he looked handsome in a suit while broadcasting, he looked even better in evening wear. Not as good as Adam, of course. He had his blond hair cut shorter than I was used to, but with his hazel eyes smiling whenever he looked at me, Adam would always be the best-looking man in any crowd. Still, I'm sure Ed Murrow turned lots of heads.

"Thank you again for going with me on that condolence call," Janet said. Her long-sleeved green gown was stylish, but her husband was the one who caught everyone's eye with his good looks and outsize personality.

"I was glad to do it," I replied. She had no idea how glad,

since it made my task earlier that day at the Kennedy house a little easier.

We went into the dining room to find more greenery on the table and over the doorways and on the mantel. Candlelight gave dinner an old-fashioned charm as it was reflected back from the crystal wine glasses, gleaming white linens, and antique French mirrors.

"Your grandson has taken to hiding in cabinets and frightening us all when we can't find him," Esther told her father.

Sir Henry said, "My Johnny would never misbehave. I'm sure he is as good a child as I was." Then he laughed uproariously.

"I believe he is," his son-in-law James replied and gave Sir Henry a smile.

The food was prepared well, but the quality of the ingredients wasn't quite as good as before the war. Not bad, just not up to Sir Henry's usual standards for a dinner party. Blander, for one thing, since spices were getting harder to come by.

Even here, I could see little changes due to the war. I suspected it was more than just the differences we saw every winter.

Adam didn't seem to notice, but he didn't eat here as often as I did. We all, even the widow of the conductor, talked about the changes we'd seen in London since the war had begun. Ed Murrow wasn't writing down notes, but I felt certain he was paying attention to everything we said.

"What do the Americans make of your broadcasts?" I asked him. "I know since we've gone to war that you've been painting word pictures of England for your listeners in the United States. What do they think?"

"Individually, they sympathize, they're heartened, they wish you well. But as a country, they are a long way from coming to your aid. They have no intention of leaving their neutrality."

"They may find the ocean isn't as wide as they think," Sir Henry said.

"As they hope," Janet Murrow added. "I don't know what it will take to shake them out of their certainty that this has nothing to do with them."

"And in the meantime," James Powell said, "things will only get worse here." He looked at his wife, Esther, with such love and fear in his eyes I felt as if I were a peeping Tom.

Esther's late mother had been Jewish. If the Germans invaded, she and the children would be in danger. We weren't in a shooting war yet, but James had every reason to worry.

In the last two years, I'd been to Germany and Austria helping Esther's mother's relatives and other Jews escape. I'd seen evidence that James had every right to be frightened on behalf of his family.

Everyone in England, deep down, feared an invasion by the Nazis.

We talked of how the shops had changed in just four months, our hopes for 1940, which would begin in little more than forty-eight hours, and how tiny a chance we could see for peace in the coming year.

Murrow asked Adam about the army and how ready they felt.

"I don't think I can answer any of your questions," Adam immediately replied.

"Why not?" Murrow asked, sounding as if he genuinely wanted to know.

"I'm a serving officer in the British army. If I say anything that might be construed as giving aid and comfort to the enemy, I'll spend the war in a jail cell or I'll be shot. You're an American. Your country is still neutral. Ask me again after the United States gets into this war." Adam grinned at him. "But I think by then you'll already understand."

"Will you serve if America goes to war?" I asked the broadcaster.

"I imagine I'll be drafted," Ed Murrow said, "but I expect I'll be doing some sort of broadcasting work for our army."

"And you, Janet? Will you stay if England finds itself directly in the line of fire?" Esther asked.

"I have a feeling it will be safer to stay than to cross the Atlantic," Janet Murrow replied with a nod.

As the soup bowls were collected and we went on to the fish course and the main course, we covered the general topics that everyone was discussing. When would Hitler strike? What was the cabinet thinking? Would the King stay in Buckingham Palace or leave for Balmoral in the highlands of Scotland? Or Canada? How would the war between the

British navy and the German U-boats end?

By the time we reached coffee and dessert, the women were discussing Esther's two young children, who were at home about a mile away, and the conductor's widow's school-aged grandchildren, who were in Switzerland. Janet was an aunt, so she had something to bring to the conversation. I had little to add since I hadn't seen Sir John and Abby Summersby's boys in two months.

We left the table and went into the drawing room for drinks and coffee, where we broke into smaller groups to talk. Janet pulled me aside. "Derek Coward said he saw you at Broadcasting House yesterday afternoon. You remember Derek?"

"The engineer. Yes. He seems to be a very nice young man."

"He saw you coming out of the restaurant in the basement. He thought you might have been looking for me."

"No. I was just having a cup of tea. I'm sorry I didn't see him. I would have stopped and spoken to him if I had." How much longer would I be able to avoid saying anything about why I was there?

"I didn't think you'd have been looking for me at Broadcasting House at that time of day. Ed is still working at home until much later to match New York time."

"That has to make for long days, or should I say, long evenings." I could sense the question coming that I wasn't sure I could answer.

Janet studied me for a moment and then asked, "I

learned you have quite a reputation for solving crimes. Are you investigating Frank Kennedy's murder?"

Chapter Nine

"Why would you think that?" I looked at Janet with what I hoped was an innocent expression.

"Ed did some asking around about you. You have a reputation for solving murders, starting with your first husband's."

Ed Murrow was a reporter looking for a story. I couldn't ever forget that. Especially since this was not a story I wanted announced all over. "I do not want to become a story on your husband's radio show. Even unnamed." Sir Malcolm would kill me.

"He hasn't, and he won't. I told him you were my friend and off limits." Janet gave me a small smile. "But I feel sorry for Christa Kennedy. Losing her brother. Maybe losing her home—"

"I helped her brother Dermot search Frank's room. We found a will hidden in there that gives the house to Dermot, who seems pretty determined to keep Christa in her home. I hope they'll both be all right."

"She seemed to think the sun rose and set on Frank," Janet said. "I hope you haven't said anything to ruin her memories of him."

I stared at her. I felt guilty about what I'd been forced to tell Christa about the blackmail.

"I see," Janet said with a small nod. "Well, is there anything I can do to help you find his killer?" When I didn't immediately respond, she added, "I think Christa will be glad to see her brother's murder avenged."

"If I find something you can help me with, I'll let you know." When I saw her hurt expression, I added, "I've just started, and already this investigation is going in various directions. For right now, keep your ears open for anything said about Kennedy at Broadcasting House. Oh, or about someone named Peter O'Malley."

"Who's he?"

"I don't know, but I'm afraid he's involved in the IRA and was possibly a friend of Frank Kennedy's and is possibly a priest. The IRA is dangerous. Don't mention him, just listen for the name and anything said about him."

"Do you think he's the killer?"

"Not any more than a dozen other people. However, the IRA are killers. I don't want you putting yourself, or me, in any danger."

"What are you girls doing whispering in the corner?" Ed Murrow said as he joined his wife and me.

"I'm learning some ways to get around the rationing that starts on the eighth of January. If you want to continue to eat well, you will disappear," Janet told him and then smiled brightly.

Fortunately, Ed didn't see the expression on Adam's face. He knew that wasn't true, which made him wonder what we were talking about. He knew about my investigations. He wasn't happy about them, but he wouldn't try to stop me.

Adam knew I wouldn't shop on the black market, because I only broke laws and rules when I had an overpowering reason. A little extra butter wasn't a reason I cared about, especially since I ate out as often as possible and restaurants had different rationing rules.

He came over and I heard him say to Ed, "I hope you didn't think I was being rude about your questions. There are things I simply can't talk about because of my position."

"Not at all." Ed smiled as if his questions were all part of a game. "I had to try, I'm a reporter, but being told no never bothers me. If it did, I wouldn't last long in my job."

"What are you doing New Year's Eve?" Adam asked. I supposed that was to show there were no hard feelings.

"Any suggestions?"

"Livvy and I are going to one of the nightclubs to go dancing." Adam turned to me. "At least I think we are."

"I hope so," I said. "Although it will seem strange celebrating the New Year in the dark, what with the blackout and all."

"But it'll be fun to get dressed up and go dancing," Janet said with enthusiasm.

"I can take you dancing tomorrow night," Ed Murrow said, "but New Year's Eve I'll be broadcasting from a hotel ballroom and there won't be any time for dancing. Not by me."

"You've never been fond of dancing at any time," his wife replied.

I had to add my bit of local knowledge. "There is ordinarily a service of sorts on the steps of St. Paul's Cathedral at about two on New Year's morning, but this year, the police will be dispersing any group that tries to assemble there. The police are afraid they'll make too much noise and confuse the air raid wardens."

"That must be some good hymn singing if it can be mistaken for an air raid," Murrow said with a laugh.

The Murrows, Esther and James Powell, and the conductor's widow left soon after, at which point Sir Henry said, "You don't mind if I confer with your wife for a few minutes, do you, Adam?"

Adam smiled as he walked over and sat in front of the fire. "Talk all you want. I'll be comfortable here. Wake me up when you're ready to go home."

Sir Henry and I moved to his study. "I've heard rumors that the body you tripped over was involved with the IRA."

"I've heard those same rumors. I've also heard rumors he was a bully and a blackmailer. A thoroughly rotten individual, but there's no proof of any of this that I've found." I hated lying to Sir Henry, but I had to because of the Official Secrets Act.

I suspected Sir Henry also knew I was lying. He always seemed to. I guess he knew me too well. "Have you found anything I can print?"

"No. Nothing. If I find a link to the IRA, I'll let you know what I can as soon as I can."

"You can't say fairer than that," Sir Henry said. "Any idea when you'll be back to the *Daily Premier*?"

I shook my head. "And if I may wish you a peaceful and prosperous 1940, I'd better get my poor husband off to bed."

"How's he doing?"

"All right, so far. This phony war is wearing on his nerves more than on ours, I imagine. When the shooting starts, he'll be in danger every second until peace is declared." I choked out the last few words and blinked back tears.

I had to put on a brave front for Adam. I suspected he did the same for me.

* * *

We had a quiet morning the next day and then went to the cinema. We returned home in time for me to promise Adam I'd be back as soon as I carried out one interview that couldn't wait. I was sorry I could only tell him "Official Secrets Act" when he asked what I was investigating.

"Sir Malcolm. Of course," he grumbled.

There wasn't anything I could say to make the situation better. I hurried over to Broadcasting House and rode the lift to the sixth floor. When I reached the broadcast theater, the director, Keith Bates, was one of the few people there. "May I have a private word with you?" I asked him in a quiet tone.

He nodded and walked out into the hallway. "We have to make this quick. We go live in half an hour," he told me.

"This won't take long. I found where Frank Kennedy was hiding your correspondence. The letters have been destroyed."

Relief flashed across his face followed by doubt. "How can I be certain?"

"Probably when you won't get any more demands for money or whatever he wanted."

"Money. With Frank it was always money."

"Why did you write those letters?"

He leaned against the wall and lit a cigarette. "I don't know. I really don't know anymore. I haven't seen her in ages."

"Who was she, and when did you write the letters?"

"Last year. Before the war. I was directing a touring company with a two-week stop in Leeds and another in Manchester. She was one of the actors. She took me over body and soul as if she were the flu. I was powerless against it. I even offered to leave my wife for her." He shook his head. "I was a fool."

I could see where this was going. "She broke it off?"

He nodded. "She met the backer of our tour. A middle-aged, titled, wealthy man. Within a day, we had broken off our relationship and she was on his arm."

"He wasn't married?"

"Oh, yes, he was, still is, but his wife has no desire to spend time with him. He's set my friend up quite well. Theater roles, a nice flat. She's done quite well. Much better than if she'd stayed with me."

"And she sold Frank Kennedy your letters to her." She seemed as odious as Kennedy, and as grubby.

"She swears they were stolen. I don't know. I can't prove anything."

"Where do you and your wife stand?"

He grimaced and put out his cigarette on the tile floor under his shoe. "On shaky ground. I had to pay. If he'd shown them to my wife, I'd never see my children again."

"A good reason for murder."

"I didn't kill him," he said in a raised voice. He glanced around and then added in a quieter tone, "With him dead, I would have guessed Mimi would find the letters, and then she'd start blackmailing me. There was no reason to think I'd be any better off having him dead."

"Do you think Mimi killed him?"

"No." He considered a moment. "Blackmail? Sure. Theft? Yes. But not murder. That's quite a big step." After another moment, he said, "Unless it was an accident. She and Frank were both physical. Expressive. Frank was pretty handy with his fists. She might have killed him trying to defend herself."

"But then why not tell someone? Scream? Why leave him there and walk off?"

"Fear of hanging. It was night, wasn't it? Dark out? I'd have walked away if I could under those circumstances. Why wouldn't Mimi?"

"Would you say the same thing of Clarissa Northfield or Paul White?"

"Clarissa would panic over a spilled cup of coffee. Paul has a cool head. He'd walk away, I'm sure, whether it was an accident or deliberate. And I'm not sure which it would be if

Paul was the killer."

"But you don't think Clarissa would walk away?"

"She'd be too busy being hysterical. She's a sweet, innocent girl, without an ounce of nerve. If anything goes wrong, she breaks down and cries."

I remembered the content of the letters she was blackmailed over. She appeared to be anything but innocent, but that might have been a side of her she showed while she dealt with her relatives and a murder. Innocent, sheltered, and quiet was certainly the character she displayed now, on the radio and in life.

I'd have to get her alone to question her more closely about Frank Kennedy and his death. That would be the only way I could get her to drop what I now suspected was an act and find out the truth. "I need to talk to Clarissa on her own. When would be the best time?"

"You really don't think—"

"I have to remove the unlikely suspects before I can get to the truth."

"I saw her go into our stage with Paul a few minutes ago. I'll keep him busy while you talk to her."

"Thank you."

We went inside and Bates called Paul White over to go through a section of the script for that evening's broadcast. I tried to herd Clarissa out into the hall. Not a hard trick, since she must have known what subject we would discuss.

"Did you act in Yorkshire?"

"Yes, in Leeds."

"In your aunt's theater?"

"It wasn't hers, but she wouldn't have believed that. She figured the money she put in made her the final decision maker, and she was loud enough and pushy enough that no one could stand up against her."

"Please, we don't have much time to talk. Was it in that theater?"

Clarissa nodded, giving me her best sweet expression. "Aunt Althea got me involved in the theater in Leeds that she was a patron of."

"And her murder. Were you involved in the investigation?"

"How could I not get involved in her murder? She was part of my family and the police were constantly around asking questions. Prying, showing up at our doors at all hours. I couldn't wait to get away to London." She shivered delicately.

I wondered if this Althea was the same woman Peter O'Malley had been writing to.

"Where were you at eleven Tuesday night? Boxing Day Night."

"As it happens, when I arrived home from Broadcasting House, they were having a party at my rooming house. We were having cocoa and hearing about the family Christmas celebrations of some of the girls who live there. The ones who got away for Christmas." She gave me a big smile. "I couldn't have killed Frank."

"So you weren't with Paul?"

Her voice and attitude changed. I found myself looking at a woman of the world. "We don't live in each other's hip pockets. I have no idea where he was. Nor do I care. It makes no difference to me as long as I have an alibi. And I no longer have to pay blackmail for my family's murderous tendencies."

She swung around toward the door to the studio, seeing what I'd already seen. Paul White was staring at her with a mixture of sorrow and fury. He turned his back on her and limped back into the studio, leaning on his crutches.

Clarissa turned and looked at me with an expression of horror. "How long was he standing there?"

I shrugged.

She rushed to the studio door.

"Wait," I called after her. "I still need to tell you..."

I wanted to tell her I'd destroyed her letters. She needed to know. "Your letters are gone..."

I was too late. She had already hurried inside.

Chapter Ten

I slipped inside the studio and looked around. Keith Bates was checking over the script and glancing up to confirm if the actors for the various parts were in the room. Clarissa, having been outspoken in her disdain for Paul, was now whispering in his ear, forcing him to move about the studio in an effort to get away from her.

"Right. Mimi is officially late. Sarah, read Mimi's part as well as your own. Everyone ready? Begin," Bates said as Mimi dashed in. "I've had it with you being tardy," he told her.

"With transit foul-ups and the blackout, you can't get anywhere on time in this city," Mimi responded as she dashed over to Sarah and took her script.

I stayed for a few minutes by the doorway and listened. The players sounded flawless. Nothing showed that Mimi had run into the room at the last moment or that Paul and Clarissa had had a falling-out.

After a few minutes, I left as quietly as I could.

Adam and I went out to dinner. It was then he told me about his plans for the next night, New Year's Eve. "A couple of my fellow officers and their wives, and the two of us, are going to the nightclub set up in the ballroom of the Hamilton Hotel. They're from out of town and staying at the hotel, so I thought we would, too. As a treat, so we don't have to find our way home in the middle of the night since the buses and trains won't be running that late, the blackout is on, and it would be too far to walk in your dancing shoes."

My opinion that my husband was the most romantic man ever only strengthened.

He told me a little about his colleagues and practically nothing about their wives, since he'd not met them. I'd have to make my own impressions of these people. Adam was keen that I meet them, and that was the important bit.

The next day, we met my father at his favorite hotel dining room where we met once a week to prove we were still alive. Otherwise, we tried to never contact each other. My father was overjoyed to see Adam, and only talked to him. Once again, I was reminded that my father had wanted a son.

There had been no changes in the food or the décor in this dining room. The clientele still looked as elegant, bejeweled, and well fed as they had before war was declared. The tablecloths were as snowy white, the chandeliers as sparklingly free of dust, and the waiters moving as silently as they ever had.

Adam thanked my father for taking us to eat at such a pleasant restaurant.

My father said, "It's to remind you of what you are fighting to preserve."

Adam glanced at me and said, "No. Hitler reminds me of that every time he opens his mouth."

The rest of the meal was frosty. I waited until we had said our goodbyes before I told Adam how proud I was of him.

"I didn't say that to annoy him, Liv. I believe we're fighting for a great deal more than white linen tablecloths and five-course meals." He took my hand and gave it a squeeze. "If you ever need your father, I hope you won't be too proud to go to him and ask for help."

"I hope it never comes to that."

Once we returned home, we dressed in our best evening wear, which meant my bias-cut, sleeveless, deep green satin with the scooped back, packed our overnight bags, and took the Underground to the stop across the road and down to the next crossroads from the hotel. My evening cape hid a good deal of my evening gown, but there was enough showing that we would have drawn strange looks on any other night. On New Year's Eve, no one gave us a second glance.

Half the people we passed were dressed in evening wear and shouting holiday greetings to everyone nearby.

At the hotel, I waited with Adam while he signed us in, and almost immediately after, we were joined by three men and two women.

I was introduced before Adam could say we'd drop off our things in our room and be right back down. They said they'd wait for us by the dining room and we hurried up in the lift.

"Somebody's wife was missing," I said.

"Oh, Miles. He's not married."

"Won't he feel a little bored with us married couples?"

"Not Miles. And he won't be alone for long. Just watch."

The seven of us enjoyed a leisurely dinner in the festively decorated hotel dining room with champagne and painted domino masks, courtesy of the hotel and the hefty price tag I'm sure went with our meal.

I learned Rob and Eileen Thompson had been married in late 1938 after he had come back from some secret mission for the army. Whenever it was mentioned, the guys put on very blank expressions that didn't fool any of us for a second. From my work with Sir Malcolm, I knew the mission had been either illegal or bloody. Probably both. Eileen had come down from York for the weekend to join Rob for his leave.

Jack and Marcie Quinn came from some unpronounceable town in Wales where they'd been married the preceding spring and where she still lived.

Miles didn't claim any life before university, and didn't reveal many details. I realized when he mentioned the Mathematical Bridge that he must have attended Cambridge, followed by the army. I suspected from his accent that his family was upper crust, but he steered all talk about him away to another topic. Any other topic.

It was nice to see us all in civilian formal evening wear. I had the feeling in the back of my mind that this would be the last time we'd all be dressed up as civilians out enjoying the evening for a very long time. I pushed the feeling away.

Eileen, Marcie, and I laughed about the amount of sugar, butter, and meat that went into our dinner, since rationing would begin on the eighth of January and we knew we wouldn't taste anything as rich as this for a long time. The men, all normally eating in the officers' mess and unaware of rationing, had no idea why we were laughing.

After dinner, we went into the nightclub set up in the ballroom. The lighting and the acoustics were all wrong for a nightclub, being too bright and not noisy or smoky enough, but the jazz orchestra they had put together was fabulous. The people coming in were a young crowd. There was plenty of room to dance, and dance we did.

Then the lights dimmed, the noise and smoke level rose, and the party began in earnest.

When I whispered into Adam's ear that maybe I should dance with Miles so he wouldn't feel left out, he said for me to wait. Half an hour later, Miles returned to our table with a young blonde in a slightly worn, pale blue gown.

She had her hair swept up and she wore blue glass jewels strung with silver around her neck, but she was definitely the Roxanne Scott who was a violinist with the Broadcasting House chamber orchestra. Roxanne with the letters about a career in prostitution that had been used by Frank Kennedy for blackmail.

I recognized her before Miles began introducing her around the table. When she saw me, she took a half-step backward and said to Miles, "Let's dance."

He led her out onto the dance floor.

Adam asked quietly, "What happened with her? One of your investigations?"

"The current one."

He growled at me with a disgusted expression. "No working tonight."

I had to practically shout in his ear, since the room was now very loud with music and laughter. "I didn't go looking for her."

"I mean it. Not one word."

There was nothing else I could do. I didn't want to lie, and I didn't want to fight. "Let's dance."

When we returned after a few dances, Miles and Roxanne were sitting at the other end of the string of tiny tables we had commandeered. Too far away for me to be able to speak to her or hear what she said.

But I could observe her. She was getting along well with Miles, who seemed to treat her better than Frank Kennedy had. She appeared pleasant and fun-loving, a perfectly normal young woman. Once again, I hoped the IRA was behind the murder.

The gaiety went on well past midnight. I knew pubs had been given special approval to stay open until twelve-fifteen, since New Year's Eve was a Sunday night. However, private gatherings held in, and by, nightclubs and hotels could stay open much later. The Hamilton called for last orders a few minutes before two in the morning. Shortly after that, the dance orchestra went into a final, long, frenzied tune that we all danced to. As they concluded, with the band leader wishing us a peaceful and prosperous 1940, all the lights again shone brightly. The magic vanished. The musicians began packing up and the waiters hurried to clear empty glasses and full ashtrays.

Miles seemed to be trying to convince Roxanne of something, to which she shook her head. She gestured toward the bandstand, picked up her tiny bag, and walked away. She turned back once and looked at him with regret in her eyes. He called after her but she turned away with slumped shoulders.

Miles watched as she joined the orchestra. A trumpet player gestured to her to carry the sheet music without giving her a glance. She did as she was told. No one in the orchestra spoke to her.

I walked over to Miles. "She came with one of the musicians?"

"The trumpet player. Her brother."

She'd told me she had no family in London. Which one of us had she been lying to?

The fellows seemed to be ready to party longer, even if the wives were tired. At three, we finally went upstairs from the lobby to our rooms with promises to meet for breakfast.

We met in the restaurant about nine-thirty the next morning, or rather that morning, with all of us in good spirits except Miles. Having met Adam's colleagues and their wives in evening wear, it was a jolt to see them in day wear, and the Welsh couple in slightly old-fashioned day wear at that.

I was sitting next to Miles at our large table. I asked, "Why do you look so glum? Nineteen forty may turn out to be a great year."

"Do you truly believe that?"

"Well, it's possible," I said, feeling cornered. We were at war, but not really. It could become peace if it didn't turn into all-out war.

"And there's Roxanne. I feel as if I've known her all my life, but I know nothing about her. It feels so unsettled. So unfinished." Looking downhearted, Miles stirred his coffee.

"She didn't tell you where to reach her?"

"She wanted to. I could tell. But she said it would be better if I just forgot about her."

"Did she tell you she's a violinist?"

"Yes, but do you know how many violinists live in London?" He sank his head into his hands.

"How many play for the BBC Chamber Orchestra?"

He looked up at me and I smiled.

"How do you know that?" he demanded.

"I was doing a piece on the wife of an American broadcaster who uses the BBC facilities. I met Roxanne while I was at Broadcasting House." That certainly left out a lot of details, such as murder and blackmail.

Miles didn't seem to notice. "Could you get a message to her?"

"I suppose, but what's so special about Roxanne? There must be hundreds of girls out there who would fall at your feet." I thought Miles was quite handsome and a good talker and a good dancer. Maybe not as good as Adam, but still good.

"I don't know. Maybe we'd end up hating each other." He shrugged. "But there's something about her. Something mysterious. Intriguing. I'll write up a note for her right after breakfast. You'll give it to her, won't you?"

"Of course. I don't guarantee she'll respond, but I'll deliver your message."

"Why wouldn't she?" Miles asked, his cheery demeanor returning.

Why was she so hesitant to tell him anything as basic as where she worked? Especially since she had looked at him so wistfully when she left him. The young blackmail victim was hiding something besides her former career. I needed to talk to her.

* * *

Once we returned to the flat, Adam and I took a long walk in the cold New Year's air. A lot of people were doing the same thing, walking around the parks, enjoying the sunshine, and pretending we were at peace. The pretense was difficult since deep trenches had been dug into the park lawn. Now they were protected by sandbags and the turf was spread over the top in huge ridges.

As we stood looking over a lake, Adam sighed.

"What are you thinking, dearest?"

"I was wondering how long it could be until I see all this, see London, again."

I squeezed his arm a little harder. There was nothing I could say. The only answer was to be there. To always be there.

"Thank you for not pushing Roxanne last night."

I was surprised at his words. "What?"

"Roxanne is a suspect or a witness or something to you, but I have to trust Miles, and Rob and Jack, with my life until this war is over. Thank you for not making that difficult for us."

"I wouldn't, darling. Never." It was hard to talk with my heart in my throat. I had to be careful not to complicate Adam's life. That was the last thing I wanted to do.

"What did Miles give you?"

"A note to pass to Roxanne."

"Will you?"

"Of course. I told him I couldn't promise that she'd answer, but I would give it to her." From the longing look she had given him as she left us the night before, I was sure she would answer.

He nodded. "Did you read it?"

"No. And I won't."

I don't know how long we stood there in silence until I heard, "Livvy. Adam. Hello," in an American accent.

Turning my head, I saw Janet and Ed Murrow had almost reached us.

"Gorgeous day, isn't it?" I asked.

"It is. We've been enjoying the sunny weather," Janet replied.

We chatted a minute before Ed said, "How long until you go back?"

"In the morning," Adam replied. His voice sounded stiff.

"How long until you get leave again?"

"That depends on Herr Hitler."

"I wish you luck." Ed Murrow held out his hand, and Adam shook it. Murrow then neatly steered his wife away as she and I called goodbye.

It was growing dark and windy and the blackout had begun by the time we reached our building.

"It looks like they've painted every curb in London white," Adam muttered, glancing around.

"I'm grateful for it," I told him. The white paint on the curbs had been added after the blackout began to help pedestrians negotiate at night without lights.

We went up to our flat, discussing which local restaurant we wanted to eat at.

We'd only been inside for a few minutes when the telephone rang. I picked it up on the second ring, hoping Adam wouldn't be called back in early.

"Olivia, I need you to go to Clapham," Sir Malcolm's voice boomed out of the receiver at me.

"Why? When?" If I sounded startled, it was because I was. My thoughts had all been on Adam.

"Right away. The police are in Mimi's rooming house and I want you down there to find out what they've discovered."

"Tomorrow. Adam goes back to his unit tomorrow morning and I'll be all yours then." I only had my husband for a few more hours. I wasn't going to leave him.

"I need you down there now. Mimi's been murdered. Stabbed, the same as Kennedy. I want to know if she was killed by the same person who killed Kennedy. If the police have any leads." He sounded threatening. He rattled off her address and I wrote it on the back of an envelope.

"Tomorrow morning, I'll go down and see what I can learn." I put a cheery note in my voice.

"Now." He made it sound as if it were the final word.

It wasn't. I decided the worst that could happen was Sir Malcolm would fire me. I enjoyed my work for him, but I seldom got to spend time with Adam. "She'll still be dead tomorrow, and I can't learn anything tonight I won't learn tomorrow. Now, I am spending the evening with my husband. Good night, Sir Malcolm."

Adam was standing in the hallway as I hung up the receiver. "Can you do that? Refuse an order?"

Chapter Eleven

"I can this time. I just better not try it again for the next, say, hundred years," I told him.

"I don't want to get you into trouble." Adam watched me closely. He knew how much my job meant to me.

"You're only here one more night this visit. I'm not going to waste it on a corpse." I walked up to him and put my arms around his neck. "So, what shall we do tonight?"

Adam smiled.

* * *

After a fond farewell and a hearty breakfast, I saw Adam off on his train. We held hands on the platform the whole way to the door to his carriage. Then we lingered until the last moment, when Adam gave me a quick kiss and hurried aboard. I stood on the platform and watched as the train left the station until it took a bend in the tracks and disappeared from sight.

Then I took a deep breath, fought back my tears, and traveled to Clapham. The whole way there, I blamed myself for Mimi's death. I'd only told two of the five blackmail victims that their letters had been destroyed, Gerald Fitzroy and Keith Bates. Well, maybe three if Clarissa had heard me tell her I had found her letters and had destroyed them. The remaining two would definitely have a reason to learn if Mimi had the letters since they weren't in Kennedy's locker or in his house and I hadn't told them the letters had been destroyed.

Mimi's blood was on my hands for not moving faster.

How did Sir Malcolm live with himself after all the possibly wrong decisions he must have made in his career?

I found Mimi's boarding house was a semidetached on a tired street of tall Victorian red brick houses that loomed over the tiny front gardens. Her front door, I thought, had once been blue. Now it was a dirty beige, the color of every other door on both sides of the street.

When I knocked, a woman in her mid-twenties answered. "We're not talking to reporters."

Was I that obviously with the *Daily Premier?* "No. I had an appointment with Mimi this morning. And then I read she was murdered. Is it true?" I widened my eyes to look surprised. Actually, I was surprised at how fast the lie had sprung to my lips.

The woman, a dyed redhead, softened slightly. "It's true. So, what's your interest then?"

"Mimi's fiancé's brother asked me to talk to her." I looked at the woman. "He was murdered, too. Her fiancé, I mean." I looked up and down the street. "May I come in?"

She paused, then opened the door wider. "Sure. I'm Trixie Enlow."

"Livvy Redmond. What happened to Mimi? All I know is

what I read in the morning newspapers."

"Apparently, she let someone in and took them up to her room. New Year's Eve, when everyone was either celebrating or performing."

When I looked blank, Trixie continued. "This is a performing artists' boarding house. Dancers, actresses, musicians, and all women. I'm a dancer at the Olympian. Our landlady was an actress before she inherited a little money and bought this place. Anyway, Mimi must have been here alone when whoever came in, killed her, and searched her room. Made a right mess of it."

"And no one heard a thing?"

"Nothing. We didn't even know she was in there, and dead, until yesterday afternoon when I went in to borrow an eyeliner pencil."

She shuddered, and I understood what a shock it must have been.

"I'm sorry. That had to be awful."

She nodded.

"Any idea when everyone had left for the evening?" I hoped I could learn a few details. The question was, would the answers help?

"I left at six and I was about the last one to leave. We did two shows on New Year's Eve. Usually, we get a rest on Sundays, but not this past Sunday since it was New Year's Eve. I'm exhausted already, and it's only Tuesday."

"Did you hear Mimi go out?"

Trixie scowled for a moment. "I think so, but I couldn't

swear to it. There were lots of shouts of 'Happy New Year' as the girls left. Come to think of it, when I left and called out, no one replied." She smiled reluctantly. "So, I must have been the last one out and Mimi had already left."

"And when did everyone return?"

"Oh, I see. You're trying to narrow down the time when Mimi must have been killed." She nodded, not looking at all surprised. Did I look as if I had an official reason to ask, or did she not mind nosy people?

"It could be helpful," I told her.

"Some of the dancers and I went out to grab a bite and a drink after the last show. I got back here a little before two, and I heard our landlady talking in her flat to one of the other girls. I'd guess no one returned until after midnight because none of the shows would have ended before then."

"And hopefully, no one's date ended before midnight, either," I said, meaning the comment to be jovial.

"I haven't heard of anyone breaking up that night," Trixie said with complete seriousness. "And we all would have heard. I heard the police say they think she was killed early evening."

"Mimi could have been killed any time in that six-hour window," I said. "But why did she return? Do you know what she had planned for New Year's Eve?"

"She had a panto in the afternoon. I saw her after that because she had an evening performance—you know, scenes and things, with an acting troupe at a large private party, and she wanted to know if she could borrow my red scarf."

"Did she take your red scarf with her?"

"Yes. Well, I thought so, but it was in her room when I found her." Trixie appeared doubtful.

"When was she supposed to return?"

"She told me the group was booked from seven fifteen until eleven forty-five. Restoration comedy and Victorian Christmas cheer. She said the party would be lavish and they'd been promised to be fed well besides their pay. The promise of good food would assure that Mimi would be on time."

"She seemed to arrive at the last minute for her rehearsals with the BBC group," I told her.

"She couldn't afford to miss a performance. None of us can. We all need our money." Trixie stopped and then looked at me before nodding to herself. "Unless someone was offering her more money for something else."

"Oh, you don't mean…" I tried to sound more shocked by the possibility of some other employment than disgusted.

"Not Mimi. She'd have only missed a show for the chance to appear in a bigger show for more money. Nothing at Broadcasting House is certain since they started moving performances to studios in the countryside, and Mimi wanted to stay in London. We all do."

"If she'd met someone who'd offered her a role in a stage play or something, why would she have come back here? Why not schedule a time to talk later and go on to the party with the rest of the troupe?" I asked.

Trixie shook her head, looking perplexed. "Unless she

only came back here for a moment to give someone something and then planned to run back out to meet her acting troupe."

"Instead, they killed her. But what were they looking for?" I wondered aloud.

Trixie studied me. "Maybe what you're looking for."

"I'm not looking for anything but Frank Kennedy's killer. Who may be Mimi's killer, too."

"How come we never heard about this brother who's involved you? All Mimi talked about was his toffee-nosed sister."

"Christa." I smiled. "She's something else. Dermot's all right. He and Frank had a falling-out a while ago and Dermot left. He returned on some holiday leave to find his brother had been murdered."

"Did the brother kill him?"

"I don't think so." I dismissed the idea quickly. Then I reconsidered. "He didn't have a good motive and I don't think Dermot has it in him. And I really don't believe he could be a killer."

"What about Christa?" Trixie asked.

"Christa wouldn't kill Frank. He was in charge of the house and her life, and she believes that is the way it should be. She's busy leaning on Dermot now." Poor kid, I thought. And he was still a child.

Or was he?

Dermot had to be in at least his mid-twenties, possibly nearly thirty. I was falling into the trap of thinking of him as a child because that was how Christa thought of him, besides Dermot's own natural reticence. I needed to stop.

We were still standing in the front hall, which was decorated in faded, now pale-pink paper with an illegible design and a well-waxed parquet floor. "Would it be all right if I saw her room?"

"Why?"

What could I say that might make Trixie agree to show me Mimi's room? "Has it been straightened already?"

"No. The police won't let anyone in until they finish. The landlady is beside herself, because she can rent the room as soon as the police let her clean it up."

"Surely we can take a peek?" I said.

"Don't touch anything," Trixie warned me.

We went up two flights of stairs on dirty carpet and then stopped in front of a door on the landing. Trixie slipped a key out of her pocket and unlocked the door.

"The police don't know every key fits every door," she told me as she turned the knob with her handkerchief over her hand.

"Have they checked for fingerprints?" I asked as I followed her inside.

"Yesterday was New Year's Day. A holiday. Most everyone was off, including the police. They took some photographs and took her away, and that was about all they could manage."

I took a couple of steps into the room, looking around. The wallpaper here had a pattern of green vines and pink blooms with a pale background that looked recently hung or freshly cleaned. A large rug covered most of the scarred wooden floor. There was a single bed with an iron bedstand, a wardrobe that must have predated Victoria's reign, and a dressing table, mirror, and chair. Every surface, from the dirty pink rug to the freshly laundered pink bedcover, was an inch deep in her belongings. Except in one area.

"Someone could do this while she lay dead?" I shook my head. People could be shocking.

"She was lying over there," Trixie said, pointing to a spot near the window while not looking at it. Papers, clothes, and jewelry were heaped up. Mimi's belongings had been shoved aside when they moved the body, showing a huge area of the rug where a thick, rust-colored stain indicated where Mimi died of her stab wound. Splatters of the same deep red color were spread also on clothes and the wall near where the body lay. One drop had slid down the blackout curtains.

Therefore, the blackout curtains had been in place. And that meant no one would have seen anything from the outside even if they'd been looking.

"Her stuff had just been tossed on top of her while she bled to death?" My stomach churned from the callousness of her killer.

"You could barely see her for the clothes dumped on top of her." Trixie looked at me and slowly nodded, tears in her eyes. "Yes, it is sick. How could someone treat another human being as if they were a piece of furniture?"

"Maybe they were in a hurry. Maybe they'd heard

someone returning?" I suggested.

"It was New Year's Eve. I would have thought no one returned, although Mimi did. I can't believe one of the other girls did as well. I think they would have mentioned it."

"Why didn't Mimi go to the party where she was supposed to perform?" I looked at all the stuff scattered around her room. "Does anything here strike you as odd?"

"Everything she owned was tossed around on every surface. Even if she was on her way to an audition, she wouldn't have everything out. Not this way."

"What made you mention an audition?" I asked.

"Her photo, there on top of the clothes on the bed. Actresses take headshots with them to auditions. Dancers take full-length photographs. Musicians don't need photos. No one cares about their looks." Trixie waved the need for photos away with a single gesture.

"If Mimi left before you that evening to get to the party on time, she would have to have been dressed and on her way at what time? Do you know who else was in the acting group or where the party was held?"

"Why are you so interested in whether she went to this party where she was supposed to perform?" Trixie asked, suspicion written on her face.

"Because it should make clear when she was murdered. Or at least, I hope it does. Who was she supposed to be acting with?"

"Why did you want to see her room?" Trixie asked, frowning.

"I don't know. I hoped seeing it would make everything clear." *Blast.* It told me someone was searching for those letters and that narrowed the list to two. Or three. I smiled wistfully. "No such luck."

Trixie stepped carefully across the floor to a small book on top of some costume jewelry and picked it up with her handkerchief. "His address is in here." She brought it back so I could read it.

I pulled my notebook and pencil from my bag and copied down Will Mason-Twigg, Restoration Players, and his address and telephone number. "Thank you."

Trixie carried it back and carefully placed it on the jewelry where it sat before. "Come on. Let's go."

We went out, still not touching anything, and Trixie used her handkerchief to close the door and then lock it.

As we walked down the stairs, I asked, "There were no new boyfriends?"

"No, and with Mimi, if there was someone, we all would have heard."

"Thank you for speaking to me, Trixie," I said as I reached the front hallway again.

"Will this satisfy Frank's brother?" she asked.

"I don't know. I hope so. There's no—"

At that moment, a door on the ground floor opened and an older woman in a housedress came into the hall. Her hair was in curlers under a scarf but she had rings on all of her pudgy fingers. "Who's this, Trixie? One of your dancer friends?"

"A friend of Frank Kennedy's brother." She nearly spit out the name. "Wants to know who killed Frank, and now Mimi."

"Oh, my. I'm sure I don't know, love. It must have happened New Year's Eve."

This woman had to be the landlady. "What time did you leave the house? Was Mimi still here then?" I hoped I hadn't made her suspicious.

"I saw Mimi leave at five-thirty or just a little after. I left for my sister's place about ten minutes later. The same as I told the police." She raised her eyebrows at me as she finished speaking.

She was suspicious, all right. "And you didn't see her again until Trixie found her dead the next afternoon. That must have been a shock for you both."

"Not as much for me as it was for Trixie. She screamed the house down."

"I don't think I was as bad as all that," Trixie said in an indignant tone.

The landlady nodded that it had been. "She came running down shrieking that Mimi was dead and her room torn up," she said, turning to me. "We all went up and had a look from the doorway. Then I came down and called the police."

"I imagine you're the one with the cool head around here." I smiled and hoped I'd said the right thing.

"I should hope so with a houseful of trusting young ladies. That's why I have the rule, 'No men inside the door.'

It had to have been a woman who killed Mimi." The landlady gave an emphatic nod.

Chapter Twelve

I didn't know if Mimi's landlady was right about her killer having to be a woman, but I didn't have time to debate it. I needed to head back to Broadcasting House and speak to Roxanne before the chamber orchestra performance that night. I also needed to finish my talk with Clarissa before rehearsal. I gave Trixie and the landlady each one of my cards, in case something strange turned up in Mimi's room.

As I left, I decided I needed to stop at a tea shop.

The more I thought about the murder over a scone and a pot of tea, the more I knew I needed to call on Sir Malcolm first. He was the one who'd sent me down there, after all.

If Peter O'Malley was part of the IRA, Sir Malcolm would know a great deal about him. And I needed to report to him on Mimi's murder since I'd refused to do what he wanted the night before.

I arrived at the entrance to the red brick building, once a block of Edwardian service flats, and stated who I wanted to see to the military guard. Then I waited until he called upstairs and then had another armed guard escort me to Sir Malcolm's office.

The tops of the trees outside were bare as they

disappeared into the low-hanging clouds. A few feet lower and those clouds would become fog. I had time to debate exactly at what height they became ground fog as I watched out the window beyond Sir Malcolm's head while he read reports and made notations on them.

Finally, when I thought I'd have time for a short nap, he put down the final report and said, "Yes?"

"Who's Peter O'Malley?"

"Oh, now there's a question. Why are you asking?"

"Frank Kennedy was blackmailing him, as well as others. What can you tell me about him?"

Sir Malcolm drummed his pen on the desktop. "What have you learned so far?"

"Unlike the rest of Kennedy's blackmailing targets, I've never seen O'Malley, nor do I know where he works. From the name, I can guess he's with the IRA, but the contents of the letters are innocuous."

"You have them? You've seen them?"

"I did."

"You did?" he bellowed. "Where are they now?"

"Burned. They're ashes."

"Good heavens, Olivia. How could you do something so foolish?" His face was turning an unhealthy red.

I held up one hand. "That's what I've told everyone. It gives me a measure of safety if the killer thinks I don't have the letters he or she was being blackmailed for and the killer thinks they've been destroyed. Especially after Mimi was killed and her room searched."

Sir Malcolm frowned. "What have you learned?"

"Frank Kennedy was a blackmailer. He had letters written by five victims that I know about. I'm not certain his killer searched his house, but his sister says someone broke in. The killer did go through his ex-fiancée's room and Frank's locker at work. Or someone did."

"What did you learn at the murder scene?"

I told him what I'd learned about the time when the crime could have been committed and the vast amount of blood spilled in the bedroom.

"And you think this killer was one of the five blackmail victims?" Sir Malcolm asked when I'd finished.

I put up my hands palms out. "Frank Kennedy was a vile piece of work. He harassed, groped, and threatened every woman he came across, and that's just the ones at Broadcasting House that I know about."

"His death might not have had anything to do with the IRA?"

"I hope it did. If not, I'd be in favor of a mild sentence for his killer. Except…"

"Except?" Sir Malcolm looked shocked.

"Except I think Frank's killer also killed Mimi in the search for those letters, and she didn't deserve to die. Especially for something she didn't possess. Something she wasn't involved in."

"Thank goodness. For a moment, I thought you had become a pacifist. And that would never do, Olivia."

"If that's all it takes to leave your service, I will keep it in mind," I told him with a furious glare. My expression didn't faze Sir Malcolm at all. "Now, Peter O'Malley. Who is he?"

"He's a priest. We think. We also have reports that he's an actor. There may be two of them and one of them has nothing to do with this. It's a common-enough name."

I felt air leak from my lungs. "If he can be a priest, a man of God, and aid the IRA in blowing up people, and stab Mimi just to search her room, I don't think I want to deal with him."

"Bring me the letters this afternoon, and I'll set someone onto trying to learn as much as we can about this man. Don't worry about Peter O'Malley until you have exhausted other avenues." He stared at me a moment and then said, "Go on. I need O'Malley's letters."

"While I do that, I need you to find out some things for me."

"Go on," he said, giving me a frosty look.

"I'd appreciate Keith Bates's home address and information on his family, and I want to know if Dermot Kennedy did arrive in England on the overnight ferry from Ireland early on the morning of the twenty-seventh."

"You think one of them is guilty?"

"No, I don't. But I don't want to miss a murderer by not checking his alibi."

"Fine." Sir Malcolm waved me off to do his bidding.

I rushed home, crossing the center of London. With the holidays over and a cold wind buffeting people about, everyone moved with speed and purpose, hindering my progress. Traffic, Underground schedules, everything was against me. I retrieved what Sir Malcolm wanted, and with O'Malley's letters in my inside coat pocket, I struggled against pedestrians on every pavement and through the beginnings of fog back to the spymaster's building and went through the same procedure as before. When I arrived in Sir Malcolm's office, he continued to talk on the telephone while holding out his hand to me.

I pulled out the two letters, still in their envelopes, and handed them over.

He cradled the receiver between his shoulder and his cheek as he used both hands to study the first envelope and then pull out the letter. To my amazement, he never hesitated over a single word in his telephone conversation.

I sat down without an invitation and tried not to listen in, waiting for him to finish and turn his attention to the letters he'd wanted me to bring in such a hurry.

When he said the name "O'Malley," I looked up and met his eyes. "He mentions various locations in the Bible and some verses in Song of Solomon. If these letters of his are in book code, we have our source."

I had to ask. "Were there more letters than just the couple that Frank Kennedy had? That you know of?" I asked Sir Malcolm.

"No. And here's the file we have on O'Malley."

He handed it over and I picked it up. It was thin. When I opened it, the first page I came to was a clear close-up photograph. The photo reminded me of the shot of Mimi on top of the mess in her room.

Peter O'Malley was handsome, with pale eyes, dark hair, and a square face. He was of average height and weight, which meant he would never stand out in a crowd. The pages after the photo gave me his details and told me he was from Yorkshire recently but born in Ireland, and had earned his living as an actor in various cities.

Otherwise, I'd learned nothing. I set the file down on the desk.

Sir Malcolm lay a piece of paper on top of the file. Dermot Kennedy had arrived in England exactly as he'd said, and I now had Keith Bates's address as well as his wife's name and the children's names and ages. I put the paper in my bag.

The spymaster put his hand over the receiver. "Are you still here?"

* * *

When I arrived at Broadcasting House before the Tuesday night concert, a week since I tripped over Frank Kennedy's body, I nearly ran into Gerald Fitzroy in the lobby. "Excuse me. I'm doing a review on the chamber orchestra program," he said by way of greeting as he moved to push past me.

"Fine. I'm here to speak to someone, but I need to speak to you as well." If I talked to Fitzroy quickly, I might still have time to talk to Roxanne.

"Yes. What is it?" He walked over to the lift and we rode up together to the eighth floor. There were others with us, so I didn't say anything.

Then we were standing in the middle of a busy hallway.

I gestured to the side of the hall and Fitzroy followed me. "Where were you New Year's Eve in the early evening?"

"That, young lady, is none of your business." He strutted to the entrance of the concert hall, where he greeted the BBC employee who was directing the small audience to their seats in the listening area.

"Thank you," I muttered. When I reached the door he'd entered, I could hear the orchestra tuning up. Too late to talk to Roxanne now. I'd have to come back for the next rehearsal on Thursday, or later tonight if I timed it right.

I went down to the sixth floor and found Clarissa. She walked over to meet me, probably wanting to finish our last talk as much as I did.

"How was your New Year's Eve?" I asked.

"I went out with a group of actors to a series of pubs. As a New Year's Eve, it wasn't memorable, but it was fun. Almost as if there wasn't a war on. Why?"

"You've heard about Mimi?"

"Yes. How awful. Keith Bates told us." Clarissa narrowed her eyes. "Why? Did she have my letters?"

"No. That was what I was going to tell you the other day when you ran off after Paul White. Your letters were found and destroyed."

"You're sure they're destroyed?" she asked me in a surprised tone.

"Certain. Burned to ashes."

Clarissa gave me a dazzling smile and said, "I appreciate all your help."

"Glad I could be of assistance."

"I'd appreciate it if you never mentioned it again."

"Mention what?" I said, wide-eyed. I could act as innocent as she could.

Looking pleased, Clarissa went into the studio for rehearsal and I went back down, planning to attempt to catch Roxanne later after her performance.

I would have thought I was too early, but when I reached the main doors from the lobby to the street, Janet Murrow was coming into Broadcasting House. No doubt she was here to listen to her husband's report to America.

She greeted me warmly and asked if I wanted to listen in. I didn't have anything else I had to do at that time, so I agreed and went upstairs with her.

Once we were off the lift and in the corridor by ourselves, Janet said, "I found out who Father O'Malley is. He's a priest at Our Lady of Peace in Kilburn."

I was impressed. Janet Murrow was a terrific investigator to find O'Malley so quickly. "How did you find out?"

"I met him. I went to see Christa Kennedy to see how she was doing, and he was there. I asked Christa if he was her priest. She said no and told me where he preaches. It's her cousin Patrick's church. Patrick and his wife have a new baby, and Patrick sent the priest to convince Christa to come to the christening."

"Was Dermot there, too?" I wasn't certain why I asked, but who knew what might be important.

"No. At least I didn't see him." Then she looked at me

closely. "I knew you wanted to know who O'Malley is. Is it important?"

"I don't know," I told her in complete honesty. "Thank you. Now I know where to go to talk to him." I took her arm and we waved to her husband before Janet Murrow and I headed into the engineer's listening room to hear the broadcast.

"Why is your husband broadcasting so early today?" I was curious about everything concerning radio programs.

Janet greeted the engineer and then turned to me. "Something important is going on back in the States, so Ed's broadcast needed to be transmitted ahead of time. They'll tape it in New York. Who knows when it will be broadcast in the U.S."

"Didn't you ever want to be a broadcaster?" I asked her.

"The very idea of a woman broadcaster causes heart attacks in the halls of CBS." Then Janet smiled. "Ed does have me write some of his scripts, unknown to the front office. I like to think they're his best."

I smiled in return. "I imagine they are." Derek Coward was the engineer again that night, and I turned to him. "Did you manage to stay out of trouble from the last time I saw you?" I asked him with a smile to show I didn't mean anything rude.

"Oh, no trouble. Mr. Murrow saw to that. He's a nice fellow," Derek said.

"I think he is," Janet said. "He—"

Derek held up a hand. "Live in 5, 4, 3…" He turned some

knobs and flipped switches. Janet and I took chairs along the side of the room out of the way and listened as Derek finished setting up the transmission and then joined us.

Then we heard Ed Murrow's voice come out of the speaker. "This is Edward R. Murrow, reporting from London for the CBS network. Tonight..."

"Have they figured out what happened to Kennedy?" Derek whispered when he sat next to me.

"No. And now they suspect his fiancée was killed by the same person," I told him while Janet focused on her husband's voice.

"I'll have to tell him that."

That was an odd reaction. "Who?"

"Father O'Toole. He asked me about Kennedy's killing. Apparently, they had a mutual friend. Well, I guess 'acquaintance' is the right word."

What? Derek had surprised me.

Over the loudspeaker, Ed Murrow was talking about dance halls. "Places are jammed nearly every night. People come early and stay late. Uniforms and civilian clothes are about evenly divided, but practically no one wears formal evening dress. That's a change."

I pulled my attention back to Derek. "Who is Father O'Toole, and who is their mutual friend?"

"Father O'Toole is our parish priest. St. Matthew's. I went to late mass on Sunday, and afterward Father O'Toole called me over."

"Is his friend Father O'Malley?" Could this be another

link?

"I don't know. Why?" Derek looked confused.

Chapter Thirteen

Derek might have a vital clue, but it felt as if I'd have to pull it out of him to find out if it was important. "Please tell me what happened after mass on Sunday."

"Father O'Toole called me over. He had been talking to another priest I've not seen before. He said he'd heard we'd had a tragedy and one of my colleagues had been killed. He hoped I was all right, since I had lost a friend under such terrible circumstances."

"Was Frank Kennedy a friend?" I had to ask.

"No." He sounded as if he thought I was crazy to ask that.

"Why was Father O'Toole so concerned if he wasn't your friend?"

"Father O'Toole christened me, and he confirmed me. He buried my father a few months ago and he knows how upset I was to lose him. I guess he was worried that I'd be as...numbed by a friend's death as I was by my father's." Derek looked at me and shrugged.

"It sounds as if Father O'Toole is very kind to you and your family."

"He is. He and my father were good friends."

"Then I'm surprised you didn't know the priest who brought him the bad news about Frank Kennedy. What was the other priest's appearance?" I was digging, but I had to bring the conversation back to the investigation. I had no idea what I might learn or where I might learn it.

"His appearance? Well, he's definitely older than me, with dark hair, I think. Maybe. Just an average build. Average. I really didn't notice." He shrugged. "My father might have known him, but I didn't. Whoever the other priest was, he knew Frank. He hoped I knew more about his death than he, the priest, had learned because I worked with him."

"Had you learned more?" This priest sounded similar to the photo and description Sir Malcolm had for Peter O'Malley in his file. Or about a million other men.

"No." He slumped in his chair. "I didn't want to know. I really didn't care. That's a terrible thing to say about a colleague, isn't it?"

"You can't carry the troubles of the whole world on your shoulders," I told him. I really didn't want Derek to be involved in murder. He seemed as if he was too nice a person. But then, so did everyone who'd had the misfortune to know Frank Kennedy.

Suddenly, Derek jumped up and ran for his headset, his eyes on the dials. During the rest of Ed Murrow's broadcast, Derek was fiddling with the controls but static seemed to grow relentlessly. By the end of the program, the sound quality was much poorer.

"And we're off the air," Derek said into his headset and flipped some switches. He pulled off his headset, looking disappointed.

Ed Murrow strode in a minute later, papers in hand.

"Sorry, Mr. Murrow," Derek said immediately. "It would still be daylight over part of the Atlantic, plus there's supposed to be rain out at sea. They were both working against us."

"Not your fault, Derek. You can't control the weather any more than I can." Then he looked at his wife. "How was I?"

"Brilliant as always. Shall we go out for a drink?" Janet looked from her husband to me.

"Count me out, I'm afraid. I have someone I want to catch after the chamber orchestra performance."

We said our farewells and then the Murrows left. I turned to Derek. "Anything else you can think of that might help?"

"Do you want me to find out from Father O'Toole who the other priest was?"

"Only if you can ask him without raising his suspicions or annoying anyone."

"Shouldn't be a problem," he said. "Who are you going to see in the chamber orchestra?"

"Roxanne Scott. She's a violinist. Do you know anyone in the orchestra?"

"I went to school with one of the French horns." Derek gave me a brief smile. "This lot has moved the biggest orchestra to Bedford. Musicians are scrambling to find other jobs if they want to stay in London. And everyone does, especially with no sign of shooting yet."

"What about you, Derek? Do you want to stay in

London?"

"I do. My family's here, although I'm the only one still living at home with my mum. And since she just lost Dad... But most of the engineering jobs are headed to Bristol and Bedford and Daventry. I'm struggling to stay on here."

"I wish you luck."

"Thank you. I'll see you at another broadcast," he said and began to clear up his work.

I went upstairs to the concert studio to find the chamber concert orchestra was still playing. I waited until they finished and began to leave the studio in a clump. Then I followed several of the female musicians downstairs to the women's cloakroom and stood outside, knowing there was only one way out.

Most of the musicians had left before Celeste and Roxanne finally came out. When I saw her, I said, "Roxanne, I need to talk to you."

She pressed her lips together and shook her head.

"Can't you leave her alone?" Celeste demanded. A couple of the other musicians looked at me strangely as they walked by.

"Roxanne is going to want to hear what I have to say."

"I don't think so," Celeste said.

"This is for her ears only," I said. "And it should be her decision."

Roxanne looked around for an exit with a panicked expression, but I was between her and both the stairs and the lift.

"Leave her alone," Celeste said, sounding frustrated with me.

Only the three of us were left in the hallway. "I burned the letters Frank Kennedy had," I said, ignoring Celeste and looking directly at Roxanne.

Roxanne suddenly relaxed, tension flooding out of her with a deep sigh. Celeste looked from one of us to the other, clearly wondering what had happened.

"They're gone?" Roxanne asked.

"Completely. Turned to ash."

She gave a long sigh and leaned against the wall. "I've been so foolish."

"Tell me about it," I said.

She stared at the tile floor and shook her head.

"How did Frank get your letters?"

She just kept shaking her head. "I don't know."

"How did you come to get into that—line of work?"

She glanced at me and sighed. "Now that I've come to London and things are going better, I don't want to be reminded of those days again. So, not another word." Roxanne turned and began to walk away.

"Would you have killed to stop Frank Kennedy from revealing your past?"

"Not before I met Miles. It didn't matter so much before I met him." I knew she hadn't met Miles until New Year's Eve. "I'm grateful to you for burning those letters. Now I can forget about that whole terrible time and never speak of it again." She gave me a big smile and began to walk past me.

"When you lived in Leeds, did you know a woman a few years younger than you named Clarissa Northfield?"

"No, but I didn't live in Leeds. We lived in a village a few miles outside of town. And I was too busy working and taking care of my family to socialize."

At the last moment I remembered my other reason for seeing her and said, "I have a note for you. From Miles."

Roxanne froze for a moment before she held out her hand. I gave her the note. She looked at the outside of the paper and then slipped it into a pocket of her coat.

With a dreamy smile I suspected was brought on by thinking of Miles, Roxanne thanked me and hurried away. Celeste pushed past me and hurried to follow her friend.

I followed them out, hoping that Roxanne wasn't hiding a fear that might have driven her to kill Frank Kennedy. But she was the only one of the blackmail victims at Broadcasting House who was unlikely to know Mimi Randall or where she lived.

* * *

The next morning, I went to the Kilburn Tube station and after asking twice as I walked along, I found Our Lady of Peace at a distance from the Underground station. It appeared to have been planned and built from stone during Victoria's reign and now was blackened by decades of coal fires.

I went inside and walked down the main aisle, stopping to sit in a pew near the front. The stone carvings all along the front of the church were magnificent and the expressions on the statues were either blissful or agonized. The thick white candles cast a flickering glow on the stained-glass windows. I watched as two priests prayed at the altar rail and then went about their business. One noticed me and came over.

"May I help you?"

"I was hoping to speak to Father O'Malley."

He smiled. "Just a moment." He walked away and then out a side door.

I waited almost long enough to think he had forgotten about me when another priest, as I guessed from his clerical collar, came in, looked around, and then came toward me. He was short and rotund with a thatch of white hair and faded blue eyes. In a vigorous voice he said, "I'm Father O'Malley. Were you looking for me?"

I supposed that even older priests could be involved in the IRA. He would have been twenty-five years younger when the insurrection began in Dublin. A young man then, and possibly a firebrand who still burned to do something for his homeland. He wasn't the man in the photo Sir Malcolm had, but it was possible Sir Malcolm was wrong this time. "I burned the letters Frank Kennedy was blackmailing you with."

He looked genuinely startled. "No one has been blackmailing me. Certainly not over any letters."

"They were letters you signed. They concerned locations mentioned in the Bible and verses from the Song of Solomon."

He wore a puzzled frown. "How could anyone be blackmailed over a letter about the Bible?" Then his frown smoothed. "I don't recall writing anyone about any particular locations in the Bible. I haven't discussed Song of Solomon in thirty years, and I'm quite certain no one has been blackmailing me."

"You are Father Peter O'Malley?"

"No. I'm Father Timothy O'Malley. Timothy John O'Malley."

Oh, dear. I felt I had definitely blotted my copybook. "This is Our Lady of Peace?"

"Yes." He looked mystified, but not worried or upset.

"Is there a Father Peter O'Malley here?"

"No. I've been here a dozen years, and there's never been a Father Peter O'Malley assigned here, or helping out, or anywhere in this part of London to my knowledge." He had a definite Irish accent, even if blurred by years of living in London.

"Then where is Father Peter O'Malley?" I asked in frustration.

"I have no idea. Are you certain he's a priest? O'Malley is a common surname."

"He signed his letters as Father Peter O'Malley."

"That's clear from what you've said," the older man told me, "but what makes you think someone was blackmailing a priest over a letter about the Bible?"

"The other writers of the letters I found with Father O'Malley's were being blackmailed over the contents of their letters. It stands to reason there was something about Peter O'Malley's letters that made him subject to blackmail, as well."

Why I was telling this priest about something he knew nothing about, I didn't know. Maybe because I was frustrated. Or it might have been his soothing tone of voice.

"Perhaps it was the person he was writing to, or his particular interpretation of the Bible that might lead to trouble."

It was my turn to be surprised. "How could an interpretation of the Bible cause trouble?"

"My dear young woman, there are interpretations of the Bible that cause nothing but trouble. Biblical scholars can argue over a single word for centuries." Then his face brightened. "Perhaps your Father O'Malley is a Biblical scholar."

"It's possible." Then I decided to mention the IRA and see what reaction I got from this Father O'Malley. "It's thought his letters were in some kind of code for the IRA and that's why he was being blackmailed."

Father Timothy O'Malley's Irish accent grew thicker and his tone sterner. "There isn't a son of Ireland who doesn't want to see her totally free, but if a priest is involved with those who harm and kill innocent people, he is failing at his calling. And make no mistake. It is a calling."

"And you're still certain you don't know where I might find Peter O'Malley?"

"No, I don't." He must have seen something in my expression, because he added, "I'm not lying to you. That's an easy sin to avoid if you've faced up to the consequences of always telling the truth. I have."

"I appreciate your help," I said as I rose.

"I'll pray you find him, and that he's innocent of whatever sin he's been blackmailed for."

"Thank you, Father." I walked out of the church, aware he had never asked for my name or who Frank Kennedy was.

I needed to find a way to talk to someone in the IRA who would answer my questions. I needed to find out if Frank Kennedy's death was associated with the IRA so I could convince Sir Malcolm to allow me to return to my regular job on the *Daily Premier*. I knew the spymaster had told me to leave the IRA alone, but if I waited for Sir Malcolm to act and then release me, when he had so many other investigations to manage, I'd be on this for the entire war.

There was another way to approach this, but there was something else I wanted to do first. Something even farther out on the Tube.

The Bates house was in a newer suburb in the far northwest of London. The address was only a few minutes' walk from the station.

I walked through the short front garden to the door and rang the bell. Half a minute later, a dark-haired woman with a pinched expression answered the door. Her "Yes?" was not welcoming.

"Mr. Bates, please."

"Why?" She crossed her arms and blocked the entrance to her home with the door only slightly ajar.

"Livvy Redmond, the *Daily Premier*. We understand that

Mr. Bates is the director for a group of actors that the murdered girl, Mimi Randall, was part of. I'm looking for a quote from Mr. Bates that we can use in our article on the murder." Well, it sounded believable.

"Keith," she called into the house, and I caught a glimpse of a well-polished wooden floor and a coat tree with a man's overcoat and a boy's jacket. A pair of wellies that should have fit the woman were on a rug just inside the door.

Keith Bates appeared a moment later with a young boy of four or five riding on his back, the child's arms around his father's neck. Before he had a chance to say anything and reveal that we'd already met, standing completely still with a startled expression, I said, "Mr. Bates? I'm Livvy Redmond of the *Daily Premier*. I'm looking for a quote on the actress Mimi Randall for our article on her murder. You're the director for the radio plays she was in?"

"Yes, I'm the director." He slid the boy off his back, down the side of his leg, before he rolled down his sleeves. It was chilly in the wind, although the sun was bright. I hoped his wife would attribute his evident tension to being put on the spot. "You want a quote?"

"You know. The usual. She was a valued member of our acting troupe. She'll be universally missed. Her Lady MacBeth was well-received."

"She never played Lady MacBeth." He sounded confused.

Keith Bates might be a good director, but he wasn't much of an actor. "In your own words, sir, something I can use for the newspaper story."

"Ah." He looked at the stoop. "She was a member of our group for over a year. Everyone liked her. I can't imagine why anyone would want to kill her."

"And her acting?"

"She had good timing for comedic roles." He looked at his wife. "That sounds so feeble."

His wife picked up the boy and carried him into the house with a *humpf,* shutting the door behind her.

"She could adjust her role to the circumstances when things went wrong. Is that good?" He raised his eyebrows at me.

"Very good, sir."

"What are you doing here?" he whispered, looking panicked.

"I think that covers it. Thank you, Mr. Bates." I turned and walked away.

I couldn't be sure Keith Bates's alibi held for the nights Frank Kennedy and Mimi Randall were killed, but after seeing him with his son, I was sure he wouldn't have gone out without his wife's approval and risked his home life.

And his wife didn't seem the type to grant her approval easily.

I headed to the *Daily Premier* building and went up to the news floor, where Mr. Colinswood had his editor's office. I found him the way I'd left him months before. He was on the phone, the receiver cradled against his ear, while he typed. A cigarette burned in the full ashtray.

The thought passed through my mind as I knocked on the doorframe that Ed Murrow was the only person I could think of who smoked as much as Mr. Colinswood. What was it about newsmen?

The editor looked up and gestured to a chair. I entered and sat, waiting for a break in the nonstop flood of news coming from the telephone. He hung up, finished typing, and took a drag on his cigarette. "Olivia, I haven't seen you in ages. What's going on? Still working for the government?"

"For the moment, although with luck you can help me get back here while you end up with a great story. Do you have a contact in the IRA who might be willing to talk to me, since I have no interest in bombings or strikes or sabotage?"

"What's this about?"

"Murder."

Chapter Fourteen

Mr. Colinswood stubbed out his cigarette and reached for a pencil. "Oh, that will make you popular with the IRA. Whose murder?"

"Frank Kennedy's. Followed by Mimi Randall's."

He glanced up in surprise. "We reported on both of those deaths. It sounds as if the police are stumped. Random attacks in the blackout, they're calling it. And you think IRA?"

"I hope IRA," I told him. "If it's not the IRA, it would be a nice person who somehow ended up being blackmailed by Kennedy. Mimi was a suspected holder of the stolen letters used for the blackmail once Kennedy was killed."

"You want to ask the IRA if they had them killed?"

"Not exactly. I want to know how far up in the organization Frank Kennedy was, and who Father Peter O'Malley is, and why he was being blackmailed."

Mr. Colinswood ran a hand through his sandy hair. It was even thinner than the last time I'd seen him. He gave me a rueful smile and said, "You don't want much, do you?"

"Just a contact. You must have someone who doesn't mind talking about things he can't possibly be thought responsible for."

He studied me for a moment. "I do. I don't know if he'll

talk to you, but let me send out some feelers. You'll be home tonight after eight?" His phone began to ring again.

"I'll make certain I am. And can you see if you can find a story or photo of any Peter O'Malley in regard to anything?" He was the only one of the five I knew nothing definite about.

I asked if I could use a phone in the newsroom and Mr. Colinswood nodded as he answered his telephone.

I called the number I had for Will Mason-Twigg from Mimi's room. It was apparently a rooming house, as a woman answered and when I asked for him, shouted, "Will! It's a woman."

A nice, posh-sounding baritone answered, "Will Mason-Twigg, Restoration Players. How may I help you?"

"I want to talk to you about Mimi Randall."

"Well, I don't want to talk about her," came back in a louder and less upper-crust voice.

"What happened?"

"How would I know? She knew we were meeting at six-fifteen to set our roles for our engagement, and she never showed." He sounded as if he were a man at the end of his rope. Since this had happened over two days before, I decided he was trying out various roles on me in this conversation.

That answered some of my questions. "This was New Year's Eve?"

"Yes."

"How many of you were performing that night?"

"It was supposed to be five, and Mimi's absence left us

very shorthanded. We only had one female among the four of us, so we had to shuffle around all sorts of roles and lines. We pulled it off, we're professionals, but she can forget working with the Restoration Players again." He sounded as if the lord of the manor was annoyed with a servant.

"Were you certain she wasn't running late?"

"We waited an extra ten minutes before we left, but in the end, we had to go on without her." When I didn't say anything, he said, "Why are you calling about her?"

"I wondered if you had seen her before she was murdered."

"What?" he gasped out. "Oh, no. Not New Year's Eve?" I couldn't tell if he was playing a role or he was sincerely shocked.

"New Year's Eve," I told him. "I think she'd planned to join you when she was killed."

Will Mason-Twigg was crying when I got off the phone.

After that conversation, I couldn't think of anything else I could do to find a murderer, and definitely not when I was so focused on Father Peter O'Malley. When I left the *Daily Premier* building, I went home and cleaned my flat, wondering how long it would be before I could earn a salary that would let me hire an occasional cleaner. Thanks to Sir Malcolm frequently borrowing my services, Sir Henry wasn't paying me any more than before the war, and wages had gone up for practically everyone else, including daily maids.

Frustrated with Adam's absence with the army, Sir Malcolm's cavalier attitude toward my availability, and the need to reach someone willing to talk about IRA personnel, I scrubbed and cleaned my flat until it gleamed. I wasn't happy that I couldn't hire someone to clean, but my mood had improved.

I also needed a cook, but that night I decided to reward myself with a meal in a nearby restaurant. At least I wouldn't starve.

By nine o'clock, I was bored with the program on the wireless, tired of reading, and annoyed with waiting for a telephone call. A half-hour later, I was dozing in a chair when the telephone finally rang.

I jumped up and rushed into the hall to answer. A man's voice with an Irish accent asked for me and then said, "Come to the Kilburn Park Underground station. Walk down to Kilburn High Road, turn left, and continue until you come to the Tin Whistle Arms. Ask for Tommy."

The line went dead.

I put on stout, low-heeled shoes, bundled up, left a note saying where I had gone, and headed out to the closest Underground station. After the cold wind and the darkness of the blackout, the Underground was bright and cheery. But once I reached ground level outside the Kilburn Park station, the night felt much darker and chillier in unfamiliar surroundings.

I found what I guessed was Kilburn High Road, there being no street signs in order to confuse the Germans and anyone not local, and headed left. The Tin Whistle Arms turned out to be a good distance down the high street.

Coming in from the blackout, I was surprised that the inside of the pub was as gloomy as the streets, with low lighting and dark paneled walls. It appeared all the customers were male, and every one of them stopped talking to stare at me.

"I think you're in the wrong place, doll," one of the men said in a not-unkind voice.

"I was told I could find Tommy here."

More silence, as a few of the men nodded to each other. Then the one who had spoken finished his beer in a gulp, set his mug on the bar, and gestured for me to follow him as he headed toward the back.

I hoped I'd live to leave this place in one piece. Following this man felt as if it were a stupid thing to do. I took a hesitant step forward. These men were hardened killers if they were members of the IRA, and this could easily be a trap.

Sir Malcolm had warned me to leave this part of the investigation alone, but I had decided I had no choice except to take a chance if I wanted answers and get back to work at the newspaper.

This felt as if it were a dumb idea, coming here to question the IRA. I could hear Sir Malcolm saying "I told her so" over my grave. Right now, I hoped to live to go back to work at the *Daily Premier*.

I walked toward the back of the building down a narrow hallway. When the man pushed open a door, cold air blasted my face as we entered an alley. There was no direct light and with the buildings cutting off any light from the sky except directly overhead, I could make out little more than vague shapes.

"This way." The figure who was slightly more than a smudge moved down the alley and then in through a doorway on the opposite side. The doorway appeared slightly lighter than the rest of the alleyway, and I hoped that meant it was welcoming.

I followed the man closely, not certain if it was more foolish to go forward or to go back. Mr. Colinswood set this up, and I knew I could trust him. I went through the doorway.

Inside, I saw I was in a workshop of some sort. There was a long wooden table in the center and a half-dozen stools around it. Two men sat there drinking out of coffee mugs. A kerosene lamp threw off a smoky light from the center of the table that didn't spread as far as the walls of the room.

"Tell us what you want, Mrs. Redmond," the man I had followed across the alley said. He sat on a stool on the far side of the table and gestured for me to sit across from him. He'd spoken enough that I could hear a thick Irish accent.

I sat and asked, "Is Father Peter O'Malley one of yours?"

This struck all three men as amusing. At least they laughed.

I was cold, tired, and scared. I didn't see anything to laugh at. "Mr. Colinswood said you would know if Father O'Malley was a member of the IRA, and if he is, how I can get a message to him." I stared at all three men in turn. "I guess he was wrong."

As I stood and turned to retrace my steps, another man

said, "Sit down." His tone was cold and commanding. I had no doubt he was the man in charge. He was about forty, sandy haired, and his accent was very faint.

I walked to the table and sat on an empty stool, leaving my hat and coat on. I didn't plan to be there long.

"What is your message for Peter O'Malley?" the spokesman asked. In this wavering light, I could see every line etched on his face. He must have been at least fifty, and I was now certain he was not the leader. Elder statesman, perhaps?

"Is Peter O'Malley a member of the Irish Republican Army?"

"Does that make a difference in your message?" the one I thought of as the leader asked.

"Yes. Tell me about him."

"Why should I?" His tone and the expressions of the three men reminded me of just how dangerous they were. At least two people had been murdered, probably by them.

I tried to sound brave. "Because he was being blackmailed by Frank Kennedy, who is now dead."

All three pairs of eyes around the table bore into me. I had nothing to back it up, except for a certain stillness in their postures, but I was certain they were surprised.

"You didn't know that, did you?" I said, hoping I had bought myself some credibility with these men.

"How do you know O'Malley was being blackmailed?" the spokesman asked.

"I found letters signed by Father Peter O'Malley along

with other people's letters in Kennedy's house after he was killed. I've talked to the other people. They admit Kennedy was blackmailing them."

"He signs himself that way, but Peter O'Malley is no priest," the man I thought was the leader said.

"What is he then?"

"A chameleon." The leader smiled. It wasn't a friendly expression. His gaze reminded me that this group was expert at assassination and sabotage and I should be very careful.

"Dressing up as a priest would be a good disguise," I said, nodding.

"He's a flimflam man. A trickster. An actor," the spokesman said. "He's spent his life on the stage. A Yorkshire Irishman, pretending to love our homeland."

"So how can I get in touch with him?"

"We don't know."

"What?" That made no sense.

"We don't know where he is," the spokesman replied.

"Is he dead? In jail? In Ireland?" I asked. They must have some idea. These ferocious men were supposed to be highly disciplined.

The spokesman shrugged. "We don't know."

"You could have just told me that to begin with," I said, annoyed. Then I had another thought. "Unless you don't want to admit he isn't one of yours."

"Maybe we don't want to admit he is one of ours," the leader said.

"Which is it? Is he a member or not?"

I met with a wall of silence.

I opened my bag and pulled out one of my calling cards. I tossed the card on the table as I rose. "When you hear from him, have him get in touch with me."

I managed one step toward the door leading to the alley when the youngest of the three men was suddenly standing before me, blocking my path. He was red haired, freckled, and big, and I had no hope of getting around him since he appeared to be a wall of muscle who would be able to pick me up with ease. I looked over my shoulder at the leader.

"Where are his letters now?" he asked me.

"I don't know. With O'Malley, perhaps?" I'd lie, cheat, anything to get out of there alive.

"Don't play games with me," came out in a growl.

"Then don't play games with me," I snapped at him.

We stared at each other for a full minute before he said, "You need to trust us."

"Trust is a two-way street." My position felt stronger when I was defiant. I watched them for a sign of what was to come.

"I'm going to trust you," the leader said. "Heaven help you if you break that trust. Sit down."

I sat back down on the wooden stool and waited.

The leader gave the muscle a nod that sent the younger man striding back to his own stool. Then the spokesman and the leader sent each other a series of glances that eventually ended with the spokesman saying, "Tell us what you know about O'Malley."

"Not much. I think he's been pretending to be Father O'Malley of Our Lady of Peace here in Kilburn. There is a Father O'Malley at the church, but he's Timothy O'Malley and he's an older man than the person I saw a photograph of."

"Photograph?"

Oops. I didn't want to say I saw it courtesy of Sir Malcolm. "He looked very ordinary. Dark hair, average size."

The leader seemed focused on finding O'Malley. "Peter O'Malley conned us. We want what is ours." From his tone and reputation, I wouldn't want to stand in his way.

"Did O'Malley know Frank Kennedy?" If O'Malley stole from the IRA, that could explain why Kennedy thought he'd pay blackmail, but not why Kennedy was the corpse.

"Yes. They'd both worked at the BBC. And then O'Malley used Kennedy to steal from us," the spokesman said.

O'Malley worked at the BBC? In what role? I decided to follow up on the theft first. "How did he do that?"

"You don't need to know," the leader said. "You might want to remember how much trouble O'Malley is in if you plan to double-cross us."

"I wouldn't think of doing that. I just want to talk to Peter O'Malley and find out if he knows how Frank Kennedy ended up with his letters and how much he was charging for them. And what did you mean, 'They'd both worked at the BBC'?"

"O'Malley's an actor. Kennedy's an engineer. They met at Broadcasting House. Now, what if those letters were part of O'Malley's con? If Kennedy had them, he might not be using them for blackmail, he might have been bringing them to us to decide what we should do with Mr. O'Malley." The leader looked at me with a gaze that pierced through the smoky, wavering light.

The smell of the burning kerosene didn't quite mask the odor of the room. Leather. I suspected if I went out the front door onto the street, I would find a sign saying this was a cobbler's shop.

"What was his con? He must have been trying to trick money out of you," I said, "and from your anger with him, I suspect he robbed you of a tidy sum."

"Imagine what you want," the leader said. The spokesman shot him a glance that I couldn't read. Another good reason to use a lantern. The weak light prevented me from gathering clues from the looks they gave one another.

"I don't care what O'Malley used for bait, I just want to know how he managed to take you in. What is the importance of those letters I found in Kennedy's home?"

"He—" the spokesman began.

"Don't tell her anything," the leader broke in.

"If you don't want my help, fine." I started to rise.

"Your help?" the leader asked, scorn in his tone.

"The fact that you're speaking to me tells me you haven't found out where O'Malley or your money is, or even if the letters Kennedy possessed are useful for your purposes." Seeing the look on the leader's face as I spoke, I sat back down on trembling legs.

"I think we can use her help," the spokesman said.

"O'Malley wouldn't fear her. And she seems to have some knowledge of what he was doing."

"All right," the leader said. "But nothing specific."

I nodded, even though neither man was looking at me.

"We wanted to obtain some materials that are hard to acquire. O'Malley approached Kennedy with an offer of some material in exchange for money. We agreed," the spokesman said.

"You paid for the material?" I asked.

"In part, but when we tried to collect, we couldn't because O'Malley had slipped away."

"Did the letters Frank Kennedy were holding have any bearing on the deal between O'Malley and Kennedy? And how could Kennedy make a deal for the IRA?"

The leader laughed mirthlessly. "She hasn't figured any of it out."

I looked from one man to the other.

"Frank Kennedy," the spokesman said, "was part of our inner council. We don't know anything about any letters from O'Malley, nor do we care. All we want from him is the material."

Chapter Fifteen

"But Frank Kennedy disparaged the Irish," I said. What I didn't add was that he was also an informant for Sir Malcolm and the government against the IRA. And yet he was part of the IRA inner circle.

"Great cover, isn't it?" the man I believed to be the leader said.

"So, Kennedy was an engineer for the BBC, no doubt having some skills you could use. He was a member of your inner council, and he was a blackmailer, probably for his own gain." I shook my head. "No wonder Kennedy was killed. I wonder if he shared in the money O'Malley received when he stole from you."

I could sense the leader stiffen, but his grim expression never changed. I guessed they hadn't thought of that. Or maybe they had, and that was why Kennedy had been killed.

Trusting a blackmailer was never a smart move. Especially a blackmailer who was selling you out to the government. Did they know that?

I didn't want to think what would happen if I told them.

"Where are the letters?" the leader asked.

"Oh, dear."

"What?" It was a demand rather than a question.

I decided to go with my story. "I burned them when I burned the other letters Kennedy was using to blackmail his fellow BBC employees."

For a moment, I feared I would be strangled.

"You. Did. What?" The leader's voice rose until it filled the room. At least he didn't move toward me.

A shiver slid down my backbone and my insides twisted into knots. "I burned them," I repeated. "It seemed the fairest thing to do with letters that were being used for blackmail. The senders were embarrassed enough to pay money so the messages wouldn't see the light of day. I doubt they wanted to pay more if their letters had fallen into the hands of someone else with a criminal streak."

"The letters from O'Malley weren't used for blackmail," the leader said, sounding as if he were hanging on to his temper by a thread. "They couldn't have been."

"How was I supposed to know that?" I asked, sounding annoyed to my ears. I hoped it was a good bluff. Could they tell how frightened I was?

"You shouldn't meddle in other people's business." His voice was frosty.

"Everyone else was glad to hear their letters had been destroyed. How was I supposed to know you'd want to keep letters that didn't belong to you?"

"Get out," the leader said. His voice was as icy as the air outdoors.

He didn't have to tell me twice. I rose and hurried toward the door to the alley I'd entered from. No one tried to stop me and I didn't feel any sharp pains from knives, so I kept going. Once I entered the dark alley, I had to let my eyes adjust. As soon as I could make out which way to go for the closest cross-street, I would hurry in that direction.

"Oi, this way."

I recognized the voice of the spokesman, as I'd named him in my mind. Was he being helpful, or was I being set up?

He turned on a dim torch and aimed it at the ground. I followed the light, and him, wordlessly out of the alley and over to Kilburn High Road. He walked with me until we were in sight of the Tube station, when he turned off his light. In a stern voice, he said, "Don't come back here without an invitation," and vanished into the dark.

I rushed into the well-lit, safe station and breathed hard in relief until I caught my breath. Then I headed for the trains on shaky legs.

* * *

I woke up the next morning to the sound of a ringing telephone. Frightened of what it might mean, I ran on bare feet down the cold hall floor and picked up the receiver. I was relieved and thrilled when I heard Adam's voice come out of the telephone. "Livvy? How are you?"

"Wonderful now that I hear your voice."

"Miles made me call you to—"

"Miles has to make you call me? We've been married too long." Still worried what the message might be, I tried to make a joke about it.

"You know how young love is," Adam said, and I heard

another male voice in the background.

"He's with you, insisting you tell me something."

"Yes. He heard back from Roxanne, and he wants you to tell her he's writing her a long letter, but he hopes to get a pass in the next few weeks and he'll come straight to London to see her."

"And you? Will you get a pass in the next few weeks and come straight to London to see me?"

"You know I'll try my hardest. There's not much going on, so I have been daily since I came back after New Year's." Then I heard Adam say, "Get lost," before he came back on the phone and said, "I miss you so much."

"I love you, Adam. Write me."

"I will. You write me, too." I heard a noise on the line as he said, "We're out of time. Love—"

I shouted "Love you," as the line went dead. I hoped he heard me.

After I washed, dressed, and had weak tea and burned toast for breakfast, I pulled Roxanne's letters from the book where I'd hidden them. Something about them was bothering me.

Most of the letters were about money and not finding paying musical employment or about her other, shameful, "performances." There were wistful comments, too. *If my father hadn't died owing so much money* or *Mother lingered, leaving us with debts and so many mouths to feed and shelter.* She rejoiced over every small part in a Leeds orchestra concert or role in an afternoon tea trio.

There was no hint as to who took over the task of taking care of the "mouths to feed and shelter" when she escaped to London. Or whether she was able to give up her sideline when she came here.

While I was looking at the letters, I pulled out Clarissa's. I read them through once, then more slowly a second time. It sounded as if Clarissa and her whole family lived in a small town just outside of Leeds. Her aunt, who sounded as if she was wealthy, was a sponsor of the theater in Leeds, and a leading man befriended her. Even though the aunt was several years older than the actor, he kept sweet-talking the woman by mentioning how much he wanted to spend all his time with her and how youthful she was.

The aunt gave the actor a sizable gift of jewelry, and he pawned it. Furious, she told him she wanted the jewelry returned, they had an argument, and soon thereafter, she was murdered.

Clarissa clearly said in one letter that the actor had killed her aunt. She also said how much she herself liked him in what sounded to me as if it were unrequited love. She wrote that he told her she was too young and, she suspected, too poor. She shifted between vindictive spurned lover and enamored youngster.

Nowhere did she give his name. He was always referred to as P O. I wondered if the actor was Peter O'Malley.

If the case was this clear, why didn't the police arrest him? Who else were they investigating?

In the next letter, Clarissa said she knew who had killed

her aunt, but she'd never tell. She made it clear the killer was someone other than P O.

This time, it sounded as if she was certain the killer was a close relative.

I dug out the telephone number to Will Mason-Twigg's boarding house and dialed the number. A man answered this time and set the receiver down. A full minute later, Will came on the line and answered my questions.

"Yes, I've run into an actor named Peter O'Malley in London a couple of times, but I've never acted with him....He's average height, dark hair, blue eyes maybe. I guess he's in his thirties, but he could play anything from early twenties to late forties without much effort....I've heard he's quite versatile, but lazy....No, I have no idea where he lives or how to reach him....No, I don't know where he comes from. Somewhere north. Now, if you have no more questions and you don't plan to hire me, I have to leave. Some of us have a living to earn."

He rang off, leaving me with answers that were too general to be of any help.

My phone rang a moment later. "Livvy, can you come over and help me? I'm at my wits' end." Esther's voice came out of the receiver sounding unnerved.

"What's wrong?"

"I have two babies and no help. Chanah has had to go to the school where her younger son is a boarder. He was injured quite badly in a student prank that went wrong. Her older son just left for the army, so he's no help, and our housekeeper has her hands full with the cooking and all it takes to run this place."

"And James?" I asked, knowing the answer to my question.

"The country can't survive without him doing whatever it is he does. I'm going mad. Please come and help me."

"What about your grandmother?" Mrs. Neugard had lived with Esther when Johnny was a baby after the old lady had finally been tugged and prodded out of Berlin.

"I'd rather slit my wrists."

What else could I say? "I'll have to leave in the afternoon to speak to someone at Broadcasting House, but I can help you for a while."

"Oh, thank you, Livvy. I'll see you soon. No! Don't—oh, get here quickly." Esther hung up on me.

Suspecting I'd be spending time with an exuberant two-year-old, I bundled up and headed out to Esther's home on the north side of London.

When I arrived, I could tell Esther was at the end of her tether. The woman who never had a hair out of place now had no lipstick on and she'd pulled her hair back in a messy braid. Her skirt was twisted around sideways. A food-stained cloth was draped over one shoulder. She carried Becca in her arms and Johnny hung from her hem.

"Livvy. Do something!"

I picked Johnny up, swung him over my head and said, "How's my favorite man?"

He giggled, and I said to Esther, "May I take him for a

walk to the park?"

"He'll freeze."

"It's sunny and not too terrible out today."

She sighed. "Whatever you want." Esther had fixed rules about her children. She had to be exhausted to let me have free rein with her son.

"All right, Johnny. We're going on an adventure," I told the little boy. "Where's your coat and hat?"

He led me to them and helped me dress him for the outdoors. The only things visible on him when I finished were his face and his knees. His outfit was mismatched, but all his mother said after a long sigh was, "Go."

Knowing where the Powells kept their tennis gear, I grabbed a ball, winked at Johnny, and off we went. Rather, off he went with me trying to keep up. The RAF could fuel one of their aeroplanes with his energy.

Johnny headed straight for the park four streets away, stopping at every corner to take my hand to walk across the road. Chanah had trained him well.

There were a few children in the park, most a few years older than Johnny. They would all, Johnny included, be sent to the country with their mothers when the war began in earnest. Or perhaps sent with the nannies who were in the park with them this blustery day. I knew Esther planned to take Chanah and the housekeeper with her when she moved to the house Sir Henry had bought in Oxfordshire.

From what I'd seen that day, she'd need all the help she could get.

After Johnny became bored with running up and down hills, we began to play catch, or chase the tennis ball as I thought of it. I could play this with half my mind while the other half chastised myself. How would I manage if Adam and I had a child while this war was on and he was away on some battlefield?

I couldn't imagine.

Eventually, Johnny tired and we trudged the distance back to the house, the little boy whining that he wanted to be carried. I distracted him with a delivery wagon's horse and a flock of pigeons as we walked along before delivering him home to be fed by the housekeeper. I said goodbye to Esther and fled to Broadcasting House.

I needed a rest.

Arriving early, I found some of the musicians tuning up, but there was no sign of Roxanne or Celeste. I asked Harriet Berg, who said they'd be along in a few minutes. She'd seen them in the ladies' dressing room.

When I saw Roxanne, Celeste was at her side. Roxanne said something and Celeste came over to me. "She says she doesn't want to speak to you."

"Then I suppose she doesn't want the message from Miles either." I turned to leave.

Roxanne caught up to me within two steps. "What did Miles say?"

"Did Kennedy find out you were up to your old tricks after you came to London?"

She reddened. "I thought you said those letters were

destroyed."

"I read them first. Have you continued with your sideline? And did Frank Kennedy know?"

"Did you really destroy those letters?" Roxanne asked in a loud voice. People in the hallway turned to look at us.

"Of course I did," I whispered.

She walked over to lean on the wall. "What did Miles say?"

"Did you continue your sideline? Yes or no."

"No, I didn't. I had a position already lined up in the chamber orchestra group when I came here. I could get by without the extra money. And Miles? Did you tell him?"

What kind of an ogre did she think I was? "No. I would never tell him. But he did say he is writing you a long letter in reply. And he will try to get a pass to visit London in the next few weeks." I studied her for a moment, afraid to hear the answer to my question. "Who is taking care of the many mouths to feed after your mother died?"

"Oh, for...." She sighed. "They moved in with other relatives. Or they died."

Chapter Sixteen

I hoped this didn't mean Roxanne Scott was mixed up in other murders. "Who died?"

"My father's mother and my mother's mother and aunt. They were all old and in poor health. Ordinarily, no one would have expected my parents to die first, but…" She shrugged. "When is Rem going to mail me a letter?"

"Rem?"

"Remington Miles. Didn't you know his first name?"

"My husband never told me." Why did that name sound familiar? "Who moved away?"

"My younger brother and sister moved near York to live with our aunt and uncle on their farm."

I nodded, hurrying my questions and answers before her rehearsal began. "Why did you do it? How did you end up forced into that position?"

"I needed money. We were poor. Musician jobs were hard to come by. One of the women on my street showed me the ropes at a time when things were particularly tough. When it was particularly cold and we needed more coal for heat and medicine for weak lungs."

"Your letters make it out to be quite easy."

"I pretended I was acting a part. You know?"

"As the ingenue prostitute?" I remembered what the letters had said.

She glared at me. "Yeah."

"Miles didn't say when he'd mail his letter," I told her. "Why did you tell him the trumpet player is your brother?"

"I don't know. He's someone from home. A cousin. He's hard to explain." Celeste tugged on Roxanne's arm and the two girls scurried into the rehearsal hall.

I walked away wondering where I'd heard of Remington Miles. And who was Roxanne's cousin from home, the trumpet player?

I went to the *Daily Premier* building and rode up to the newsroom in search of Mr. Colinswood. He was in his office, tie askew, shirtsleeves rolled up, cigarette burning in the ashtray, and banging on his typewriter. "How can I help you, Olivia?" he asked without pausing in his typing.

"Where would I have heard the name Remington Miles?"

He glanced at the window, his face scrunched in thought. "Eighth Earl of Winterbyre. Died two years ago at some advanced age."

My mouth dropped open. After I shut it, I said, "There must be a grandson with the same name."

"The current earl is married to an American heiress. A real stunner. They have an heir and a couple of spares. I imagine one of them is named after the old man."

"Could you do me a favor? Have someone pull out the story about the murder of a woman named Althea Northfield a year ago."

"Already done." He opened a drawer and pulled out some newsprint. Slapping it on his desktop, he took a drag on his cigarette and turned back to his typewriter.

"How did you know I needed this?" Mr. Colinswood was a bigger magician than I had thought.

"You asked for it. You wanted a photo of a Peter O'Malley." He glanced back at me with a puzzled look.

"I did, yes."

"He was the prime suspect in the Northfield murder for a time. His picture, and hers, were appearing in every newspaper in the country. Including ours."

I looked at the date on the cutting. A little over a year ago. The story gave the basic facts about the murder. She was found by her sister, Phyllis Thackey, who called the police. Althea Northfield was well known in theatrical circles in the Leeds area as a patron of the arts, leading fundraising efforts and subscription campaigns for the local theater.

Her photo showed a heavily made-up dark-haired woman in her late forties. Peter O'Malley was in front of a group of actors dressed for a Shakespearean production. He was dark haired and smiling, looking several years younger than the murdered woman.

He looked as if he were the man in Sir Malcolm's file on Peter O'Malley.

I wondered if he killed her, and then went on to kill Frank Kennedy and Mimi Randall.

"That raises more questions," I told him.

"I do what I can." He grinned and began to strike the typewriter keys again.

"Thanks. I'll run upstairs and see if Sir Henry has any message for Esther. I'll see you later."

Mr. Colinswood fully looked at me for the first time. "You owe me a front-page story."

"Soon. I'm trying."

He smiled and I waved to him on my way out.

I went upstairs to Sir Henry's office. When his secretary waved me through, I knocked on the door and walked in. "I've been using Mr. Colinswood to find some information for me on this investigation. In the meantime, I've been drafted to babysit Johnny."

"My Johnny?" I didn't think Grandpa Sir Henry would hear anything except his grandson's name. I was right. "What happened?"

"Chanah's younger son was badly injured at school. Chanah went down to see him and I'm filling in. If anyone's looking for me, I suspect I'll be at your daughter's tonight."

"If this keeps up, Esther may have to have her grandmother come help out again."

I looked at him in surprise and saw barely contained amusement. "Esther's trying very hard to avoid that. Mrs. Neugard is getting too old for the hard work of dealing with babies. And toddlers."

Sir Henry cringed when I mentioned his mother-in-law's name. "I don't want to be there when she learns she wasn't called to help out."

"Neither do I," I admitted. "Maybe she won't find out." Changing subjects, I said, "Tell me about Gerald Fitzroy."

"A pain in my rump, but a very useful pain. He knows everyone in the music and theater communities in London. He always gets his copy in on time and it rarely needs to be corrected."

Unlike my articles, I could hear him thinking. "So why is he such a problem?"

"He's a know-it-all, vindictive, and he always has to have the last word. No humility. I can't stand him." He tapped his fingers on the desktop. "I've also heard the *Daily Premier* referred to as Fitzroy's tame paper. Apparently, he features friends of his in every review, and it's becoming obvious to other venues and artists. I'm going to have to speak to Mr. Fitzroy."

I'd remember that if I had to deal with Fitzroy more during this investigation. I said goodbye and went home to pack a small overnight bag and traveled to Esther's leafy area of good-size detached houses.

Esther greeted me with "Thank goodness you're here. I've not heard from Chanah and Johnny has been a terror. I never had any brothers. I don't know what to do." She'd straightened her skirt, but her hair was still sticking out from her messy braid and she had yet to apply lipstick.

"I didn't have any brothers either," I reminded her. "I try to keep him busy, and that usually works."

"I hope Becca doesn't act this way in another year or two." Esther looked down at her sleeping daughter and shuddered.

"Do you want me to stay the night?"

"Yes, please. At least I'll have adult conversation after they go to bed."

"What about James?"

"They sent him to the coast for a few days. Don't ask me which coast."

"Britain certainly has coastlines," I replied, knowing how we all had to keep quiet about anything and everything.

I set my bag down and dressed Johnny in his heavy outerwear to play in the back garden. When we came in, it was time for my tea and his dinner. Esther and Becca joined us in the kitchen for our meals, where Johnny showed more interest in my tea than his own food. Apparently, the housekeeper, Mrs. Blum, was used to this behavior from Johnny, and she had an extra tea meal ready for the little boy.

"How long has he been refusing to eat his strained food?" Esther asked.

"Since he developed a full set of teeth," the housekeeper replied. "You might try this on Becca." She handed over Johnny's bowl and Esther tried feeding a small spoonful to Becca.

The little girl swallowed it greedily and gestured to the bowl as she made noises.

"I wish Chanah would tell me about these changes," Esther said.

"Then it's a blessing she was called away so you can find out exactly what your children are up to," I said. I knew I wouldn't be able to afford a nurse when Adam and I had our children. This was one problem I was certain I wouldn't have.

Esther stared at me for a moment, and then after feeding Becca another mouthful, said, "You think I'm not paying enough attention to my children."

"No. I think you have a great deal on your shoulders and you're trying to cope with new problems using old solutions. It's good that you have Chanah, but you need to oversee what is going on more closely."

"I was afraid she'd feel I was interfering," Esther said.

"Nonsense," Mrs. Blum said. "We've been wondering why you haven't shown more interest in those precious babies."

"Well," Esther said, squaring her shoulders, "it sounds as if I need to do more with my children."

"It'll get easier," I told her, "once Becca is a toddler and can follow Johnny around a little." Actually, I had no idea, but it sounded good, and Mrs. Blum nodded, so it must have had some merit.

After that, the mood lightened, Esther didn't appear to be so stressed, and in response, Johnny calmed down. Well, he calmed down some.

I guessed bath time would be boisterous and decided now would be a good time to talk to Clarissa before rehearsal. I went back to Broadcasting House and went up to the sixth floor.

Fortunately, Clarissa had already arrived and willingly came over when I waved to her.

"I want to ask you about those accusations in your letters Frank Kennedy had," I said.

"I don't want to talk about it." She turned to leave.

Her attitude told me this wouldn't be easy. "Please reassure me they had nothing to do with a police matter."

"I had nothing to do with it." She put her hands in the air and took a step away from me.

"But you suspected someone," I said, still blocking her way to the studio.

"And that was unfair. And it doesn't matter. The only thing important was what the police thought. The police didn't think so, otherwise they would have investigated and charged him."

"This person you didn't like, it was Peter O'Malley, wasn't it?"

"What if it was. So?" She shrugged. "Anyway, it was a long way away from here, back in Yorkshire."

"Did you know someone in Leeds, or in Yorkshire, named Roxanne Scott?"

"No. Should I have?" There was something hard in her gaze.

"I don't know. I wondered if you were both from the same village."

She shook her head. "Never heard of her. And what does it matter? It's all behind me. Behind all of us. And now that my letters are gone, I'm free."

"You weren't free as long as Kennedy had those letters?" I asked.

"Kennedy threatened to take them to the police. I was afraid they'd use them to charge someone, anyone, with her murder. The whole family just wants to let the matter lie."

"But it's murder," I said. "Someone died. Your aunt died."

She took a step toward me. "Then let the police solve the crime. It's none of your business. You've already become involved in Frank Kennedy's death and his blackmailing. Why don't you just stick with that? Or do you think you're some kind of Sherlock Holmes?"

* * *

When I returned to Esther's, it was bedtime, and I didn't think either child would ever settle down. Finally, Esther used her no-nonsense tone of voice and both children curled up and stopped fussing.

We didn't dress for dinner. We were both too exhausted. Mrs. Blum's soup, followed by a Welsh rarebit and a salad, was excellent. We finished with a pudding and then took our coffee and wine into the drawing room, where Mrs. Blum had lit a fire while we were eating. It was cozy and we kicked off our shoes and snuggled into the large beige-and-red plaid chairs on either side of the fire, our feet tucked under us.

"I'm afraid Chanah will come back with her son," Esther told me.

"Why? I thought he was at a good school. Didn't he get his admission by coming here on the Kindertransport?" I remembered Esther telling me both of Chanah's sons came over from Germany on the plan to get Jewish children out of the country. Then Esther obtained a visa for Chanah to work as her nursery maid, one of the few categories that adult German Jews could apply for to get sanctuary.

"She doesn't trust the English any more than the Germans. Germans incarcerated her husband and then killed him. They beat up her older son. The German government confiscated their home, their money, their valuables. And now English boys have harmed her younger son."

"How does the son feel about it?" I asked.

"The older son went into the army to fight Hitler quite willingly, despite his mother's tears. The younger son? I guess it depends on how well he fits into the school and how many friends he's made." Esther shook her head. "Let's not talk about the war. Not tonight."

Instead, we talked only of life before the war. Times before Esther had children. Life before the world had forced us to be grown-up.

We had a wonderful evening, and I slept as if I were a rock for the first time since Adam had gone back to his unit after New Year's.

After a long and involved morning routine with Johnny telling us how things should be done, I dressed him warmly and once again we walked to the park. By the time he was cold and tired and willing to walk home, it was nearly lunch time.

"We'll eat in the kitchen," Esther told me as I was peeling layers off her son. "Chanah should be on her way back now. Her son's leg was broken, but otherwise, he only suffered scrapes and bruises. The miscreants have been punished."

"What happened?"

Esther glanced at her son. "Go into the kitchen for your lunch," she told him. "We'll be there in a minute."

Johnny ran off happily, and after Esther watched him go, said, "He's German. Some of the boys took exception to that. When they learned he was German and Jewish, a few of the boys were even more upset with him and everything he represents. One of the older boys, the ringleader, who'd been in trouble for bullying before, was sent down. The rest understand that world events are not the fault of anyone at the school, including Chanah's son."

"Is Chanah all right with him staying in school there?"

"She doesn't have much choice. Her son made the decision, and his English is much better than hers. Apparently, the other boys involved were properly embarrassed and are making efforts to be friendly, and the boys not involved stood up for her son, saved him from more harm, and have since been visiting him. Chanah's son has told her he doesn't want to leave the school and his friends."

"In that case, after luncheon, I'll head off to work if you'll be all right."

"Of course, Livvy. I overreacted."

"I'm glad you did. I had fun. Particularly last night talking over old times."

She smiled. "I did, too. I can't believe we were ever that young."

I gathered up my things and after lunch, said farewell

and went home. I went up in the lift, unlocked the door of my flat, and walked into a pile of destruction.

Blast! Someone had torn my flat apart. I kicked a book and a pillow, furious with the person who invaded my home. If I could get my hands on them...

Books covered the floor of the drawing room, clothes covered the floor of the bedrooms, but the kitchen was untouched. Why would...? In a flash, I was checking the books I'd hidden the blackmail letters in.

They were gone. All but one of Keith Bates'.

I doubted Bates had searched my flat and left behind one of his own letters while taking all of the three other victims'. Peter O'Malley's letters had already been taken to Sir Malcolm, so anyone looking for his letters wouldn't have bothered taking the others when they didn't find his. I was left with three possibilities, all of them possibly desperate enough to upend my flat.

Nothing else appeared to be missing. I decided there was no point in contacting the overtaxed police and began to put everything back where it belonged. That necessitated dusting and hoovering. When I finished, two hours had passed and I was now certain nothing else had been taken.

I went down to the basement. Fortunately, our storage unit was untouched. I removed the copies I'd made of the letters and took them up to my flat.

After I made myself a cup of tea, I read through all the letters again. Roxanne would get all sorts of attention of the wrong sort if her letters became public and be highly embarrassed, but I doubted she would face any legal consequences now. She would, however, probably lose Miles, and I guessed that would be painful.

Gerald Fitzroy could face criminal prosecution if these letters, and his homosexuality, were made public, and Sir Henry would be forced to fire him. If Sir Henry was truly unhappy about Fitzroy favoring his friends, he might be glad of an excuse to fire his chief reviewer.

Clarissa was the tricky case. A murder had been committed and never solved. She worded the letters to sound as if she had knowledge of what happened, information she had not shared with the police, but it was not clear exactly what she had seen and heard. She openly accused other people. Could these letters get her in trouble with the police for withholding evidence? Maybe. Could they get her in trouble with the killer? Definitely.

There was one way to find out if any of them had searched my home. Ask them and then figure out who lied. I needed to get to Broadcasting House before tonight's performance to ask Roxanne.

First, I would store the copies of the letters back in the storage unit. Apparently, my flat wasn't safe from burglars, even with Sutton guarding the lobby.

It was windy, cold, cloudy, and very dark on the streets as I made my way to Broadcasting House. I was glad I had strips of reflective material on my coat, making it easier for buses and autos to avoid me, but it was so dark that night I wasn't certain even that would help.

I kept looking over my shoulder, although I couldn't see more than a few feet in any direction because of the blackout. If the killer was following me, the reflective strips would help him or her track me. Frightened, I ran the last few steps to enter Broadcasting House.

Just as I stepped into the lift, Janet Murrow came up behind me. "I have news for you," she said with a smile. "I've found Peter O'Malley."

Chapter Seventeen

"Where?" I asked, blowing on my cold hands.

"Here," Janet Murrow said, joining me in the lift. "He's performing in tomorrow night's play."

"Did you hear if someone was called up? Whose place did he take?" It would be getting harder for the BBC to replace young men as the military call-ups continued. This wouldn't be a problem with musicians and behind-the-scenes talent, but actors' voices were more specific.

"Paul White. The government needed a good broadcasting voice for some position, but they didn't want to take anyone who could serve in an able-bodied capacity. With his crutches, Paul is perfect."

I looked at Janet in surprise. "How did you learn all this?"

"I talked to the director, a Mr. Bates. I mentioned CBS broadcasting from the fourth floor and that I write scripts for them. He answered all my questions." She looked proud of her sleuthing.

I gave her a smile, happy that she'd been helping me. "Why hasn't O'Malley been called up?"

"He's an Irish citizen. They're neutral."

"I thought he was from the north of England." Or perhaps that was just my assumption, remembering what the

Irishmen in Kilburn had said. I needed to get over to the *Daily Premier* building tomorrow to see if I could find a review that mentioned Peter O'Malley. If he'd acted in any large production in London, our newspaper would have mentioned him.

"He said he's been working in Yorkshire for the last few years."

"Janet, how did you manage to learn so much about O'Malley?" I was impressed.

"He signed in just ahead of me last night. I saw his name, knew you wanted to find him, and so I started talking to him. He invited me to watch the rehearsal, and that's when I also began to question the director."

"Tell me what you learned."

She laughed and pulled me out through the open doors of the lift when it stopped on the fourth floor. There was no one in the hallway. "He said he was born in Ireland and came here as a child. He's always worked in the theater. His parents think that is a disgrace. No way to make a living."

"Any comments on the IRA?"

She shook her head.

"Did he say why he came to London?"

"He said he came to seek his fortune." Janet laughed again. "He's quite a glib character. Don't expect to get a straight answer out of him."

"I have to go upstairs to speak to one of the musicians. May I talk to you later?"

"Come back here. I'll be in the usual place."

"I will," I told her and smiled. Then I hopped back on the lift and headed for the Friday night chamber music concert.

When I looked in the studio, neither Roxanne nor Celeste were inside. I stationed myself near the door and waited. Within a couple of minutes, the two young women appeared.

"That was a nasty trick, tearing my home apart," I told Roxanne. I hoped shocking her might bring out the truth. I couldn't imagine anyone else knowing which flat was mine, while she could have learned the location from Miles.

"What? Tear your house apart? Why would...?" Roxanne looked surprised, and I thought truthfully. Maybe.

"Perhaps you didn't believe I burned the letters, and so you wrecked my home looking for them." I hoped I sounded as annoyed as I felt.

"But I believed you when you said you destroyed them. And now are you telling me you didn't?" Roxanne started to storm away.

I put out my hand to stop her. "They're destroyed, but someone tore my house apart looking for them anyway. I think it was you."

"It wasn't. How would I even know where you live?" She pushed my hand away and started to march toward the studio.

"From Miles."

"We have better things to talk about." Roxanne disappeared into the studio, Celeste on her heels.

She had a point. The telephone and the flat were still in my first married name, and I doubted anyone at Broadcasting

House would know that. Miles probably knew, but that wouldn't be what he would talk to Roxanne about.

No one would know unless someone was interested enough to follow me home and then find a way past our doorman, Sutton, to discover my flat number.

I groaned at my own stupidity. I'd never considered that possibility and hadn't watched for anyone trailing me.

Roxanne was the only one who wondered if I still had the letters, wasn't she? Who was standing outside the concert studio when we'd argued about the existence of the letters?

I tried to dredge up the memory, but I'd been focused on Roxanne and Celeste and never noticed who else was in the hallway before Thursday's rehearsal. I thought there were other people standing around, but it was all a blur.

I gave up trying and turned around, bumping into Gerald Fitzroy, who seemed to be in a hurry to enter the chamber orchestra studio. "You're spending a lot of time around here where you can't cover a story," he told me.

"You didn't need to burgle my flat," I told him. "Your letters weren't there."

"Quiet. Ssh. Ssh. Not so loud," he replied, forcing me toward the opposite wall by walking into me. "I thought you burned them."

"I did. So why did you burgle my flat?"

"My dear lady, it wasn't me. You sound paranoid."

"Someone who didn't believe I burned the letters searched my flat. They didn't find anything, but they made a mess." I looked down an inch or so on him. "It looked as if it was something someone as untrusting as you would have done."

I let my anger show in my voice.

"Not me, Mrs. Redmond. Goodbye." He hurried into the studio.

I took the lift back to the fourth floor to join Janet while we listened to Ed Murrow's broadcast. He was just beginning as I slipped in and took a seat next to her.

Murrow spoke on the cold and dark and quiet outside and how few people were out and about. But if he went into the Tube, the pubs, the restaurants, the theaters, the dance halls, there was plenty of light and people and music and laughter. It was as if we were in two different worlds.

"Don't get the idea these people are discouraged or defeated. They are confident of winning this war somehow or other," we heard him say over the speaker in the listening room.

He was speaking not only to his American audience tonight. He was speaking to those who lived in England. It was a shame most of my countrymen wouldn't get to hear this.

Derek was so mesmerized by his words he didn't realize I'd come in until after Murrow stopped speaking and Derek finished flipping switches and checking gauges. "Hello, Livvy. When did you arrive?"

"Just after the broadcast began. That was really good."

"Wasn't it?" Janet said. "You could see the streets of London."

"Which I am just sick of," Ed Murrow said as he came in. "I think I'm going to have Bill Shirer meet me in Amsterdam soon so we can exchange notes on how things are going. They're neutral in the Netherlands. The lights should still be on over there."

"And the heat?" Janet asked.

"I don't think Europe has heard of heat," her husband said before giving her a grin. "This is going to be all work. You might as well stay here where I know you're safe. You'll keep an eye out for her, won't you, Livvy?"

"Of course. That's no guarantee that she'll be safe, however. I don't have the best reputation for staying out of trouble," I told them.

"Now, why do I believe that?" he asked me.

Janet laughed. "Do you want to go out for a drink, Livvy? What about you, Derek?"

We both agreed and the four of us went downstairs and walked along the road to the Pen and Whistle. "Good name for a pub near Broadcasting House," Ed said.

"Oh, no," Derek told him. "This was originally owned by a retired Peeler. Pen as in jail, and whistle for a bobby's whistle."

The inside looked Victorian, with dark paneling and red fabric-covered benches. I discovered when I ordered a half that their ale was quite good despite the shortages. Janet and I sat on a bench along a side wall and Derek and Ed sat across the table from us on dark wooden stools that matched the dented and scratched table and the paneling, the dark color seeming to suck the light out of the pub.

"Janet, do you know where I live?" I asked.

"No. Where?" She sounded as if it was a social query.

"I'm wondering how many people know. My flat was searched earlier today."

"Good heavens. Was anything stolen?"

I shook my head, not wanting to lie and not wanting to explain about the letters. "The odd thing is, the name on my flat is my first husband's. He died over two years ago. But the way it was searched made it clear they knew it was my flat."

"If it wasn't random—"

Ed, who'd been glancing behind him, said, "Excuse me, ladies. Derek, you know those men over there, don't you?"

"Yes."

"Introduce me, will you? Won't be long." Ed and Derek left our table to join some men across the pub.

"It wasn't random," I told Janet when it was the two of us.

"Then it must have been someone who knew you before you married Adam. How long ago was that?"

"This past July." I looked at her. "Or I was burgled by someone who followed me."

She held my gaze and nodded. "It would have to be someone who followed you into your building and right up to your door."

"Our doorman is so conscientious that someone following a resident in seems unlikely."

"You're lucky," she told me. "We just have a key to the

outside door for nights. During the day, the door is left unlocked most of the time. We have a woman who manages the place, but she's just for packages and letting in cleaners and repairmen and things."

"How is that working out?" I asked, diverted from my troubles.

"No break-ins so far," she told me. "Did you report it to the police?"

"There didn't seem to be any point since nothing was taken."

"What do you plan to do?"

"I don't know." That at least was honest.

"Do you think it has something to do with Frank Kennedy's murder and Peter O'Malley?"

"Yes. I plan to invite myself to tomorrow night's performance of the play. Who knows what I might learn?"

"Do you want me to come, too?" Janet asked.

"Please don't feel that you need to." I didn't want her to feel obligated.

"I want to. My life is a little bit boring with Ed off talking to everyone else." By this time, Ed had been introduced by Derek to a group of BBC engineers and office workers and the two of them were now in the middle of a large group of laughing, chattering people.

"We could join them," I suggested.

As I started to rise, Janet held out a hand to stop me. "No. Ed wouldn't appreciate that. There's work and there's life away from work. He doesn't want to see the two combined."

"Are you all right with that?"

"What you are watching is Ed getting ideas for his broadcasts. He's brilliant. And I love him. We've learned that if we split up and talk to different people, we learn twice as much. And I write articles and radio scripts of my own." She smiled warmly, her gaze apparently focused on the distance where her thoughts resided. Then she stared at me, back in the present. "Mind you, Ed does want to have things his own way, and not everyone loves him the way I do."

I laughed at her tone of voice, showing she understood him and wasn't blinded to his faults. "I'd love to have you meet me at Studio 6A tomorrow evening. I'll have to question a few people before they begin, but once they go onto the sound stage, we can hear them from the 'listening room' outside the door."

* * *

The next morning, I went to the *Daily Premier* building and went upstairs to the newsroom, where Mr. Colinswood's office was. He was behind his desk as usual when I arrived, reading copy while talking on the telephone.

He gestured me to sit while he continued to talk. Once he hung up the receiver, he said, "It's grainy, but I was able to get a copy of a photo of Peter O'Malley by himself for you along with the rest of our coverage on the murder."

He handed it over, and I looked at it carefully. The story listed Peter O'Malley as an actor helping the police with their inquiries. It listed a few plays he was in where he'd received good reviews in the local press. The photograph was slightly blurred and at an angle, showing mostly the right-hand side of his face, but I felt confident that this was the same man in the photo Sir Malcolm had shown me. "May I keep this?"

"I don't want it. What I do want is a good story out of this."

"Do you know anyone on a Leeds newspaper?"

He thought for a moment. "No. I don't think we've ever hired from there, either. At least not in the past five years." His phone rang again and he picked it up.

We waved to each other and I left, putting the photo into my bag.

Sir Malcolm was also at his desk, as usual, when I reached his office. The guard who walked me to his door knocked and then turned the handle as the spymaster called out "Come."

I walked in and found him reading from two different reports spread on his desk.

"Sit down, Olivia."

I did so and then retrieved O'Malley's photo and article out of my bag. I set them on top of the reports Sir Malcolm had been reading. "I believe O'Malley is an actor and not a priest."

Sir Malcolm glanced over the newsprint. "That seems to be the logical conclusion from what we've now learned."

I wish he'd known this earlier. And had shared the information with me. "Did he kill that woman in Yorkshire?"

"My, you are well informed."

"That's what you don't pay me for. Someday, Sir Henry will say no and then you'll have to make a decision."

He looked at me from under his bushy eyebrows. "Hope that day never comes. We don't pay as well as Sir Henry pays you."

I didn't know how he knew my salary, but I was sure he, and the government, didn't pay as well. "Is O'Malley a murderer?"

"The local police couldn't build a case against him or anyone else. It might have been that young actress you've been talking to. Have you considered that?"

"Yes." It seemed unlikely, but it was possible. "How sure are you that O'Malley is IRA?"

"I'm not."

Now I was confused. The men I'd talked to indicated a connection, but I didn't want to tell Sir Malcolm what I'd been up to. "Then what is this about?"

"The Nazi sympathizers hiding out, waiting for the expected invasion, are not our only threat. The IRA have been in contact with Germany and have decided to aid our enemies.

"The IRA started a bombing campaign on English soil starting last January. They only stopped at the end of November with the arrest of five Irish men and women. Now that the trial has been held and two of the men are scheduled to be hanged, we expect the bombing campaign to begin again, only worse in retaliation.

"We've had some of our best people trying to infiltrate

the IRA since the bombings began, and we've learned nothing. We think this O'Malley is important, but we don't know why, and Kennedy was no help while he was alive.

"We know we didn't round up all the IRA members. And since there were several significant bombings by the IRA during those ten months, we know that if they want, they can inflict significant casualties as well as damage. The only questions are when will they begin again, where, and how do they get their explosives?"

Where did O'Malley fit into this, and did I really want to chase after someone that dangerous?

Chapter Eighteen

"All right," I said. "I understand the government is afraid the IRA will start another bombing campaign to protest two of their own being sentenced to death. Where does O'Malley come into this?"

Sir Malcolm gave me a gloomy look. "He came to London to avoid the nasty publicity of being suspected for a murder in Leeds. Then he tried to sell Kennedy nonexistent explosives, which means the IRA are after him for theft."

That fit in with what I had learned from the men in Kilburn. "And O'Malley's letters that Kennedy had?"

"I think Kennedy was using the letters to try to force O'Malley to deliver the explosives. Although there's no reason to think O'Malley could get his hands on something as hard to obtain as explosives." Sir Malcolm sat behind his desk glowering at me.

"Somehow O'Malley must have convinced the IRA that he could procure explosives," I pointed out.

"Yes, but then, he's an actor." Sir Malcolm made it sound as if he had leprosy.

"Why did he tell Kennedy this story, if you're right and he couldn't deliver?" That seemed as if it were the strangest part of Sir Malcolm's explanation, and I didn't believe it.

"I have no idea. Why don't you ask him that when you find him?"

"I will. Are you certain O'Malley doesn't have explosives stored away somewhere?"

"Where could he have obtained them?"

"I don't know, but are you absolutely certain?"

Sir Malcolm made a growling sound. "No, not absolutely. I wish I were."

"I do know where O'Malley's supposed to be at six this evening. And you really don't know if he's a member of the IRA?" I gave Sir Malcolm a smile. He was usually certain of the people he was after.

"I don't think O'Malley's a member. I do know he said he's trying to aid them with explosives." He shrugged. "Unless he's just picking their pockets. But it's a dangerous game he's playing, not trying to hide his identity with the IRA looking for him."

"Maybe he can get the explosives. Maybe he wasn't fleecing the IRA. Maybe Kennedy's death has nothing to do with O'Malley." Another possibility that needed to be studied.

"I hope you're wrong. We don't need the IRA with any more ammunition. But why would you think O'Malley's claim is true?" Sir Malcolm studied me with a look that said he wanted to be convinced.

"He's working as an actor, which he's done before up north. Working as an actor, he wouldn't want to hide his identity." I started counting on my fingers. "No one is looking for him for the murder now. His reviews weren't bad. If he were trying to steal from the IRA, you'd think once they realized they'd been taken, he'd want to hide. But he's working here, under his own name, at the same place Kennedy worked."

If I were Sir Malcolm, I would seriously consider trying to figure out where O'Malley would have hidden explosives. Sir Malcolm, however, seemed unimpressed with my logic as he appeared stone-faced and waved me out.

I stopped at an ABC restaurant for root vegetable soup and a cheese sandwich, knowing I might not have a chance to get dinner that night. Then I went back to the flat.

Within a minute of my arrival, the telephone rang. When I answered, my father's voice boomed out, sounding dignified and annoyed. "I've been trying to reach you for an hour. Where were you?"

"I had an errand to run. Are we meeting for Sunday dinner tomorrow?"

"Of course. I have a reservation for two o'clock at the Ritz. Plenty of time to go to church first. Is Adam home this weekend?"

"Not so far. Why?"

"I was hoping to see him. I value his company." My father sounded fonder of my husband than of me. But then, I knew this was the truth.

"I miss him, too," I told him.

"Of course, Olivia. Well, I'll see you tomorrow." He didn't sound eager for our meeting as he rang off.

It took all my control not to throw the phone at the wall.

* * *

I arrived at Broadcasting House a little after five, but it already felt as if it had been dark outside for several hours. When I signed in, I saw that Peter O'Malley had signed in quite a while ahead of me. I headed straight for the sixth floor, and was surprised to meet Roxanne, Celeste, Harriet Berg, and several others carrying their instrument cases out of the radio actors' studio.

"You've gone into acting?" I asked them jovially.

"They wanted to hear new introductory music for the radio plays," Roxanne told me.

"They paid us extra to come in tonight," Celeste added as they walked on.

I walked into the studio to find O'Malley standing close to Clarissa Northfield, head bent to catch her words. The discussion had an air of intimacy. Gerald Fitzroy was in conference with three other men I didn't know. Two technicians were moving microphones and wires into another configuration. With the actors spread about reading scripts or talking, the room seemed more crowded than usual.

To one side, I found Keith Bates marking up a script. "I hear you have a new actor. You must miss Paul White. He was quite good," I said.

"Oh, hello. Wondered if you'd be back after checking my alibi. Thank you for not upsetting my wife. That was what you were doing?" he asked.

"It always pays to make sure," I told him. I was glad all the signs pointed to him not being a killer.

"I'm glad to be there with my children. I'm not going to mess up my family life again." He nodded and added, "Yes, Paul has a great voice. The government did well by taking him on. We were lucky to find anyone to replace him."

"Did you get someone who's just above the age limit for the moment?" I was curious as to what he'd told the director.

"He's Irish. Since they're neutral, we should be able to hang onto him for a while. He was on the stage in Manchester and Leeds, so he has some experience. Better than we can hope for, these days." Bates looked toward O'Malley with a scowl.

Leeds again. But why did Bates look unhappy? "And Mimi's replacement?"

"A good local stage performer. Of course, with women we have more to choose from."

I had recognized Peter O'Malley and as soon as Clarissa walked off, I walked over and greeted him. He gave me a slimy smile and said, "Are you my leading lady?"

I smiled back at him. "No, I'm the lady who was told by the IRA that you owe them something explosive."

"Not so loud," he murmured, glancing around. "Let's go out in the hall."

I followed him out and down the hallway to an alcove with a bench. "Well? Are you going to deliver or were you just after quick riches?"

He looked over his shoulder before he faced me and said,

"I don't go after riches if it means a slit throat."

"Then you need to hand over the goods soon or your customers will come to their own conclusions." *And Sir Malcolm will want to get his hands on those explosives when you hand them over,* I added silently.

"Kennedy was my contact. Once he was killed, I didn't know what to do or whom to trust. Since you appear to be in touch with them, tell my friends from Dublin to send me a contact so we can finish our deal."

"You already received your money?"

He gave me a grim smile. "A down payment, nothing more, but enough to get me killed."

There was something I wondered. "Why did Frank Kennedy have a couple of your letters?"

"Do you know who they were to?"

I shook my head.

"Althea Northfield. A woman who was murdered last year in Leeds. The woman people thought I'd killed."

"Why did Kennedy have them?"

"He was trying to blackmail me, the rat. He thought they showed I killed her."

"Why were they signed 'Father' Peter O'Malley?"

"She liked to act. I think that's why she was a patron of the theater in Leeds." He looked at me and said, "You don't get it, do you? She chose her lovers from the leading men who'd pass through town, but she wanted them to pretend to be someone else. Father Peter O'Malley was the role she chose for me."

"Those were love letters?" I kept my voice lowered with effort.

"In code for the location of our trysts."

Sir Malcolm would not be happy when I told him he was diverting people to decipher love letters. Before I could ask anything else, we heard two men loudly arguing. Within a minute, several people came out into the hallway and walked off.

Bates followed them out of the studio and said to the actors, "Everybody onstage for last-minute instructions."

"That's my cue. Tell the IRA what I said. I want to get this over with." O'Malley hurried through the door as I saw Janet Murrow walking down the hallway. Clarissa Northfield raced past her and ducked inside the studio.

As Gerald Fitzroy walked out, I stopped him. "Are you doing a review on this play?"

"No, I came up to see the producer and find out what the BBC has planned for this spring. Amazing how Bates can't keep his actors under control." He lowered his voice. "You'd better have destroyed my letters. I will come back at you if I am threatened with more blackmail. And you'd better not be working with O'Malley."

"What? Why would I be working with O'Malley?" I said, but Fitzroy had already made his speedy way to the lift despite his limp while I stood there in shock.

I didn't understand why the director looked at O'Malley with such a sour face or why the theater critic was so angry with him. Or what Fitzroy thought O'Malley and I could be working on together.

Janet arrived then. She and I sat in the listening room and enjoyed the play. Afterward, we told Keith Bates how well the performance went while I kept an eye on O'Malley. Unfortunately, I couldn't approach him with more questions because Clarissa Northfield had latched on to him and wasn't letting him out of her sight. That also meant I couldn't question her.

Finally, she had to let him go to retrieve her bag. As I headed toward O'Malley, he shook his head just enough that I got the message. Not now. Then he said in a voice that carried to me, "I'm looking forward to the play on Monday. Since it's such an old standard, will we have a rehearsal first?"

Keith Bates heard him too. "Everyone arrive at five Monday for a run-through before the performance."

There were various responses as all the actors gathered their things and left. Clarissa snared O'Malley's arm and nearly dragged him off.

Bates watched them leave and shook his head.

"What's wrong?" I asked him.

"Clarissa. As soon as one actor leaves, she grabs hold of another. She's such an innocent, I don't think she realizes how much trouble this one could be."

"What do you mean?"

Bates shook his head and then gave me a smile. "Nothing. He just has a peculiar sense of humor."

He walked off and Janet told me, "Ed is dining with some sources tonight. Have you had dinner yet?"

"No, and dinner sounds like a great idea," I told her as we headed downstairs.

We went across Oxford Street and headed into Soho. Despite the blackout and cold, there were people out everywhere, going to dinner or to clubs. Janet and I agreed on practically the first restaurant we came to and went inside, where we were promptly seated.

We had ordered from what felt as if it were a limited menu, another effect of the war, when I looked up and saw Roxanne and Miles walking toward me.

My first thought was of Adam? How did Miles get the weekend off when Adam had to stay with his regiment? As Miles grew closer, his focus on Roxanne, I blurted out, "Where's Adam?"

Miles looked down, came to a stop, and blinked. "He's in camp," he said and reddened.

I stared at him, waiting for an explanation while Roxanne turned around to look from one of us to the other.

"My father needed me for an official ceremony this afternoon. Ghastly boring thing." Miles looked uncomfortable. "The army sets great store by these things, even if I don't."

"You have my condolences," I said in a dry tone. He was here with Roxanne, while Adam was with the army somewhere else, somewhere not with me.

That wasn't Miles's fault, I reminded myself. It was Hitler's. And Adam would expect me to be kind to his friend. Adam was a much nicer person than I was. I tried to sound sincere when I said, "But lucky for you that you're getting a break."

"It should have been my older brother at the ceremony, but the army has him off someplace unreachable, so I had to stand in."

Roxanne stood listening to this with widening eyes. She mustn't have known Miles's standing in the aristocracy.

"The army gave me a pass until tomorrow afternoon, but my family doesn't need to see me again until morning when I go back." He gave me a fleeting smile. "I would have invited Adam to come to London if I could, but it doesn't work that way."

"Something to do with your father's title?" I kept my voice lowered, trying not to glare at him. "Some new post in the government?"

Miles nodded.

"Roxanne," I said, turning toward her, "you're from Leeds. Did you ever play violin for Althea Northfield or the theater there?"

She jumped.

"What is it?" Miles asked, putting a hand on her back and pulling her closer to him.

She nodded. "She—she ran the theater."

"Look, they want us to sit down and order. We'll talk later," Miles said and nudged Roxanne away from our table.

"He's in your husband's unit and he has leave this weekend while your husband doesn't?" Janet asked.

"Afraid so."

"That doesn't seem fair."

"There's nothing remotely fair about this war for anyone. Not us. Not the Germans. Not the rest of the world." I didn't mind admitting my anger to Janet. She was kind and even-tempered.

"I suspect America will learn that before it's over," she replied before we both fell silent.

We had eaten, talking of random topics, and were drinking our coffee when Miles and Roxanne came past us again. "We're going to a dance hall not far from here if you have more questions," Miles said.

"I don't want to interfere with your evening, but I do need to ask Roxanne some questions. Monday morning before rehearsal?"

"The Broadcasting House café at noon for a cup of tea?" she suggested reluctantly. She looked as if I had mentioned drawing and quartering her. Or perhaps she thought I'd poison her tea.

"I'll see you there." I gave the two of them a smile and tried not to sound threatening. Roxanne looked petrified. Miles looked puzzled at Roxanne's reaction.

Then Roxanne bolted from the restaurant, with Miles on her heels saying, "What's wrong? Tell me."

* * *

Sunday was a day of waiting. I went to church with my father, ate lunch with him, talked to Adam on the telephone, and then went for a long walk. I was in before the blackout started.

I was reading in the drawing room and having a cup of tea when the lights went out. Were power cuts going to be another effect of the war? I went to the window and peeked out. Because of the blackout, I couldn't tell if the power cut was only my flat or the entire city.

Then I felt my way to my door and opened it to look out. Immediately, I was pushed back in with a torch shining in my face.

I heard the door click behind my assailant, but in the darkness with my eyes dazzled, I couldn't see anything of him or her.

"Where is he?" a man's voice said.

"Who?" My voice shook a little.

"O'Malley." A second man's voice. I hadn't realized a second man had come into my flat.

"He told me he has the explosives and he needs another contact now that Kennedy is dead so he can give them to you."

"Where is he?" The man asked.

Where was Sutton? was my question. "I'm meeting him at five tomorrow afternoon if you want to go with me."

"Where?" One of the men had moved around me and now grabbed me from behind, one hand pulling my hair, and my head, back. The other man moved closer to crowd me from the front.

I was pinned between them and didn't trust them to leave me alive. "So that once I tell you then you can kill me? No."

"Where?"

I felt something narrow and cold glide along my neck.

Chapter Nineteen

I tried to lean away from what I guessed was a knife blade, but the person behind me, a man I thought, blocked my movement. I tried not to tremble. I felt my only chance was to not show my fear. My voice squeaked as I said, "I'm only dealing with the two men I dealt with before."

"Now you're dealing with us."

"I could trust them to meet me and talk to O'Malley without these theatrics." I didn't want to die, but I certainly wasn't going to make it easy for them now that my fear was becoming tinged with annoyance.

Compared to the IRA men I had dealt with before, these two were common thugs.

"Tell me," the man in front of me with the knife, crowding against me, demanded.

"Let's go and talk to your leaders and see what they say." They must have been able to feel me tremble, but I was going to try to hang on to the only thing I believed would keep me alive. My meeting place with Peter O'Malley.

There was a pause, and then something, a hood or cap perhaps, went over my eyes and nose, leaving my mouth free. The hood smelled of smoke. Coal smoke. I was shoved back into a chair and held in place by one meaty hand.

At least I could no longer feel the knife or the presence of the man holding the blade standing directly in front of me.

I sat there for a minute or more before I heard a knock on my front door. Footsteps, then a click as the door opened, then more footsteps into my drawing room. "All right, Mrs. Redmond. We know you've been talking to O'Malley. Where is he?"

The voice was familiar, but I wasn't certain. "Who are you? How do I know you aren't someone other than the people he's been dealing with? Or that I've been dealing with?"

The speaker must have signaled my jailer, because the hood came off. By the torchlight, I could see the leader and the spokesman from the other night seated facing me. "Recognize me?" the spokesman asked.

I nodded. "At a quarter to five tomorrow evening, meet me on the north side of Oxford Street by the Oxford Circus Underground station."

"Why don't we just meet you at five outside Broadcasting House? We know he's working there."

"If you know that, why have you put on this theater production?"

"Not everyone believed you would be willing to help us discuss things with O'Malley," the spokesman said with a touch of annoyance in his voice. Apparently, the IRA wasn't as unified as they claimed.

"And this was how you decided whether you could trust me? By threatening me? Good grief." Now that I was feeling less frightened, I let my anger show in my voice. Their behavior was juvenile at best, stupid and dangerous at worst.

Especially dangerous for me.

"Don't get cheeky with me, my lass, or we will show you our thoughts in a tangible way," the leader said, speaking for the first time.

"I'm not trying to harm you." Not yet. "Don't threaten me."

"We will meet you at five tomorrow evening on the pavement in front of Broadcasting House," the spokesman said.

"Don't try to double-cross us," the leader said. Both men rose and walked out of my flat, leaving me with the two thugs. Ten seconds later, they left, taking their hood and their knife with them.

I trembled with relief before I rose on shaky legs and walked to my front door. I opened it a crack and a moment later, the lights came back on both in the building hallway and in my flat.

They must have a way to shut down the mains power to our building. They were frightening in their abilities.

I rushed down to the lobby to look for Sutton. He arrived a moment later from the basement, where the storage cabinets were accessed as well as the utilities for the building.

"Hello," I greeted him. "Did we blow a fuse?"

"No," he said, looking around. "Someone sneaked downstairs and pulled the mains switch. That's what caused the fuses to blow."

"Did you see who it was?"

"No. It happened while someone came in to ask for a person who doesn't live here. Someone I've never heard of." Sutton looked glum at being used so poorly.

"I'm sorry someone would pull such a trick on you. Still, not so bad as this past Friday afternoon, when someone ransacked my flat."

"What?" Sutton's gaze shot to my face. "Why didn't you tell me? Did you report it to the police?"

"Nothing was taken. There was nothing you could do. But it seems as if someone is playing tricks on us. Was it someone looking for a resident that let this person get upstairs to my flat?"

"What time was this?"

"Before two in the afternoon on Friday."

Sutton nodded. "A pretty young lady asked for directions to the Tube station. I was telling her when a delivery came for Mrs. Shaw on the sixth floor. And Mrs. Lawrence returned from shopping with the baby, causing commotion in the lobby until you couldn't hear yourself think. When I finished with all that, you know how particular Mrs. Shaw is, the young lady was gone. Gave up, I thought. But anyone could have slipped by me with all that going on."

"How would anyone have known which flat was mine? It's still in Reggie Denis's name."

"That's my fault." He looked at the floor and reddened.

I looked at him. "Sutton? What's going on?"

"Someone called around New Year's and asked for Mrs. Redmond's flat number. Said they were doing a delivery for a late Christmas present. I told them. But nothing ever showed up." He gestured, palms up. "I'm sorry."

"You couldn't know. I'm sorry I've brought all this trouble to our door."

"I'm sorry it's so easy to get by me these days."

"Sutton, you're as sharp as ever," I told him. "Someone very clever is playing us for fools."

I went upstairs to my flat, now definitely known to someone. The killer, probably. Someone female? Still shaken and chilled by the experience, I went to bed and piled the covers over me.

* * *

The next morning, a bright and cold Monday, I went first to the *Daily Premier* building to talk to Mr. Colinswood. It was too early for the fog of tobacco smoke to have filled his office when I arrived, but not too early that he wasn't already on the telephone. "What can I do for you, Olivia?" he asked when he set down the telephone receiver.

"I'm going to write up an account of my dealings with the IRA and O'Malley, who are about to trade explosives for cash."

"Good grief, Olivia. That's a front-page story. If this O'Malley hands over explosives to the IRA, people will get hurt. People will get killed. I can't sit on a story this big," Mr. Colinswood said, forcefully stubbing out his cigarette in the empty ashtray.

"You have to trust me. He needs to hand over the explosives. All you have to do is sit on what I write until I give you the go-ahead to publish."

"Can you promise me no one will get hurt?"

"Unless something goes very wrong. And then the story you'll be able to write will be even better," I told him. I smiled, hiding the reality that I couldn't promise.

"What if you're the one who gets killed?" Mr. Colinswood sounded both annoyed and worried.

"Then give what I've written to Scotland Yard." I had a second thought. "No, give it to Sir Malcolm. Sir Henry knows how to reach him. And if you're holding it, no one will be looking for it here."

"You'd better write it all down. Every detail," Mr. Colinswood said, shaking his head as he answered his telephone again.

I found the nearest free typewriter and typed up my tale. Then I called Sir Malcolm from one of the telephones in the newsroom. When he answered, I told him, "O'Malley does have the package. He's meeting the recipients at five. From then on, it's up to you to recover it."

"And Kennedy?" came out of the telephone as a growl.

"He wasn't murdered for it. In fact, those letters you wanted? They were love letters between two people who liked to play-act. They weren't code for where the package is hidden."

"How do you know that?"

"O'Malley."

A grumble, rather than words, came out of the receiver. "Pretty odd love letters. Could be a cover story," he finally said.

I could tell he was more annoyed than doubting what I told him. "Maybe, but it is interesting that the other party is the murdered woman in Yorkshire. I think Kennedy wanted them for blackmail, not to use to find ex—the package." I stopped myself from saying "explosives" over the telephone line.

Who knew what operator might be listening in to our conversation?

"Humpf," Sir Malcolm said. "At least if we tail O'Malley, we'll be able to recover the goods. And the purchasers will be with him?"

"I suspect they'll travel to the site together. I don't know for certain." Hopefully, they would go there without me.

"Where is this meeting taking place?"

"Sixth floor, Broadcasting House."

After I hung up, I waved farewell to Mr. Colinswood. He put his hand over the mouthpiece in the receiver and said, "Promise me you'll be careful."

"I will. I have no desire to end up dead or in jail." I gave him a confident smile that I didn't feel and headed for Broadcasting House for my meeting with Roxanne.

I found her waiting for me in the basement café. After we got our tea, I leaned over the table and said, "You come from Leeds. As I was asking the other night, did you ever perform for Althea Northfield or any of the plays she was involved with?"

"I've heard of her. I was in the orchestra for a few plays and heard her name. She was a patron, a very important person in Leeds theater, but I never met her. Why? You do know she was murdered."

I nodded. "It seems that everyone involved with Frank Kennedy was from Leeds."

"Really?" She sounded surprised.

I decided to discover what I really needed to know. "Who was the trumpet player from New Year's Eve?"

"He's..." She hesitated. I suspected she was trying to come up with a story I might believe.

"Tell me the truth." *Please.*

"He's someone I don't want Miles to meet. Or for him to hear about Miles."

"Relative or pimp?" I asked quietly, staring at her.

"You're brutal." Her eyes gleamed, but she held back her tears.

"Only when people lie to me." I softened my tone. "Roxanne, what you tell Miles is up to you. I need to find Frank Kennedy's killer so I can go back to my normal life. Or as normal as anything gets these days. Now, who is this trumpet player?"

"A cousin who was already living in London when I received an offer to play in the BBC Chamber Music Orchestra. I was only offered employment since so many men were being drafted. My cousin lets me live in his flat in exchange for cleaning and paying reduced rent. It leaves me some money to send to my aunt and uncle for my brother and sister's upkeep."

"You could move out. Move into Celeste's rooming house."

"No, I can't." She looked at me over her tea. "He knows what I was doing in Leeds. He said he'd tell everyone if I move out. I'd be ruined. No one would hire me if they learn of my—past."

Blackmail again. "Were you ever arrested in Leeds or anywhere else for your former career?"

"No, and it was never my career. Just a part-time earner to supplement my part-time music positions," she snapped.

I changed my questioning. "What made you think I kept your letters? I've tried to be completely honest with you." Well, as much as I could. And it would prove true if Roxanne weren't involved in Frank Kennedy's murder.

"I was told that you might have kept them." Her voice faded out.

"Who said that?"

She shook her head.

"Please, Roxanne. Who?"

She rose. "I have to go upstairs to rehearsal."

I put out a hand to stop her. "Who are you afraid of? Is someone else blackmailing you now?"

"No, and I don't know who the man is who said it." She shoved away from me and fled.

I sat until my tea grew cold, staring into space. I doubted there was anything Roxanne could have been blackmailed over besides her previous career.

I was certain Miles didn't know. Roxanne would keep that from him. It would end their relationship if he learned of her past, and be a cloud between them if she didn't confess.

But who was this "man" that Roxanne didn't know who was somehow a threat over her letters?

Somehow, what evidence I had made me feel certain I could eliminate Roxanne and Bates from the list of suspects. Kennedy's brother and sister didn't know the people he was blackmailing. I could rule them out, too. It was just instinct, but I felt I could trust my feelings on this.

Derek and the other engineers? The rest of the musicians and actresses? There was nothing pointing to any individual one of them.

Later that day, I'd be able to talk to O'Malley and learn what he knew about Kennedy's death. I still had to speak to Clarissa, and I needed to find Gerald Fitzroy somewhere so I could question him.

* * *

I left, only to return shortly before five. Within two minutes, the leader and the spokesman of the IRA group I'd met joined me. When we signed in, I glanced at their names in the ledger. The spokesman was named Sean, his surname scrawled. The leader signed in as Michael Collins. I didn't believe him.

We went silently upstairs to the hallway outside the entrance to the studio. Both men seemed tense, and I feared they planned to attack once they had Peter O'Malley in their sights. However, they kept their hands in plain view, so perhaps it was only their reputation that had my imagination running wild.

O'Malley was talking to Clarissa in the hallway when we exited the lift. He appeared to tell her to go inside, he'd be in shortly. She made clear she wouldn't.

O'Malley shrugged and walked toward us, while Clarissa shot a stare at me that should have wounded. I guessed she thought I was a threat to her pursuit of O'Malley. She was young, pretty, and single. She had nothing to fear from me.

At the moment, though, I didn't have time to straighten her out. I followed spokesman Sean and "Michael Collins" to where they stopped in front of O'Malley.

"I have a run-through and then a performance this evening, gentlemen. Can we meet at half-past nine?" O'Malley mentioned a pub on Baker Street, a good distance to the west.

The leader nodded, and then said, "If you don't show up, we will find you, O'Malley." There was so much menace in his tone that I took a half-step away from him.

O'Malley didn't look concerned. "I want to finish our business, too, gentlemen. And get the rest of my money."

"I expect you to be there, also, Mrs. Redmond, or we'll come looking for you. Particularly if anything goes wrong." The leader's gaze was cold when he glanced back at me.

I nodded, not trusting my voice.

"Half-past nine," the spokesman said, and the two Irishmen walked back to the lift. I waited for them to leave before I said to O'Malley, "Don't keep them waiting."

"I don't intend to. I want this over as much as they do." He walked into the studio.

Clarissa and I stayed in the hallway looking at each other. Her expression was as puzzled as mine must have been.

"Clarissa, do you know anything about my flat being burgled?"

"No. Why would I? You don't have anything I want." She stalked into the studio, her nose in the air.

I was about to follow her when Gerald Fitzroy emerged from the lift. "Mr. Fitzroy, do you know anything about my flat being burgled?" This wasn't my first time asking him about this, but maybe I'd have better luck getting an answer the second time.

"You accused me of this before. Why would I?"

"Hunting for correspondence?" I guessed.

He paled. "You promised."

"There's nothing to find, but I suspect someone wanted to verify my words. I can't imagine why else anyone would break into my flat."

"Well, it wasn't me. I have no interest in learning where your flat is. You certainly aren't rich enough or interesting enough." He held out his hands to his sides. "Do I look as if I'm a burglar?" Then he paused for a moment and said, "I'm not sure I believe you destroyed my letters, not after what I heard," before he stormed into the listening room.

What had he heard? And from whom?

I followed him into the listening room. No one else was

in there at that moment. Knowing time was short, I said, "You heard what from whom?"

"O'Malley said he could start up Ken—" Fitzroy stopped as an engineer came in. He gestured for me to leave.

Restart Kennedy's blackmail scheme? How could he do that? I wished I had more time to question Fitzroy, but I needed to stop the IRA from getting the explosives first.

* * *

I arrived at the pub at the appointed time, knowing Sir Malcolm's men would already be in place. I had rung him and told him the time and place of the meeting and warned him his people would have to follow discreetly for who knew how long. I didn't see anyone I knew except for the IRA spokesman. He was with a younger man I didn't recognize.

I walked over and spoke to them, and then went to the bar and ordered a half pint. When I returned, they fell silent.

Half-past nine came and went, and I began to feel nervous. The younger IRA man began to eye me as if he were measuring me for a noose. The spokesman, though, appeared to be relaxed, as if he waited for people all day long.

Finally, O'Malley came into the pub and blinked as his eyes grew accustomed to the light after the blackout outside. When he saw us, he nodded and then went to order a pint.

The four of us did little talking as we sipped our ale and tried to look inconspicuous. At least I tried. At ten minutes to ten, the spokesman said, "Drink up."

A moment later, the four of us walked out of the pub. As

we headed up Baker Street toward the Tube station, I was aware of a skirmish behind us. I turned to see four men, fists flying, in front of the pub.

"Friends of yours?" the spokesman asked. Without waiting for a reply, he took my arm in his and hurried me along the pavement.

Chapter Twenty

From the Baker Street Tube station, we traveled to the Kilburn Park station at O'Malley's direction. I didn't see anyone on the train with us who looked as if they could be Sir Malcolm's men, so I guessed they were caught up in that fight leaving the pub. I was on my own.

How I could be expected to stop the IRA from walking away with the explosives wasn't clear.

O'Malley seemed relaxed, as if he didn't have any worries. Either he really was taking these IRA men to the explosives, or he had a very good escape plan. Maybe both.

Since I had no plan beyond surviving, I hoped it was the former.

The Underground was busy with late-night workers. I wasn't afraid enough to tremble until we left the lighted and busy train at the Kilburn Park station and I went out to face the dark streets with a slippery actor and two IRA killers. I started to lag behind before we left the station, and as soon as we stepped onto the pavement, the young IRA man grabbed hold of my arm.

I dropped my bag in such a way that everything fell out of it.

"Leave it," the spokesman snapped.

"No." I crouched down and started to pick up my things to put back in my bag. In the dark it was hard to find anything, so I groped around with my gloved hands.

"He said leave it," the big, younger man said.

"No." I picked up more of my things as he jerked my arm, making me spill everything I'd picked up in an even bigger circle. I glared at him. "See what you've done. Leave me alone."

O'Malley stood to the side, watching this comedy of errors as if it had nothing to do with him.

"Why, you…" I thought the younger man might have raised his fist, but the spokesman must have stopped him with a sign.

"People are looking, Seamus," the older man told the younger one as he helped me gather my things and then gave me a hand up. "Let's go."

We assembled along the pavement. O'Malley walked along as if he didn't have a care. The two IRA men followed him, keeping an eye on any traffic, on wheels or on foot. They told O'Malley to wait as they had me move to walk in front of them. I strolled along next to O'Malley, keeping my mouth shut so my teeth didn't chatter from fear.

We walked across the bridge over the railroad tracks and then turned away from the High Road through a gloomy area. I couldn't make out if the buildings were terrace houses or warehouses, it was so dark on the narrow streets. We finally ended up at a Victorian cemetery with low block walls around it.

O'Malley never hesitated. He followed a map in his head through the blackness that left the rest of us picking our way along paths marred by tree roots and leaning headstones. We struggled to keep up with a lack of moonlight. The next night would be a new moon.

"Where are we?" I asked after yelping when I tripped over something unseen.

"The Old Cemetery," O'Malley said. "It's just here."

We stopped in front of one of the few mausoleums. The younger IRA man turned on a torch so O'Malley could see to fit an old, ornate key into the lock. As soon as he swung the door open, cold, musty air flew out at us. Nothing could get me to go inside, but O'Malley took the torch and went in without a moment's hesitation.

I heard a couple of bumps and then he returned struggling under the weight of a large package wrapped in something that crinkled the way brown paper would. He handed the package to the younger man, shifting the heavy weight from his arms onto the other man's before turning around to shut and lock the door to the mausoleum by torch light.

"Whose is it?" I asked, glancing above the door. I couldn't read the name since the torch wasn't aimed directly at the carving.

"Curious, aren't you," the IRA spokesman said as the younger man quickly set down the package. He removed the paper and took the torch to display a large crate filled with sticks of dynamite.

I took a step back.

"The family of a friend," O'Malley said.

It took me a moment to realize he was answering my question about the mausoleum.

"I can't carry this the whole way to where you said to take it," the younger IRA man muttered to the spokesman. Then he turned to O'Malley. "How did you move this?"

"There's a wheelbarrow by the lodge. I borrowed that to move it through the cemetery."

"I'll think of someplace close," the spokesman said. "Close enough to move it the whole way in the barrow."

"I want my money. Then I'm going home," O'Malley said.

"You're going to have to help us move this," the spokesman said.

"Not part of the deal. I handed it off. It's all yours, and I want my money," O'Malley said, sounding belligerent. "I got it this far on my own. There are two of you. You should be able to take it from here."

I took two steps away from them, not wanting any part of whatever might happen next.

The spokesman pulled out a large knife and said, "You're going to help us move this someplace safe before you see your money."

"How do I know you won't take the goods and run me through to keep from paying up?" O'Malley said, his arms folded over his chest.

"That's why we brought the lass. To assure fair dealing. Show me where this barrow is kept." The spokesman put his knife away.

The two men, O'Malley in front, walked away into the darkness, leaving me with the younger IRA man and a crate full of dynamite. "Don't think about going anywhere," he told me.

"I'm not. I wouldn't." I shut my mouth on anything else I might say, since I sounded so nervous. Even now, O'Malley might be bleeding to death from a knife thrust from the IRA.

"I don't enjoy standing around this way. Those bobbies in the pub might have followed us." The younger man sounded as nervous as I felt.

The men he thought were bobbies must have been Sir Malcolm's people. "How could anyone follow us clear out here? There's no one around here except the dead."

"Don't say that."

This big, strong young man was afraid of being in a cemetery at night? I decided to rattle him. "We're in a graveyard. Everyone here is dead. What's wrong with that?"

"Just be quiet."

"Don't tell me you're afraid of ghosts." I decided I might as well make him as uncomfortable as he made me.

"Be quiet." He was nearly shouting at me now.

"Ghosts aren't going to bother you if you have a clear conscience," I told him.

"Will you—?"

"Stop shouting," the spokesman said, "and get the crate in here."

I could see the wheelbarrow in the light from the torch.

The young IRA man lifted the crate and banged it down into the wagon, making the wooden and metal contraption groan and me flinch.

I looked around. "Where's O'Malley?"

The spokesman swore. "Get this to Paddy's. Go in through the alley." Then he took off with a torch in one direction while the younger man with the other torch went another. I followed the beam of light on the ground, thinking the IRA spokesman would head for the nearest way out of the graveyard as he followed O'Malley.

I wanted to get out of there as quickly as possible and go home. At least the IRA men were no longer interested in me. I only needed to find the Tube station. I'd call Sir Malcolm from my flat and tell him what transpired.

All of a sudden, shapes moved in the darkness. The spokesman landed on the ground, his torch flying away and going out.

I was grabbed. I quickly found struggling didn't help. I couldn't break free, held from behind with my feet off the ground and all in darkness around me.

I heard shouts in the distance and a metallic crash I thought might be the wheelbarrow.

It felt as if a long time had passed, but it must have only been half a minute before torches were turned on and the shapes turned into ordinary-looking men.

"We've got a man over here with a wheelbarrow full of dynamite," one of the men bundled up in an overcoat, bowler hat, and scarf said.

"Take him and the dynamite to headquarters," another man said. This one had on a flat cap similar to what the IRA men wore. "Take these two in separate cars."

I was half-dragged, half-carried toward the entrance and the road and unceremoniously tossed into an automobile. "Who are you?" I asked for the fourth or fifth time, this time addressing the driver as well as the man sitting next to me. Neither was in a constable's uniform, but they both had that look about them. They sat rigidly with no expression on their faces, and neither said a word.

We drove through the empty, dark streets with only an occasional bus or lorry to contend with. Once we reached the official heart of London, I recognized where we were by the outline of famous buildings against the slightly paler, starlit sky.

When we drove through the gates into the courtyard of New Scotland Yard and were surrounded by what I knew were the familiar red brick Victorian buildings, I felt strangely relieved. I was sure Sir Malcolm would see I didn't languish in prison, and I was safe from the ire of the IRA.

At least for the time being.

They didn't, however, take off my iron bracelets and I was marched into a small room for questioning. I was told to sit in a straight-backed wooden chair by a large, solid wooden table. Two other wooden chairs sat on the other side of the table.

A uniformed bobby stood by the door, as if waiting for me to try to escape. What I really wanted was for someone to take my manacles off.

Or find me a more comfortable chair.

After a long, tiring wait while I wished I could go home to bed, two Scotland Yard detectives joined me in the vanilla-colored room with dull lighting and no windows. One of the men I recognized as the one in the flat cap who appeared to be in charge of the raid on the cemetery. He was medium height and thin with a long narrow nose. The other man was larger in every direction, wearing a nice three-piece gray suit and a weary air.

"Name?" Flat Cap barked.

"Olivia Redmond."

"Where did the dynamite come from?" He showed no inclination to introduce himself.

"The mausoleum."

"How did the dynamite get into the mausoleum?"

"You'll have to ask Peter O'Malley." His questioning made me curious. Shouldn't Sir Malcolm's people know that?

"Who is Peter O'Malley?"

"You didn't catch him, did you?" I asked. Their raid hadn't been successful if O'Malley had escaped.

"What's your connection to the IRA?"

"Ask Sir Malcolm Freemantle."

"Who?" Flat Cap asked.

"This interview is terminated," the larger man said, rising.

Both Flat Cap and I looked at him in amazement.

He took a key and unlocked the manacles. "You're free

to leave."

"Outside," Flat Cap said. Then he turned to me. "You stay."

"If you'll excuse us for a moment, Mrs. Redmond," the larger man said and walked out of the room. The man in the flat cap gestured to a bobby to stand guard inside the room while he followed the larger man out.

I sat, glaring at the door and wondering how long they would keep me waiting as I rubbed my wrists.

The two men returned in a few minutes, although now the larger man who also showed no interest in identifying himself was clearly in charge. "All right, Mrs. Redmond, if you would tell us how you came to be in the cemetery tonight. We have Sir Malcolm's permission to hear this."

I made the explanation as short and uncomplicated as possible. I left Mr. Colinswood out of it entirely, focusing on the pub and the mausoleum.

When I finished, the larger man said, "I see you understood our men were ambushed coming out of the pub. Clever of you to dump out the contents of your bag outside the Tube station. It gave us time to find you."

"You already knew the action would be around Kilburn?" I knew Sir Malcolm's people had been following the IRA since the bombings started a year before. They'd know possible places to stash the explosives.

"Of course. We knew the dynamite would end up there in an IRA safe house. We were patrolling the area, looking for you and your companions."

"Did you catch O'Malley?" He was the key to the whole business.

"We'll find him."

"Is he working for you?" I was suspicious since he had escaped their attempt to catch us all.

"That's all we need, Mrs. Redmond. We will give you a lift home." The larger man rose.

I rose and found myself looking up to him. "The IRA are going to think either O'Malley or I told you where to find them and the dynamite. I don't want to be murdered, and I'm certain he doesn't, either."

"Both of the IRA men are still locked up here. They have no way to communicate with their comrades, of which there are very few now," Flat Cap told me.

"Why do you think there are so few now?" I asked. One would be too many in my estimation.

"Because five of them were put on trial. Three are in prison and two more await the gallows because of their bombings. It tends to make anyone with similar beliefs either lay low or go back to Ireland." Flat Cap seemed satisfied with the results.

I wasn't, because I imagined I could still be in danger, but I doubted whether speaking out would help. I followed the larger man down brightly lit corridors until we left the building and walked to a police car. In a moment, a bobby drove me out of the New Scotland Yard forecourt.

As we rode along Portland Place just past Broadcasting House, I saw a figure in the weak light of the headlights stumble backward along the pavement and collapse clutching his chest. I thought I recognized him.

The only other person out this late was faced away from the stricken man as they strode along the pavement. A figure who was little more than a shadow vanishing in the darkness. There was no one around to help.

"Stop," I shouted at the bobby and started to open my car door.

Startled, he pulled to the curb and stopped. I jumped out and ran to the person on the pavement and turned his head, feeling for a pulse in his neck. Nothing. By now the bobby was kneeling on the other side of the man. I tried loosening the man's tie and telling him help was coming. "Blow your whistle," I commanded the driver.

"Miss. Look," the bobby said as he shone his torch on the man. Then he rose and blew on his whistle while I stared at a knife sticking out of the man's chest.

I was right when I thought I had recognized the man. Peter O'Malley.

Had the IRA found out about the dynamite and the arrests already? Or was the shadow I'd seen someone else? I looked over my shoulder, expecting to be attacked immediately.

Chapter Twenty-One

We were soon surrounded by uniformed police officers, technical officers with torches and cameras, and my interrogators Flat Cap and the larger man. It reminded me of finding Frank Kennedy's body, except it was colder this night and I'd met this dead man before.

The stronger light let me see the dark smear around the knife as the doctor rose and picked up his medical bag. "I wouldn't be surprised if the knife hit the heart or an artery. Death appears to have been sudden," he told Flat Cap, who then walked over to me.

"Did you see him get stabbed?" Flat Cap asked.

"No."

"Anyone near him on the pavement?"

"No. Just one person walking away farther up the pavement and very few vehicles about."

"Did you recognize Peter O'Malley?" the larger man asked. He was now wearing a bowler hat and a dark overcoat.

"Yes, in the headlights while we drove along Portland Place and then when the constable turned his torch toward him."

"Where did you last see him?"

I was cold, tired, and sickened by the body garishly lit up

in front of me under a tent to try to follow blackout regulations. "You know very well—"

"For the record," Flat Cap demanded.

"In the Old Cemetery in Kilburn earlier tonight." Then I asked, "Could I please go home and get out of this cold?"

"Yes," said the larger man. He waved to the bobby who'd been driving me to my building when we'd found Peter O'Malley to take me the rest of the way home.

* * *

The next morning, I woke up under six blankets to find I was finally no longer chilled. Wrapping up in an old woolen robe, I went into the kitchen to fix tea and toast. I was halfway done when the telephone rang.

When I answered, Sir Malcolm's voice boomed out of the receiver. "I need you to come to my office this morning. Immediately."

"I haven't had my tea yet."

"I'll get you a cup of tea when you get here. Now, hurry."

That didn't sound the way Sir Malcolm normally did. He never offered me anything. "What's wrong?"

"That's what I want you to tell me."

Not what I expected to hear. "I'll get down there as soon as I can." I hung up and started dressing while my tea steeped.

Bundled up against the cold from my red wool cloche hat to my sensible brown stacked-heel shoes and with a warming cup of tea and some burnt toast inside me, I traveled down to Sir Malcolm's office near Westminster.

Once more, I followed an armed soldier upstairs to Sir Malcolm's lair. When we'd been greeted with his commanding "Come," the soldier watched me enter before leaving the hallway.

I shut the door and walked over to face Sir Malcolm's desk, once more enjoying the view of bare branches and rooftops behind him. There were days when the winter view was more welcoming than the frosty man seated at the desk. Then I sat down and waited until he finished his telephone call.

"Now," he asked, hanging up the receiver, "what were you doing in a cemetery at night with the IRA and dynamite?"

I explained how I'd been asked to introduce Peter O'Malley to the men who wanted to do business with him, once more leaving Mr. Colinswood out of the tale.

"And you just happen to have developed IRA contacts." Sir Malcolm's tone was dry. "When I told you to leave it alone."

"I asked around the newspaper. Someone knew someone who—you know how it goes," I replied.

"And you had to tag along with them to get the dynamite."

This was easier. "The IRA contacts didn't want me to leave their sides until the deal was done and the dynamite could be put away safely. They didn't want me having a chance to call you. Or someone such as yourself."

"So they don't believe you called us in." Sir Malcolm looked relieved.

"And they shouldn't believe O'Malley told on them either, because he was with us until moments before Scotland Yard showed up." I stared into Sir Malcolm's dark eyes. "I don't believe the IRA killed him."

"The two men with you certainly didn't. But they have friends." Sir Malcolm was his usual glum self.

"The IRA didn't know where the explosives were until O'Malley led them to it. Nor did they know how much they weighed until O'Malley handed them off and then led them to where a wheelbarrow was kept. They'd made no plans for a heavy container." From what I'd seen, I didn't believe O'Malley had been in touch with the IRA.

"And now our only link between a supplier of dynamite and the IRA is dead." He glared at me. "We needed him alive."

"Well, don't look at me." I didn't point out I had an impeccable alibi in Scotland Yard.

"Those IRA men aren't talking. Not even to tell us they don't know who killed O'Malley."

"They don't trust you. By the way, what are their real names?" I asked.

"Sean Byrne and Seamus Phelan."

"Sean's the older one?"

Sir Malcolm nodded.

I had an idea. "Let me talk to him."

"You'll be wasting your time. They know you must be one of us now."

"I just want him to verify that they didn't kill O'Malley."

"You think he'd admit to it?" Sir Malcolm looked as if he thought I was mentally defective.

"No, but I think he'll make a good case for why they didn't kill O'Malley. And that might give us a clue as to who killed him and Kennedy and Mimi." At least, I hoped so.

"You think they were all killed by the same person? Stabbing is a common method of murder."

"Kennedy and Mimi were both murdered because of Kennedy's blackmail. O'Malley was one of the victims. I don't know the connection yet, but it's there. I am sure of it," I told him and let my certainty shine through.

"I don't see where this could be helpful. And Scotland Yard still believes the IRA was behind Kennedy's murder, since he was taking money from both the IRA and the government. Unless you know where O'Malley was getting the dynamite..."

I shook my head. "Unless it's manufactured in mausoleums."

He grumbled before he picked up one of the reports on his desk and began to study it. "You need to attack this investigation from another direction. Stay away from the IRA."

Our meeting was over.

As I rose, Sir Malcolm said, "I'm serious. Stay away from the IRA. I don't want to investigate your murder next."

"I don't want you to, either."

I marched out of his office and out of the building. I made it as far as the edge of St. James Park when an automobile stopped next to me along the white-painted curb and I was roughly hauled toward the vehicle. Elbowing my attacker didn't accomplish anything but annoy him, and I was tossed headfirst onto the floor of the back seat.

A moment later, he climbed in after me, slammed the door, and we took off with a jerky movement.

When I climbed up right side up into a sitting position, brushing dirt from the floor off my face, I didn't recognize my attacker, but I did recognize the man seated on the other side of me. The IRA leader.

"Do you know what happens to traitors?" he barked.

"I'm not the traitor, and neither was Peter O'Malley. And still your bullies held a knife to my throat in my flat." If he was going to kidnap me in broad daylight, he could listen to my grievances. I was still furious about being assaulted in my own flat on Sunday night.

The leader smiled. "The thick edge, not the sharp edge. Silly lass, you can't tell the difference."

"It was still a knife. That's no way to get cooperation." Lack of sleep and getting grabbed off the street left control of my temper in tatters and me in a bad mood.

"If you or O'Malley weren't traitors, how did things go so very wrong?" He returned my glare.

"You were being watched before either of us met you."

"Impossible."

"You don't know much about surveillance, do you?" I couldn't hide my scorn. They seemed to be long on threats and short on techniques.

"We know we can trust all of our people. That leaves only you and O'Malley knowing about the dynamite and not to be trusted."

I shook my head as I would at a dim child. "You've forgotten about Frank Kennedy. Either you found out he was working for the government and killed him, or one of his blackmail victims had had enough."

The leader glared at me. "Kennedy was trustworthy. He was part of our inner circle."

"He was on the government payroll, and he told them about O'Malley and the dynamite. However, he told the police he was on the fringes of the organization, not anything grand such as the inner circle." I held his gaze until he turned his head and looked out the window at the traffic outside.

After I thought, I added, "It seems strange that he would claim to be on the fringes of the IRA when he'd have made more money from the government by telling them he was part of the inner circle, since Frank Kennedy was interested in money most of all. Guess we'll never know why."

I continued, "It was his treachery that made the government think your people killed him. But I don't think you did."

Without turning his head to look at me, the leader said, "You're a fool to trust us."

"I don't trust you. I just don't believe you killed Kennedy. Or Mimi."

"Who?"

"Mimi Randall. Kennedy's ex-fiancée. I think her murder

proves you and the IRA didn't kill Kennedy."

He faced me then and raised his brows.

I decided I might as well explain. "If Kennedy was killed to retrieve his blackmail material and his murderer didn't find it, and we know it was searched for, then the next place to look would be Mimi's room.

"To do that, Mimi had to let him or her in. She lives— lived up a couple of flights in a rooming house. And then the only possible way to keep the murderer's identity secret was to kill her. And the only way not to be seen by the other residents was to enter when everyone else would be gone. New Year's Eve."

After a minute, he asked, "So who do you think killed Kennedy?"

"One of five people. Well, four now that O'Malley is dead."

"Who?"

"Why do you want to know?"

"To make certain they're none of mine."

"You mean IRA."

"Yes."

"Clarissa Northfield, an actress for the BBC radio players group. Keith Bates, a BBC radio play director. Roxanne Scott, a violinist in the BBC Chamber Orchestra. And Gerald Fitzroy, the head drama and music critic for the *Daily Premier*."

The leader nodded. "All of them involved in the BBC or spending time there with Kennedy. Did they all know each other?"

"Bates, O'Malley, and Clarissa Northfield all knew each other from various plays performed on the BBC, as did Mimi Randall, which means she would have recognized them. Otherwise, I don't know," I told him.

"Fitzroy knows everyone at the BBC."

I looked at the leader in surprise. "How do you know that?"

"I know Fitzroy."

When he didn't say any more, I asked, "Continue. Please."

"Fitzroy is Irish. We have relatives in the same village near the border between Free Ireland and English-held Ireland. He always was a poofta little traitor, with his nose into everyone else's business."

"Are you being derogatory, or are you telling me something?"

He smiled with a shake of his head. "Why do you think he left Ireland? We ran him out. It doesn't matter so much in a cesspool such as you find in London, but not in our Irish villages, corrupting the lads."

That matched what I gathered from Fitzroy's letters held by Kennedy, but I had wondered if the IRA man knew this for certain. Apparently, this was old news. "Have you been in touch with him recently?"

"No, and if I'd had those letters Kennedy supposedly had, I've have turned them in to the police myself. They want to put us in jail? They should lock Fitzroy up, him and all his poofta friends."

The leader would have wanted to put my first husband behind bars, and Reggie didn't deserve that. Did Fitzroy fear the IRA, or people of their ilk, would get hold of his letters and have him imprisoned?

I could understand Fitzroy being frightened. But frightened enough to kill? Instead of prison, he would have been taking his chances on hanging. Had Kennedy threatened to show the authorities Fitzroy's letters? Was that what was behind the murders of Kennedy and Mimi? But that didn't explain O'Malley's murder.

I realized the leader was watching me. "Now that you have what you want, will you let me go?" I said. I had more work to do, and no more time to waste on the IRA.

He nodded, and the driver pulled the automobile to the curb. The big man who'd grabbed me climbed out and offered me a hand to alight from the vehicle. I did and hurried away from them toward my flat.

Once I had tea and changed my clothes to something more appropriate for an evening at the BBC, nicer material and with a longer, slimmer skirt, I went to Broadcasting House. More and more curbs along my route were sporting a coat of white paint to make them more visible at night.

I wanted to watch the chamber music concert and the play rehearsal with fresh eyes, and I hoped to watch Gerald Fitzroy as he normally acted around the other blackmail victims. When I'd first talked to him, he'd known who the others were. How?

I knew the play rehearsal started first, so I went up to the sixth floor. As I walked in, Keith Bates was telling the assembled cast that one of their number had been murdered the night before. This was the second time he'd had to do that in a week.

I looked at their faces. Bates looked shocked and horrified. Clarissa looked angry for an instant, as if a favorite plaything had been taken away and crushed. Then she shifted to the pout of an innocent child. I suspected she was trying out reactions the way she'd study for a part.

"We'll try to replace him, of course, although it won't be easy with conscription growing. We'll have to double up parts for this rehearsal. Let's see…"

Where was Fitzroy? Not here.

I went upstairs to where the concert would be performed. Fitzroy was there, talking to the engineer and the conductor. A few of the musicians spoke to him as they walked by to take their seats and tune their instruments. He seemed to know many of them by name and made comments about the music they would be playing that night.

It felt as if he were one of the group. One of the regulars at Broadcasting House. I didn't see how he could be impartial in his reviews if he was friends with everyone there.

He couldn't. That was what Sir Henry had heard from various sources about his chief theater and music reviewer, and the publisher was not happy. Fitzroy's reputation was getting him in trouble.

No one at the *Daily Premier* knew what Fitzroy would be reviewing ahead of time. In the past, they had left it up to him. As his boss, Miss Westcott, said, it was easier than carrying on a protracted battle. Perhaps he designed his work that way to allow him to review his friends' performances and ignore the performances of anyone who threatened him.

Perhaps he just enjoyed the freedom of arranging his own work schedule.

My eyes widened as a voice behind me said, "I've heard one of Frank Kennedy's victims was murdered. How did they know he was being blackmailed? Did you tell them?"

Chapter Twenty-Two

I turned to find Roxanne Scott and her friend Celeste Young standing beside me. "That would be a very good thing to learn, but it wasn't me who told anyone. What have you heard?" I asked.

Roxanne looked worried. "Nothing. I just thought... I hoped..."

"You're too sensible to just dream things up and make accusations on your own. Who have you been talking to? Who's made you worry about whether the letters were destroyed?" I watched her as she backed away from me and hurried into the studio.

Celeste murmured, "It was because of one of the men in the actors' studio on Saturday, when we played the new introductory music for everyone."

"Who was it? What did this man say to her?" I asked.

"I don't know who he is. And he didn't just say it to Roxanne," she told me and followed her friend into the performance room.

I waited in the hall, and a minute later, Fitzroy walked past. I hurried over and stopped him by saying, "Were you the one who told everyone who Frank Kennedy's victims were?"

He swung around and looked up at me. "No, but all of us seem to know who's in the club. Is that because of you?"

"No. None of the others would have seen me talking to you or Roxanne. Did you tell them?"

"No. And if you're looking for a killer, it wasn't me." I followed the reviewer as he walked away from me and entered the lift, slamming the ornate metal door in my face. I needed to talk to him, certain he knew something important. I dashed down the stairs. I reached the lobby some moments behind him and started to follow him when I heard someone call out my name.

I saw Janet Murrow across the lobby waving to me. I stopped and waited for her to reach me as Fitzroy disappeared into the dark of the blackout. I'd have to find him later.

"I heard that someone else was murdered. One of Frank Kennedy's victims or an IRA member or someone," she said when she reached me.

"One of the actors here. And also a victim of Kennedy," I added in a whisper. I moved out of the stream of traffic through the lobby of Broadcasting House, and when we were away from listening ears, I added, "I still think it's because of the blackmail."

"You think the killer is someone who's angry about being blackmailed?" Janet asked.

"I think this killer is afraid that there are more letters out there and he or she wants to be certain they're all destroyed."

"Didn't you assure everyone the letters were burned?" she asked me.

I nodded.

"Then why would they think there were still letters out there?"

"Maybe there were more letters than just the ones Frank Kennedy received. Maybe the blackmail has continued." I decided to be honest. "Maybe someone discovered the letters hadn't been burned."

"Who could do that if they'd been burned?" Janet wore a puzzled frown.

"They hadn't been. Burned, that is."

"What?!" She realized she had shouted and glanced around before saying, "What?" in a quieter tone.

I drew her farther back out of the way. "I kept them in case the authorities needed them to make their case against someone. The authorities did want the letters of the man who was killed last night because of his ties to the IRA, but I'm sure it did them no good. The rest, except for one, were found and taken when my flat was burgled."

"Who did that?"

"I don't know. Maybe the killer?"

"The one letter that was left behind was not written by your killer." Janet sounded positive.

"Unless they are trying to fool us into thinking they would never have left behind their own letter." That kind of devious thinking was worthy of Sir Malcolm. I'd spent too much time with him.

Janet shook her head. "Anyone who would kill to retrieve their letters wouldn't leave one of their own behind. The person who wrote that letter is definitely not your thief or a murderer."

I found myself agreeing with her. "I've ruled him out on the basis of his alibi. That leaves three possibilities. Two of those could go to jail based on the evidence of their letters."

I thought of Roxanne. "But I doubt they'd prosecute one of them. And the third? It deals with a murder last year in Yorkshire, but it isn't evidence of anything but gossip."

"Was anyone arrested for the murder?"

"No."

"How was it carried out? Was any weapon recovered?"

"I don't know." Janet had some good ideas, and I decided to follow up on them. "I don't think it matters. Clarissa doesn't seem to be a killer."

"Why?" Janet asked. "I've never met her. What is she like?"

"She's young and frightened but she tries not to show it. She's delicate and flighty. And she seems to always need someone to lean on. A man to lean on. That's not the type of person to commit murder, let alone get away with it." I thought for a moment. "Of course, she is an actress."

"Frank Kennedy's murder was very much at close range and personal and, I imagine, took a good amount of strength. I wonder if the murder in Yorkshire was the same." Janet looked at me to see what I would do.

Why not find out? It wasn't as if I had solved any of these

murders or done anything useful. "I'll check at the *Daily Premier* in the morning. In the meantime, what are you doing here? Is Ed about to broadcast?"

"Yes. Come listen with me, and afterward let's go out to dinner."

* * *

The next morning, I crossed London in a whirl of wind and snowflakes. No one lingered outdoors. When I reached the *Daily Premier* building, I entered the lobby while shaking off the flakes sticking to my coat. Then I took the lift up to the news floor and Mr. Colinswood's office.

He was meeting with two of his colleagues, so I waited outside away from the door. About ten minutes later, the sub-editors came out and I went in before anyone else could claim Mr. Colinswood's attention.

"What can I do for you, Olivia?" he asked.

"I want to read the details of Althea Northfield's murder in Yorkshire last year. How the local papers reported it. How would I go about it?"

"Go to the Newspaper Library Reading Room in Colindale. They have copies of all the Yorkshire papers. All the British papers, really." He lit a cigarette and leaned back to look at me.

"That's where I'd have to send someone if I needed to find out the answers for you on something that happened in Yorkshire. Anyone can go in and read the newspapers there. If you have to claim a valid reason for looking at old volumes, you can mention who you work for." He grinned. "Well, who you work for most of the time."

"Thank you. The sooner I can solve this mystery, the sooner I can get back here."

"We look forward to it, but be careful. Somebody is not going to want to be accused of murder. Someone who has already killed, and more than once."

That was certain. I waved and headed off to the Underground station. Two transfers and I was on the Northern Line taking the Edgware Branch.

The snow was falling harder out on the northern edge of London when I reached Colindale. I asked for directions and found my way to the reading room, where I requested the newspapers I thought would help me.

The Leeds papers came in huge leather-bound volumes that required a large desk to hold them while I turned the pages. I sat at a desk and began to study them.

At first, the daily papers sounded as if the police had a suspect, but those early assured statements quickly faded away. In their place were vague comments about following various leads.

Then I found an article on the inquest. Althea Northfield had been poisoned with rat poison found in a meat pie. One serving had been eaten. No one admitted to knowing where the meat pie had come from.

The Yorkshire murder was done at a distance, unlike the recent stabbings here in London. Clarissa might have killed her aunt, but I couldn't see her stabbing the victims associated with the BBC in the past two weeks.

I couldn't see how she could feed poison to anyone at Broadcasting House, and no one else had died that way.

While Clarissa might have killed Frank Kennedy in a fit of anger over his financial demands, I didn't believe she would have killed anyone else. Especially not Peter O'Malley, who appeared to have replaced Paul White in her affections.

No, Clarissa Northfield didn't appear to be the killer, but I wondered if she had heard O'Malley say something that would indicate who would have a reason to kill him.

Blackmail was a good motive for Frank Kennedy's death, and a search for the letters he'd used against his victims would explain Mimi Randall's murder. O'Malley's was the death that didn't seem to fit the pattern.

And yet something told me there had to be a connection.

Even with the blackout, murder was rare. Here were three murders in a matter of days that killed people who knew each other.

A conversation with Clarissa seemed to be in order, as well as a chat with Gerald Fitzroy if I could pin either of them down. There was a play rehearsal that night, so I needed to get to Broadcasting House early to speak to her. On the other hand, Roxanne had no reason to return there until the next evening. I'd start with Clarissa and what O'Malley might have said to her.

* * *

I arrived at Broadcasting House early and rode up in the polished metal lift to the studios on the sixth floor. A minute or two later, Keith Bates arrived and froze for a moment when he saw me. "What's happened now?" he asked, clutching his script to his chest.

"I want to speak to Clarissa. She'd been constantly in O'Malley's company for the few days before his murder. I'm hoping he said something to her that might be a clue," I told him.

"I hope so. This group of players seems to be short on luck. I don't know how many more murders any of us can take." Bates had shadows under his eyes and his face had a gauntness I associated with pain.

"Everything all right at home?"

"Yes. Odd how everything here is falling apart while my family life couldn't be better." He sounded amazed and a little stunned.

At that moment, Clarissa arrived and greeted Bates. "She needs to talk to you," he said to her and walked into the studio.

"The angel of death," Clarissa said, staring at me.

"What?"

"You wanted to talk to Mimi and the next thing you know, she's dead. Then Peter goes off to meet you after a performance and the next thing you know, he's dead."

Peter? Not O'Malley? How well did she know him? "I'm trying to find out why they were killed. Did Peter O'Malley say anything odd before or after the performance?"

"That he had to go with you to meet some men he had business with and he'd see me at rehearsal the next night."

"Nothing odd there. Did he say anything that left you

wondering?" I asked.

"Yes. What men? What business? And why you?" she replied, sounding annoyed.

"I don't think that led to his death. He must have said something to you that would help."

"Why must he have? We discovered we were both blackmail victims of Frank Kennedy. And we were both glad when he turned up dead. That's all." Her expression said that she'd discovered the milk had soured.

"Did anyone try to blackmail either of you after Kennedy was killed?"

"No." Then she gave me a sharp look. "You said you'd burned all his letters."

"All that I found." That lie was surprisingly easy to tell. "I've heard people worrying that Kennedy had more letters elsewhere, but I've not heard of any other attempts to blackmail anyone."

"Peter said that he'd found more letters and would go into the blackmailing business himself, but I told him not to be a fool." She wrapped her arms around her chest.

It was a frightening thought, since one blackmailer had been murdered already. "He didn't have any letters, did he?"

She made a scoffing noise. "Of course not."

"When and where did he say this?"

"Last Saturday, in the studio before rehearsal started."

I leaned forward. "Who heard him say that?"

"Everyone."

"Clarissa. This is important. Think."

"It was a madhouse. This was our one full practice before the performance that night. All the actors were there, the special effects men, at least one engineer, maybe two, Keith of course—"

"Keith Bates, the director?"

"Yes. Some musicians practicing a new theme song to open the performances so Keith could hear it along with the producer and the engineers. Then the producer was talking to a couple of drama critics about the plans for the three different BBC wartime locations around England and what will be broadcast this spring from each one. Meanwhile, one of the engineers went upstairs and got their boss who came down and argued with the producer about frequencies."

"All this was going on at once?" She was right. It must have been a madhouse.

"Pretty much. It was noisy, the room was crowded, at least until the musicians were dismissed, and that was when the chief engineer and the producer got into a shouting match."

"When during all of this did Peter O'Malley talk about setting himself up as a blackmailer?"

Clarissa scrunched up her face as she thought, looking younger than usual. "I remember he spoke loudly. It was before the shouting match. I'm sure of that, because afterward we went straight into rehearsal, with Keith throwing everyone out except the actors and the producer. Can't throw him out, can he?"

"So, O'Malley said he'd go into the blackmailing business

with a great number of people around to hear him." Not the wisest thing he could say in that crowd.

Possibly all of Kennedy's victims were present to hear O'Malley threaten them.

Chapter Twenty-Three

"Do you know who was standing nearby when he said this?" I asked. I had to narrow my list of suspects somehow.

Clarissa shook her head. "I have no idea. It didn't seem important, and I really didn't care." Her big blue eyes gave me an innocent stare.

I thought for a moment. "Was Peter O'Malley good friends with your aunt? Did you meet him in the theater in Leeds?"

Her head seemed to swivel on her shoulders at the sound of the lift doors opening. "It's Will. He must be replacing Peter." She smiled, sounding excited to see him.

"Who? And what about—?"

"Will Mason-Twigg. I've acted with him before. He's great fun." She hurried toward him, utterly dismissing me. "Hello, Will. I'm so glad to see you here. Will you be working with us?"

She was giving him her sweet little girl smile. I'd had enough of her innocence and youthful enthusiasm for one day. I gave up on Clarissa and hurried into the studio to find Keith Bates.

"Hello, Mrs. Redmond," Bates said from behind me. "Come to watch another rehearsal?"

"No. I want to ask you something instead. Before Saturday night's rehearsal, did you hear Peter O'Malley say that he was gathering letters and was going to restart Kennedy's blackmail business? Anything along those lines?"

"Yes. The whole room could hear him. He had that kind of theater voice and this studio has that kind of acoustics."

"Did it sound as if he was joking?"

"Not at the time. My wife and I are getting on better, and I didn't want him to ruin things. I spoke to him during a break in the rehearsal and he told me then it was a joke. He looked at me as if I was crazy, worrying about those letters, but my future, my family's future..." He gave a hopeless gesture.

"Is that why you killed him?" I asked in a low voice.

"What? No. I did not kill him," he whispered, making sure his voice didn't carry the way O'Malley's had.

"Did you spend Monday night with your family?"

"Yes. The whole night. I'm not so much of a fool as to leave them again." He shook his head. "You've been out to my house already checking on my alibi, are you going to do it again? Just don't say anything to upset my wife. She looked for your story on Mimi for a few days. I don't think she'll trust you again."

I believed him, both about his being at home and his wife not trusting me or anyone.

"Was Gerald Fitzroy one of the critics who was here before rehearsal Saturday night?"

"Of course. The man seems to live in this building."

"And the musicians for the new theme music before

each performance? Were they here Monday night as well as Saturday night?"

"No. A recording was made Sunday afternoon, to be ready for the Monday performance. The engineers dealt with that."

I had another thought. "Did it seem as if O'Malley was threatening blackmail to anyone in particular?"

"He was talking to Clarissa, so if he were talking about blackmail to anyone, it would have been her. But that's ridiculous."

"Why is it ridiculous?"

"She's just a kid. Probably not even twenty."

I thanked him and walked away, knowing I'd have to talk to Roxanne tomorrow afternoon and Clarissa again tomorrow night. They would have to be very serious talks. And I needed to find Gerald Fitzroy.

* * *

I thought a lot about talking to Roxanne the next morning, enough that I was not surprised when our phone rang and I heard Adam's voice come out of the receiver. "I have a weekend pass starting tomorrow night. So you'd better get your fancy man out of the flat."

I laughed, knowing neither of us would believe such a suggestion for a second. "That's wonderful. What time do you think you'd get here?"

"Not until late, so late we'll only be able to go out for fish and chips."

"That's fine, as long as you are here." A whole weekend.

I was bouncing on my toes with excitement.

"Miles and I will leave as soon as we clean up from training."

"He's coming to London, too?" I asked, trying not to sound annoyed that he seemed to be released every weekend while Adam wasn't. I hoped he wouldn't be interfering with our time together.

"He asks if you'll let Roxanne know."

"Of course." I'd just been thinking about a way to approach her. This would let me bargain with Roxanne to get her to talk to me. I was not her favorite person, and I was still wondering why. I'd made clear I wouldn't tell about her time in Leeds.

I went over to Broadcasting House well before the chamber concert group began practicing and looked around. Roxanne wasn't there yet, so I planted myself where I could see her coming and settled in to wait.

Roxanne arrived with Celeste before the conductor Markowitz, so I knew we'd have a little time to talk. "Roxanne..."

"I don't want to talk to you." She started to hurry.

I hurried alongside of her. "Then I'll have to go to the police with what I suspect, and then Miles will find out, and then..."

She came to a halt. "All right. Celeste, wait for me inside."

Celeste looked at me with raised eyebrows, but she went into the studio.

"How do I get in touch with the trumpeter you were with on New Year's Eve?"

She faced me, hands on hips. "Oh, no. I do not want Miles to find out about him."

"He already knows. He saw him. Roxanne, why won't you make this easy for both of us so I can go on my way?"

"Do you promise not to tell Miles?"

"It's none of Miles's business if it's not illegal. Or even if it is. He's not the police. Why would I tell him?"

She stared at the ceiling for a half minute, cringing with dread, before she finally said, "Tom is my cousin. Ordinarily, he wants nothing to do with me if I'm not cleaning up after him, but on New Year's he told me I could tag along."

"So you two live together?"

"We have a flat together. I have the box room. Celeste lives in the boarding house next door. I asked her to say we lived in the same building so I wouldn't have to explain Tom, and she agreed. She gave me a spare key so Rem could drop me off there."

We had moved over to the side of the hallway, out of the way of the other musicians. "Why didn't Tom protect you from Kennedy's annoyances?"

"Because he doesn't care. Because he's mad that he can't get hired onto one of the BBC orchestras the way I did." It came out louder than she meant it to, and then she lowered her voice. "He won't let me leave because he knows my secret. He makes me help pay the rent and clean up after him. He hates cleaning up after himself, and if he didn't need my wages, he'd throw me out in a second."

Roxanne studied me for a moment before she added, "If Miles knew about my lower-class family and my background, he'd walk away. And I really care for him. Please don't tell him."

"I won't. By the way, he'll get into town late tomorrow night."

The smile that crossed her face left me in no doubt about her feelings for Miles.

"Were you in the group of musicians playing the new introductory music for the Monday night playhouse?" I asked.

"Yes." She sounded puzzled over why I would ask.

"Can you remember who was in the studio while you were playing the song for the director and producer?"

"I didn't know most of them. Actors, I guess. A couple of critics. Two of the engineers working on the sound levels." She shrugged one shoulder, holding the violin case in the other arm.

"Was Gerald Fitzroy there?"

"Yes. I know him. He always seems to be around." Then she looked sharply at me. "Why? You can't think he has anything to do with murder."

"I'm trying to find out who overheard Peter O'Malley's comments about starting Kennedy's blackmail business again."

"Everyone there heard someone say he had more letters to blackmail with. We had just finished playing and it was quiet. No one could help hearing some man—was that O'Malley?—talk about making money off of other people's indiscretions." She glared at me. "I could have killed him myself."

"But you wouldn't really have, would you? How could Peter O'Malley blackmail you over your letters about your previous career?"

She had her face close to mine, whispering angrily. "He couldn't. You had all the letters there were for Kennedy to use against me."

"In that case, I wouldn't think you'd have to worry that O'Malley could ruin you. Besides, you negotiated with Kennedy. You could do it again if there had been more letters." I held her gaze, waiting for her to tell me more.

Roxanne sighed. "Kennedy had threatened to take them to the top people here at Broadcasting House. They would have fired me. My career would have been ruined. I would never have lived down the shame. This new man, O'Malley, never approached me with a demand for money. I couldn't see how he could have come up with more letters if you burned mine."

"When he mentioned blackmail, did he seem to be speaking to anyone in particular?"

"No. Well maybe the woman he was talking to. Sort of." She walked off a step, then turned back to me. "Three people have died because of the evil Frank Kennedy did. But I didn't kill him or anyone else."

She walked into the studio to the sound of instruments

tuning up.

Leaving me two more of Frank Kennedy's victims to question.

I traveled back to the *Daily Premier* building to talk to Miss Westcott, who was at least nominally Fitzroy's superior. When I approached her desk, she asked, "When are you returning?"

"Soon, I hope. I need to speak to Gerald Fitzroy. Where might I find him?"

"Your guess is as good as mine. He's as much a free spirit as you are, except he can write a good lead." She raised her brows at the mention of my biggest failing in her eyes.

"Has he mentioned which performances he plans to cover?"

She gave a sigh followed by a grumble. "We never know until he turns them in. He's worked here forever, and I don't know of anyone who's been bold enough in ages to request prior notice of his reviews. It would cost me too much aggravation to try, and I know I wouldn't succeed."

Miss Westcott had also worked there forever, and if she didn't have the nerve to attempt to rein Fitzroy in, no one else would. Most of us were terrified of her. I certainly was.

"Unless you're going to do some work, I suggest you leave." She gave me a pointed stare. I left.

The only other place I thought I might learn Fitzroy's whereabouts was at his home in South Kensington. I boldly climbed the steps leading to his front door and rang the bell.

The gaunt butler in his black suit answered the door, his

expression saying he wanted me gone before I said a word.

"Is Mr. Fitzroy at home?"

"No."

"Do you know where I might find him?"

"No."

"Do you know what performance he is reviewing tonight?"

"No."

Wanting to see if he could say yes to anything, I asked, "Is Mr. Fitzroy still in London?"

"Of course. Now if you've finished wasting your time and mine, Mrs. Redmond, I have things to do." He shut the door in my face, telling me only that he knew who I was.

Why would Gerald Fitzroy's butler recall my name and face so clearly? Unless he was involved in the murders, either as a participant or an alibi for his master. Otherwise, why would he remember my name? Why would he care?

At this point, Fitzroy would know or soon learn that I was looking for him. If he was guilty of murder to keep the secret of his letters safe and stay out of jail, then I might be his next target.

I didn't like that thought. I wanted protection provided by the man who had set me on this course.

Next, I headed over to Sir Malcolm's office. It had been his idea for me to leave the *Daily Premier* again for a time to find Frank Kennedy's killer, particularly if it wasn't the IRA. I was now certain it wasn't the IRA, and I'd found a motive for all three deaths.

Gerald Fitzroy had everything he wanted. He chose his assignments for the *Daily Premier*, spending time reviewing his friends' performances and being paid for it. He had a nice home and servants to wait on him. If Kennedy turned his letters over to the police, it would become a scandal. He might go to jail. He would lose his easy job and the money that came with it that paid for his luxurious lifestyle.

I suspected we'd found the killer in Gerald Fitzroy, and I wanted Sir Malcolm's help in catching him without my becoming his next victim.

When I entered the small lobby where the armed soldier sat, I asked for Sir Malcolm.

"Not here."

My heart fluttered in shock at his words. Sir Malcolm was always here. "I must get a message to him." Saying that it was a matter of life and death would sound ridiculous to a soldier since we were at war, but it felt that way to me.

"He'll be back Saturday."

"Saturday will be too late." If Gerald Fitzroy had killed those three people, he wouldn't wait to silence me.

Chapter Twenty-Four

"Sorry," the soldier replied with a complete lack of expression. "He'll be back on Saturday."

I left Sir Malcolm a written message, letting him know who I suspected if I turned up dead. If I were still alive, then I wanted his help in checking out Fitzroy's alibis for all three murders.

After I gave the folded note to the disinterested soldier, I left the building, wondering where I could hide if I needed to until Saturday. I really didn't think Fitzroy would come after me, I hadn't threatened him in any way, but I knew I shouldn't be alone, at least at night when the killings had taken place.

There was no way I could endanger Sir Henry Benton or his daughter, Esther Powell, or their family. The same with Sir John and Abby Summersby. None of my friends should be subjected to the threat of a knife-wielding maniac. I had to go someplace where no one would guess I would hide out, at least that night, and I wanted to be close to London when Adam arrived late the next night.

My father's house. Perfect.

I went home and called the number I had to get in touch with Adam. A half-hour later he returned my call. "What's happened?" He sounded worried, since I knew not to call in anything less than an emergency.

"Don't come to the flat tomorrow when you reach London. Come to my father's house instead."

"Livvy? What's wrong?"

I couldn't lie to Adam, but I didn't mean to blurt everything out to him. "I believe I found a murderer for Sir Malcolm. Except Sir Malcolm is nowhere to be found until Saturday and the murderer knows I'm looking for him. All I plan to do is question him. He shouldn't see me as a threat, but I'm trying to be cautious."

I'd never heard Adam use such strong language before. He ended with, "I'll get there as soon as I can tomorrow. But the flat should be safe. Sutton's on the door and there are people there all the time."

"And yet someone ransacked our flat. Fortunately, I wasn't in at the time. Sutton had given out our flat number to someone over the telephone recently."

More cursing was followed by, "Go to your father's house and don't go out again."

"I'm safe enough during the day. It's just this blasted blackout. The killer strikes while hiding in it."

Adam ignored my reply. "Does he know about your father? Does he know where your father lives?"

"No to both. Adam, I want you to be careful. I'll be fine."

"Don't worry about me. Worry about yourself." Then there was a pause before he said, "How does this killer murder his victims?"

"With a knife. He just runs them through."

More cursing came through the receiver. "Who is this guy? What does he look like?"

"I believe the killer is Gerald Fitzroy. He's in his late sixties, small, thin, walks with a limp. And if he's the murderer, he's killed three people."

"He doesn't look threatening and he uses it to catch his victims off guard during the blackout. Understood," Adam said. "Be careful, Livvy. I don't want anything to happen to you."

"I don't want you to do anything heroic and get hurt, either. Please be careful," I told him.

"Get over there before the blackout begins," he told me.

We said goodbye and I hurried to pack a small case with what I would need for two nights and days. Then I called my father at work. "I hope you don't mind a houseguest for a few days," I said after we exchanged wary greetings.

"Who?"

"Me."

"Why?"

Why? Once again, I was annoyed with my father's warm welcome. "It would be better if Adam and I are not home for the next couple of days."

"Is Adam with you?" My father now sounded much more welcoming.

"He'll be here tomorrow."

"I look forward to seeing him."

Thanks, Father. "I'm going over to your house later

tonight."

"If you must. I won't be home until late and there's nothing there for dinner. I'm eating at my club tonight."

"I'm sure I can find myself something to eat on the way there." And then take a cab the rest of the way to protect myself in the blackout.

My father's tone turned serious. "Olivia, what trouble have you found yourself in? Does this have anything to do with Sir Malcolm?"

"Yes, and he won't be back in London to take care of the problem until Saturday."

"I told you not to get involved with that man." My father never changed his opinions or his advice.

"It was the only way I could learn where they had you locked up, if you recall."

"Yes, well, you could have left me there. That ended without any difficulties. And I did warn you—"

This was one point of contention between us. One of many. "I couldn't abandon you."

"It wouldn't have been abandoning me. I had everything well in hand. Instead—"

"Well in hand? Hardly. You were rotting in a prison cell."

"Only because the police thought I'd killed John Kenseth. Totally absurd, and it was proven to be wrong." My father used his stuffiest tone.

"Because I worked with Sir Malcolm to prove you innocent." Why could my father never see reality? "And because of your foolishness, I've had to work with Sir

Malcolm ever since."

"If you had left well enough alone—"

"You would have been hanged." We were nearly shouting over the telephone at each other.

After a long pause, my father said, "Humpf. Do you still have a key?"

"Yes. I'll be there before you get home. And please, stay away from any short men in their late sixties who walk with a limp."

He laughed. "That's what you're afraid of?"

"He's already killed three people." Well, maybe, but my father wouldn't be on his guard if I said maybe.

My father stopped laughing. "Olivia. You shouldn't be involved in this sort of thing."

"What sort of thing should I be involved in?" I snapped at him.

"You're married now. You should be making a home for you and Adam. Not chasing after murderers for Sir Malcolm. That's for men to take care of."

I could feel steam rising from my ears. "The men are all off fighting Hitler. Remember him?" Or they would be when the shooting war began.

"Of course I do. I admit with the war on, you could take on certain jobs. Working for Sir Henry's newspaper might be suitable."

I'd been working for Sir Henry for over two years, and this was the first time my father admitted my position "might" be acceptable. "Oh, my. Thank you."

"Don't be sarcastic, Olivia. It's unbecoming."

"No matter whose fault it is that I'm working for Sir Malcolm, the fact remains there is a definite danger over the next few days until Sir Malcolm sorts everything out. I'm going to pick up some fish and chips and go over to your house. Please be careful on the way home. There's no way he should be able to find a link between us, but I don't want you to take any chances."

"Be careful, Olivia. The blackout starts soon."

That was as caring as we were to each other. I was grateful that we could manage such sentiments. After we hung up, I left, locking up the flat and waving to Sutton as I walked out the door. I didn't say anything to him, so he couldn't let anyone know where I was going. Then I headed to Broadcasting House.

Darkness, and the blackout, began before I arrived carrying my little case. I signed in and went up to the sixth floor where I found Clarissa talking to Will Mason-Twigg. Giving his long, narrow face a smile, I said, "Mr. Mason-Twigg, I want a word alone with Clarissa. Won't take but a minute."

He nodded and loped off, leaving me with a sulky-looking Clarissa. "Performance tonight?" I asked.

"No. Just a rehearsal."

I decided to dive in. "Peter O'Malley was your aunt's lover," I stated rather than asked.

"Yes. It was so ridiculous. She was at least ten years older than he was. And she kept fawning over him. Buying him things." Clarissa stopped heaping scorn on the dead man and lowered her voice as she leaned toward me. "I think he killed her when she stopped buying him things."

"Why was that?"

"He became used to the presents. The attention."

"No," I told her, "I mean, why did she stop?"

"She realized how foolish she looked."

"Because you told her so?"

Clarissa shook her head. "No. My other aunt. Phyllis told her."

"Who inherited when your aunt Althea died?"

"I inherited a small sum, a very small sum, and some keepsakes, the same as two cousins in Canada." She shook off her grumbling tone and began to sound more cheerful. "The bulk of the money, and the house, went to Aunt Phyllis. Next in line was my simpering sister Louise and my giggling cousin Carol. My Canadian cousins and I received the leftovers."

Did she inherit a very small amount or did it just feel that way to her? "Was your aunt Phyllis investigated for the murder?"

"Yes, but they couldn't prove anything against her, either."

"Do you know for certain your aunt stopped giving O'Malley presents?"

Again, she shook her head. "But it must be what happened, mustn't it?"

"Maybe, maybe not. I can't see him baking her a meat

pie."

Clarissa reddened. "What about a meat pie?"

"That's what killed her."

She shrugged. "Anyone can buy a meat pie and add poison to it."

"Wouldn't your aunt be curious as to why a lover she'd had a fight with would bring her a meat pie? That would have had the police asking questions of the family, where the pie was more likely to have come from," I suggested.

"Yes," she admitted. "The police questioned all of us, the servants, everyone. But anyone could have bought that meat pie and delivered it. No one knew when or where it had come from."

"In one of your letters, you almost accused your aunt Phyllis of killing her sister."

She shrugged and glanced around as if looking for someone more interesting. "What I wrote was gossip. The police couldn't use my letters to convict anyone, or even exonerate them. I'm ashamed I wrote such nonsense, when I didn't know anything for certain. Not really."

"Your aunt wouldn't be surprised to get a pie from her sister, would she?" I asked. I had no idea what went on in the Yorkshire countryside.

"No, Aunt Althea wouldn't. Aunt Phyllis was kind. She cooked treats for the family all the time." She paused and added, "If you tell anyone I said that, I'll deny it."

"What happened between the sisters to lead one to kill the other?"

Clarissa leaned back against the wall with a sigh and began to explain. "Aunt Althea, Aunt Phyllis, and my father were siblings. He got the largest share when their parents died, and the sisters were supposed to split the remainder. However, Aunt Althea forged their father's signature on some papers and got most of Aunt Phyllis's inheritance and some of my father's. Aunt Althea was an artist. And a very good forger."

"Phyllis needed the money?"

"It wouldn't have hurt, but what she really objected to was being cheated. Althea was the favorite, and Phyllis didn't enjoy having her inheritance stolen after she'd done things for her parents only to have Althea belittle them or take credit for them. Phyllis was tired of being pushed aside. Althea was the pretty one, and she used her looks to get away with anything she wanted, before and after their parents died." Clarissa straightened and took a step away from me.

"Surely the police would have figured this out."

"Nobody was willing to speak out against Aunt Phyllis."

"Why? Were they afraid of her?" I asked.

"No. They just didn't like Aunt Althea. Or her boyfriends."

"What did you inherit from your aunt?"

"A little money. Some household goods to remember her by. Nothing special. Just kitchen goods." She sounded annoyed. Or cheated.

"Anything to help you set up housekeeping in London?"

"No. Nothing practical for now. I've left it in storage."

Keith Bates called the actors together. Clarissa gave me a nod and walked into the studio.

I had almost made up my mind to get dinner in the BBC café in the lower level when I bumped into Janet in the lobby. "It turns out Ed is going to broadcast later tonight, so we're going out to dinner now. Join us."

The killer had only struck when the victim was alone. "I'd love to."

The three of us walked to a nearby restaurant and had a good dinner even by prewar standards. When I said this, Ed Murrow began to question me about the differences between last winter and this one.

"You were here," I protested. "Why should you have to ask me what you already know?"

"Oh, but do I? I was pretty new here last winter. I know the gas masks and sandbags were new then, but you were seeing them suddenly appear after living here your whole life. It must have been a shock."

I nodded. "It still is." I looked at the plate set before me. "This is the thinnest chop I've ever seen, but it is a chop. Things are not as plentiful as they were, but we still have enough. It's the same, but different. If the war continues for too long, things will get..." I was going to say "much worse." I changed it to, "More difficult."

We talked a little longer, Ed telling us about the characters around Broadcasting House, when he said, "Do you know the theater reviewer for the *Daily Premier*?"

"You mean Gerald Fitzroy? Yes." Was I about to hear a

threat against my life?

"Is he all right?" Ed Murrow continued. "He claimed it was just the sight of blood, but I don't know. He's not a young man."

Janet and I both looked at him, puzzled, before I said, "What are you talking about?"

"I went to Broadcasting House early today to speak to my BBC scheduler about the timing of my broadcasts and found him in a hallway outside a studio. There were other people around us including your Fitzroy. An engineer got a nosebleed, apparently he gets them routinely, and Fitzroy dropped like a rock. When they brought him around, he said he faints at the sight of blood. I wondered if something was wrong with him. Fainting at the sight of a little blood is strange, I would have thought."

"Ed," Janet said, "many people faint at the sight of blood. We weren't all brought up on a farm."

"Were you brought up on a farm? I didn't know that," I said without thinking, while my mind went back to all the blood in Mimi Randall's room.

"A farm, and then I worked in logging camps. Plenty of blood around..." Ed Murrow continued to talk, but I didn't hear him.

If Gerald Fitzroy fainted at the sight of blood, he would have never been able to search Mimi's room while she lay in a pool of her own blood with more of it splattered on the walls. He couldn't be the killer. I had this all wrong.

Chapter Twenty-Five

As soon as we finished dinner, I thanked the Murrows and headed for the Underground. I was no longer frightened that Fitzroy would try to knife me since he couldn't have stabbed the victims and faced all that blood. It might be safe to travel to my father's house by cheaper methods, because neither of the women blackmail victims would think I suspected them.

Cabs had become incredibly expensive since the war began because most of the fuel was being commandeered by the military. And while cabs at least received some allocation of fuel, many people, unable to get any fuel, hadn't relicensed their cars for 1940, so they were also in need of cabs on many occasions.

And while prices for food and heat and many other things were rising along with other people's wages, neither Sir Henry nor Sir Malcolm would pay me extra.

Once I left the station nearest my girlhood home, I walked quickly through the cold and dark of the blackout. The only sounds were the wind blowing and frost crunching under my feet. Mercifully, someone had applied white paint to some of the curbs and trees and the short stone wall around the churchyard. There were few people about, and none once I passed the church my family attended and walked along my father's street.

Then I heard a crunch at a distance. Turning quickly, I saw a shadow some way behind me trudging along in the light of the new moon. Another late-night worker or partier heading home, I told myself. I don't think I believed me.

At least in the dark with my eyes adjusted to the night, the clear skies gave off enough light to show the faint outlines of buildings and people if they were nearby.

I hurried to my father's house, setting my case on the porch as I dug my key out of my bag. In the blackout it would have been hard to find the lock without white paint around the keyhole.

After trying to get the key into the lock with shaking hands, I finally got the door opened, picked up my case, and hurried inside away from the sound of those footsteps. I put the lock on the door and turned on the hall light before checking that the blackout curtains were in place around the ground floor.

The rugs, the furniture—everything looked normal. Safe. Unchanged in years. All the windows were covered and I gave a sigh of relief.

I put my case at the bottom of the stairs and went out to the kitchen, wondering if there was anything there to eat. The house felt cold, and I left my coat on. Despite my father's protectiveness about his pristine copper teakettle, I was chilled and wanted to heat some water. My father's tin-lined teakettle didn't have the first scratch on it, similar to so many of his favorite pots and pans, while mine were all dented. My father came into my kitchen once and had never returned. I filled the kettle and put it on for tea and found an old tin that contained what seemed to be fresh biscuits.

I nibbled on one as I found a cup and saucer as well as a spoon and sugar. I knew better than to look for milk. That wouldn't be delivered until morning, or maybe next week. My father seldom used it.

While I fixed tea, I tried to answer my question. Who killed Frank Kennedy, Mimi Randall, and Peter O'Malley? I felt certain all three were killed by the same knife-wielding hand. It wasn't Fitzroy because of the blood. I felt certain it wasn't Keith Bates because his wife didn't trust him and wouldn't have let him out of the house. That left the two women.

Roxanne Scott was afraid of me. She was afraid of her cousin. She wanted to keep her job and continue to see Miles. That left her in fear of blackmail. She might well have killed Kennedy out of fear, but I wasn't certain she knew who Kennedy's fiancée was, much less where the fiancée lived. Playing in the chamber group, Roxanne had little opportunity to talk to the actors working on the sixth floor. She definitely wouldn't have known O'Malley was out on the streets walking near Broadcasting House so late on Monday night. Or that he was planning to go to a pub on Baker Street after the radio players' performance.

Roxanne would have left Broadcasting House early on Monday night because it was a rehearsal day, not a performance day.

That left Clarissa Northfield. She was in the same group of players as Mimi. And O'Malley.

But how could someone so young and innocent-seeming be a killer?

The phone rang and I went into the hall munching on a biscuit, realizing belatedly I'd left the lid off the tin. When I answered, Adam's voice came out at me.

"Livvy. I was hoping you'd arrived at your father's house safely."

"I've got the wrong person," I told him.

"Who is it?"

"Clarissa Northfield."

"Are you sure? You were certain it was Fitzroy earlier."

"He faints at the sight of blood. That's a bad trait for a killer who uses a knife," I told him.

I heard him choke back laughter. "I can see where it would be a handicap. Why do you think this Clarissa went on a killing spree?"

"I think she may have killed her aunt in Yorkshire. That was what she was getting blackmailed for. Maybe."

"You need to be a little more certain," Adam said.

"At least I should be safe here." I heard a sound in the kitchen and assumed the kettle must be boiling. Or the wind scraped a branch along the back of the house. After so long, I was no longer familiar with the normal creaking of my father's house. "Clarissa shouldn't know where my father lives. And when Sir Malcolm returns on Saturday, I can drop the whole question on him and let him sort it out."

"You're sure you'll be safe until I can get there tomorrow night?"

"Yes." We signed off with endearments and while Adam must have hurried off to do army things, I went back into the kitchen for tea and biscuits. The teakettle was just beginning to boil. So what had I heard? Probably a creak from the old boards or the wind blowing against a pane of glass.

I spent the time before my father returned home worrying if I might be attacked, and afterward, defending all my choices from my father's complaints.

I left after breakfast on Friday morning at the same time as my father left for work, leaving Mrs. Johnson, who was his cook, daily, and housekeeper rolled into one, free to get on with her day.

I ran some errands and came back to my building to ask Sutton if anyone had asked after me. No one had. I hoped that meant all was well.

At the *Daily Premier,* I again went to see Mr. Colinswood, who was happy with the story someone made out of my information on the IRA. I no longer expected my stories would appear in the paper the way I had written them.

He wasn't nearly as happy with the deletions insisted on by Scotland Yard and the government censors.

Next, I went looking for Gerald Fitzroy and found him on the features floor. "Last Saturday, did you hear an actor talking about reviving Kennedy's blackmail scheme?"

"Yes," he said and gave a sniff. "I've heard O'Malley is a hooligan. Is that why he was murdered?"

"I don't know. Do you have any ideas?"

"Definitely not. I try to stay away from trouble."

"Did it seem as if he was speaking to any one person or to the entire room?"

"He had been talking to the ingenue, but no one was paying them any attention and no one could hear what they said. Then we all heard his claim of having letters to blackmail people with. The cessation of any other noise in the room made it possible for us to hear his words. I'm certain he was talking to her. He seemed shocked that everyone else had heard him. That everyone was looking at him. Now, do you mind?"

"What do you mean, he seemed shocked?"

"He glanced around, saw people were looking at him, and turned red. Is that good enough?"

I walked away confident I now knew who killed three people to protect a secret.

I went to Sir Malcolm's building and left him a second note. I would have removed the first one I'd left, but someone had taken it upstairs to his office already.

Once I reached my father's house that afternoon and found the housekeeper had left, I paced and worried while I waited for my father to return home from Whitehall and Adam to arrive on his leave. I was used to moving around London, talking to people and discovering clues, writing copy for the *Daily Premier* and visiting friends. I wasn't used to being forced to stay in one place.

I was used to streetlights. I was familiar with lights in

store windows and car headlights. I wasn't accustomed to listening for someone coming after me in the night. I wasn't accustomed to worrying about my safety. For the first time, the blackout curtains pulled against the darkness outside made me feel trapped.

That Clarissa hadn't attacked me before now told me I was worrying for no reason. My father and Adam would be here soon. Sir Malcolm would be back in the morning and this waiting, and my task for him, would end.

Bored, I once again began heating water in the teakettle and pulled out the biscuit tin. There was nothing else in the house for tea, a meal my father scorned at home and barely partook of in company. I, on the other hand, believed in every meal offered.

I leaned on the countertop munching on a biscuit while I waited for the water to boil. The kettle had been polished to a shine and I'd been warned many times over the years to be careful using it. I didn't touch it unless I was desperate for a cup of tea.

For the second time in two days, I really needed a cup of tea.

Just as the kettle started to whistle, I saw movement reflected in the shiny surface. I turned and stared open-mouthed at the woman. "How did you get in here?" I finally managed.

She didn't say a word, she just moved toward me from the direction of the back door.

I saw the knife in her hand held down by her side. "Why,

Clarissa?" Of course. She'd inherited kitchen goods after she'd killed her aunt. I picked up the lid to the biscuit tin and stepped in front of the stove.

"Stay where you are." She raised the knife.

"So you can kill me? I don't think so."

She rushed toward me.

The biscuit tin deflected her initial thrust, but the knife slid down the lid and sliced my fingers.

Seeing blood on my hand didn't slow Clarissa down, but the pain made me want to double up and shriek.

The second lunge came an instant later. Without time to think, I grabbed the teakettle and threw it at her face as the top flew off.

She dropped the knife as the burning-hot metal kettle and boiling water hit her. Scalding liquid splashed everywhere. Her hat and scarf protected her forehead and neck, but her cheeks, chin, and nose took the brunt of the attack.

She screamed as she covered her face with her hands, no doubt trying to stop the sudden pain blistering her skin from the boiling water and heated copper.

Water splashed down her clothes and mine and left a puddle on the floor. The teakettle hit the floor and bounced; I was sure it would leave a dent.

Screaming, Clarissa stumbled out of the room. I followed her to the rear hall to see her struggle with blistering hands to turn the doorknob and race out of the house.

I shut and locked the door after her and then hurried to

the telephone in the hallway, calling the police.

* * *

The police had already examined the back door and taken my statement when my father walked into the kitchen from the front hall, looking around in amazement.

"Olivia. You're getting blood on the table," he said, finally noticing me.

I tightened the handkerchief around my fingers and gasped at the pain.

"Who are you, sir?" the police sergeant asked.

"Sir Ronald Harper. This is my house."

"Well, your house was broken into by a knife-wielding madwoman," the sergeant told him, "by the name of Clarissa Northfield."

"I don't know her. Olivia?"

"She's killed three people in the last two weeks by stabbing them. When I realized she was the killer, she followed me here and broke in to kill me." That left out a lot of details that were best shared with Sir Malcolm when he returned the next day.

"Do you know where she lives, miss?"

I told him Keith Bates or the staff at Broadcasting House would know the address of her rooming house.

The sergeant told me to have a doctor look at my fingers and the police left. I hoped they'd find Clarissa at her residence, but I doubted anyone could be that lucky.

My father called his doctor and then rejoined me in the kitchen. "Olivia. There is water all over the floor. Were you making yourself a cup of tea?" Then he saw the teakettle, now terribly dented. "Olivia!"

I restrained myself from hysterical giggling. "Could you please make me a cup? I think it would help."

I could hear grumbling as my father fussed around the stove, muttering about damage to other people's property, but in a few minutes my father brought me a cup of tea, well sugared, to the kitchen table. He sat down with me, having brought himself a snifter of brandy.

The doctor patched me up before Adam arrived at my father's house to begin his weekend leave. Adam was the one who talked to the police when they rang to tell us Clarissa hadn't come home and to be on our guard.

My father's presence muted our greeting, but Adam held my uninjured hand constantly. I felt safer with Adam there, but my father felt my husband provided him with a sympathetic audience to his lecture on how my duty was to provide a home and hot meals for my husband. Adam's response was to ask if my father had ever tasted my cooking.

My father's answer was to offer to take us out to dinner.

They both, each in their own way, let me know they were not happy with a killer trying to stab me. For once, we were all in agreement.

Chapter Twenty-Six

Saturday morning, we went back to the flat before Adam escorted me to Sir Malcolm's office. He waited on the ground floor while a soldier took me upstairs to see the chief.

"You've done good work, Olivia. The police should take over now."

"Until they find her, I'm in danger." I was frightened, and it showed in my tone.

"There isn't much I can do about that, unless you want me to lock you up in a jail cell." He smiled faintly at the thought.

"No, thank you." I hoped he'd said that only to annoy me. "I want you to find her and arrest her. She needs to be locked up for killing three people."

"What about Gerald Fitzroy?" Sir Malcolm asked.

"He had motive, but it turns out he faints at the sight of blood. Not a good trait in someone who kills by stabbing."

He scowled as he said, "You almost had the wrong person arrested."

"I know. I'm sorry. And it's a mistake that nearly cost me my life. But at least I left you a second note." I stared at Sir Malcolm until I had his full attention. "You should stop using me as an investigator. As you've just pointed out, I'm not very good at finding the person who is guilty." I hoped this argument would successfully get me released from Sir Malcolm's service.

"But you keep looking until you find the right villain. And that, more than going after the wrong person first, is what is really important."

"I told you I thought the killer was Gerald Fitzroy. What if I'd been killed before I left the second note? What if one of the soldiers downstairs lost the second note? Fitzroy could have been hanged for a crime he didn't commit. And Clarissa would have gone free." I shook my head. "I want out."

"Perhaps you're right. You nearly made a mistake this time." He drummed his pen on the desktop for a moment before saying, "Yes. I'll have Clarissa Northfield pulled in for questioning, once we find her. You're excused from working for us, at least for the time being. Possibly forever."

"Thank you." I started to rise from my chair.

"Or possibly not. Understand," Sir Malcolm said as he stared at me from beneath his bushy eyebrows, "when we get into a shooting war, I may need you back at work for me again. Once the shooting and bombing starts, it will change everything. In the meantime, you're Sir Henry Benton's problem."

I nearly cheered.

Adam and I went out to lunch and then walked around Hyde Park arm in arm. It felt good to be together, enjoying familiar sights. Peaceful sights, if you ignored the bomb shelter trenches cutting through the park, now covered and making raised humps in the lawns, and how some passersby carried their gas masks with them.

"Sir Malcolm is probably done with me after I told him the wrong person was the killer," I finally told Adam.

"He told you that?"

"Yes. Well, he said maybe."

Adam was quiet for a moment before he said, "I'm glad."

I was surprised he said that. I was more surprised that I agreed with him. I gave him a smile and said, "I'm glad, too."

"Sir Henry will be ecstatic."

Adam spoke so seriously I had to laugh. "Yes, I suppose he will be."

We talked of people and places that had nothing to do with Sir Malcolm or the war as we walked back across London to the flat, enjoying the frigid, dry weather.

I heard the telephone ringing in the flat as we reached the door. I put my key in the lock and turned the handle. As I began to push the door open, a shadow of movement on the other side made me step to the side with a startled look on my face.

It must have been seeing my expression that made Adam step back against the wall on the other side of the door. I just had time to notice that before Clarissa Northfield came at me, knife first, through the doorway. My shifting away from the door forced her to turn slightly as she came flying out of the flat.

Adam came down on her shoulder with a blow that made her bones crack. Clarissa dropped the knife and began to sag toward the carpet. I scooped up the knife and Adam caught the young woman before she fell.

"Call Sir Malcolm," Adam told me.

I hurried inside and picked up the now silent phone. It was then I wondered who had telephoned before we'd entered the flat.

* * *

Sir Malcolm, along with a Scotland Yard inspector and two constables, left with an angry Clarissa. She now had her arm in a sling from the strike to her shoulder as well as red, blistery burns on her nose and cheeks from the tea kettle.

I stopped Sir Malcolm in the lobby after running to our basement storage cupboard to get my transcripts of her letters Kennedy had used for blackmail. "I want to know what she tells you."

"Why? You're done with this."

"Because she could have talked her way out of a murder charge if she hadn't broken into my flat and attacked me as I came home. I want to know why."

Sir Malcolm glanced at the pages. "Where are the originals?"

"Someone broke into the flat and stole the letters. I believe it was Clarissa, but whoever did it, I'm sure the letters have been destroyed by now."

"And not admissible in court," he told me.

"I think reading certain passages to her might provoke a reaction," I replied. "That is, if she isn't willing to talk."

"That's not my concern. Or yours." With a snort, Sir

Malcolm said, "I will give this to the inspector. How he handles this, and Miss Northfield, is his business. We're done with this, Olivia. We have been since the IRA was stopped from obtaining the explosives."

I stared at Sir Malcolm. "After she tried to kill me, you want me to stay out of this."

"I want you to stay out of it." Adam's voice came from behind me. I turned as he joined us and continued, "You told me Sir Malcolm has given you permission to stop investigating. So, please, stop. For however long we have until the war heats up, let's try to have as normal a life as possible."

"But what if she's released? What if she comes back to attack us again?" I was afraid of Clarissa and her determination to kill me.

Adam gave Sir Malcolm a hard look. I turned to see him nod to Adam. "I'll let you know if that happens."

The two men shook hands, Sir Malcolm nodded to me, and left.

Our doorman, Sutton, came over to us. "That was the young lady who came asking directions. She looks pretty banged up now, but I never forget a pretty face and figure."

"And you said she had disappeared when you finished with the delivery." She must have been following me once she killed O'Malley, knowing I was suspicious.

"Yes. Her. I wonder if she was the one who called about delivery of a late Christmas present?"

"How did she get past you today?" Adam asked.

"Must've been when the second mail delivery came. That's always a busy time with people coming and going through the lobby and asking me to do things. Take care of things." He looked from one of us to the other. "I would have stopped her if I'd known I should be watching out for her especially."

"I know you would have, Sutton." I gave him a smile.

"She doesn't get through the lobby in the future," Adam said.

Sutton nearly saluted at the bark in his voice.

When we went back upstairs, I could hear the phone ringing again. I entered the flat and answered.

Janet Murrow said, "I've been calling you all evening. Do you want to come to dinner with us after Ed finishes tonight's broadcast?"

"Adam's here. Let me ask him how tired he is."

"We have to eat," he said quietly so Janet wouldn't hear him.

"Yes, we'd love to," I said into the receiver. "What time should we meet you at Broadcasting House?"

She told me and added, "The police have been here tonight. Clarissa Northfield, you remember the ingenue for the players group, has been arrested for multiple murders. I know Ed's going to ask you about that."

"I don't know if I'll have anything useful to tell him," I answered in a weak voice. I could picture Edward R. Murrow, American broadcaster, questioning me about the investigation. I was a witness to her attack on me and the blackmail letters. I didn't think I should say anything. Or at least not much.

Chapter Twenty-Seven

It felt as if we had just returned from dinner and gone to sleep before our telephone rang. I wanted to let it ring, but Adam and I both knew Hitler might have made his move, in which case Adam's leave was over.

I listened in, bare feet frozen to the hall floor, as Adam picked up the receiver. He said, "Send him up. I'll meet him at the lift." When he hung up, he told me, "You'd better put the coffeepot on. It's Miles and he's in a right state."

I did as he asked and then went to our room to put on my robe and slippers. I was just tying the belt when I heard them, Miles speaking loudly, come into the flat. Probably annoying the neighbors.

When Miles saw me, he pointed a finger in my general direction and said, "How long have you known she was a whore?"

"When did anyone ever have to depend on you for their next meal?" I replied.

"Livvy?" Adam asked, looking perplexed.

"I loved her. Oh, God, I loved her." Miles was sobbing now. "And she betrayed me."

"She loves you. And it was all over long ago, once she was no longer desperate. Long before you met her." I wasn't sure of that, but it sounded good.

"Doesn't matter," Miles said, waving one arm. "Doesn't matter at all."

"Once you're off fighting in Europe, and the whole continent, and maybe Britain, lies in ruins, you'll learn how far people will go to keep their loved ones from starving. Then you'll learn what really matters." Roxanne must have confessed the details of her past herself. Her honesty and bravery in telling Miles all impressed me a great deal more than the aristocrat.

"Who was starving?" Adam asked.

"Roxanne, her grandparents, her great-aunt, and her younger siblings. She was the only one old enough and strong enough to work. They needed food. They needed a roof over their heads. Something Miles here can't relate to, with his London house and his country estates and his servants."

"People rely on us for their living," Miles answered.

"Your parents aren't going to starve to death if you don't earn enough every day." I glared at him.

"Livvy, of course they aren't," Adam said.

"And so he is standing in judgment on a girl without having the first idea of the horrors she's been through. How resourceful she's had to be to survive and save her family. Don't expect him to save you, Adam, if it comes down to it in battle. The only life he's concerned about is his own. The coffee is in the kitchen," I called over my shoulder as I strode off, disgusted with Miles.

"What about her brother?" Miles shouted.

I stormed back. "He's not her brother, he's a distant cousin who is letting her live in his box room in exchange for cooking and cleaning. She still has to support her young siblings with part of her earnings."

"On her back." He nearly spit out the words.

I put my face closer to his and was hit with the alcohol fumes. "No, Miles, she's not, but that's just the narrowminded garbage that wealthy men have thrown at poor women for centuries. She is a gifted musician and when she got work at the BBC, she could support them all. Good night." I was nearly yelling when I finished.

Exhausted, I went to sleep immediately with my pillow over my ears. I didn't hear any more from either of them until Adam woke me after sunup.

"Don't you think you were a little hard on him?" he asked me with a kiss on my forehead after he adjusted my pillow.

"He's judging Roxanne without understanding anything about her life or her struggles. But then, how could he? He's the son of an earl."

"I can't believe things could have been that bad. She could have found a job somewhere."

"The north of England has had the Depression a lot worse than the south. Employment is very hard to get there, even now with the war on. And she only used—that—" I dismissed Roxanne's activities with a wave of my hand— "as an extra source of funds when she couldn't get any violinist work or music teaching or church pianist positions. And there was no one else to help them."

He looked at me for a minute. "You're sure?"

"Yes."

Adam put his arms around me. "I'm glad you never had to go through that."

"So am I." Very grateful.

We both went back to sleep for a little while before we rose and went into the kitchen to make more coffee. I thought we'd need it that morning. Miles stumbled out from the guest room looking wrinkled and bleary-eyed as soon as the coffee began to spread its fragrance around the flat.

As soon as he walked in, I turned away to pull out another cup.

"I'm sorry to have dropped in on you this way," Miles said.

I thought he was talking to Adam and not me. He was, after all, Adam's colleague.

"I'm sorry I asked her what was wrong. Why she was suspected of murder. Why she was blackmailed. I kept after her, telling her it couldn't possibly make any difference. I was wrong." Miles walked into the dining room with slumped shoulders.

I looked at Adam, who stared back at me. Neither of us had any answers. He followed Miles into the dining room and I waited for the coffee to be ready. I could hear them talking too quietly to make out the words.

When the coffee was done, I carried the tray in and handed out the cups. "You told her she could trust you with the truth, but you weren't honest. What are you going to do now that you've lied to her?"

"Livvy." Adam scowled at me.

Miles glanced at him. "She's right." Then he turned to me. "I need to straighten myself up and go over to her flat, well, her cousin's flat, and talk to her. Ask her to give me some time to digest this. As soon as Hitler moves, we'll be in the thick of fighting and I won't be able to deal with anything else. When things settle down, we'll talk again. In the meantime, if she's desperate again, I'll tell her to contact me. Or actually someone I can trust. A banker."

"That's kind," I told him, "but don't expect her to accept your help. She's proud."

"I have to try. I did love her," he said, holding his hands palm up. "What else can I do?"

* * *

Sir Malcolm telephoned in the morning before we'd had our second cup of coffee. We were to meet my father for Sunday dinner at the usual hotel, but with Adam here on leave, we were taking life slowly.

"Your transcripts of the letters came in handy. Clarissa Northfield has admitted to it all. She bragged about it, in fact. She killed her aunt for the inheritance, and then it turned out not to be as much as she thought. She did, however, inherit her aunt's collection of kitchen knives." He shook his head and added, "We've verified that with the Yorkshire constabulary. An odd bequest."

"Which she put to use for the first time when Frank Kennedy tried to blackmail her."

"She saw it as a sign to eliminate her enemies by stabbing. The inspector said she would change from a sweet young woman to a snarling hag and back again as fast as he could blink his eyes."

"She's an actress," I told him.

"Apparently a very good one. She looked in Kennedy's locker and at his home before stopping Mimi Randall on the street and telling her about a play that would be opening in the West End. Clarissa said she knew the casting director. They went back to Mimi's room to get her photo for Clarissa to supposedly take to the director when Clarissa killed her and searched for the letters. Again, no luck."

"Why did she kill Peter O'Malley? He was a blackmail victim. He wouldn't have the letters."

"No. She knew you had them because she'd found them by that time. And yes, she really did destroy all of them. But O'Malley was her aunt's lover. He knew the family and he suspected Clarissa killed her aunt. He tried a little blackmail of his own, and she killed him for that."

"Was that what people heard at the radio play studio last Saturday, when O'Malley was talking about blackmail?" I asked.

"He was warning her he could blackmail her, too."

"She'll hang."

"Scotland Yard thinks she'll try her sweet young thing act on the judge and jury, but she signed a confession." Sir Malcolm added with no inflection, "She'll hang."

I remembered her as I'd first seen her with Paul White.

Young, sweet, quiet. And she'd already killed two people.

When I returned to the *Daily Premier* the following week, how would I explain this to Sir Henry? At least I wouldn't be leaving him anymore for assignments from Sir Malcolm. I hoped.

I looked forward to my regular position at the *Daily Premier*. Normal assignments. Seeing Esther and my friends on the weekends. Being here when Adam got leave from the army. Going to sleep each night knowing no one was going to break in or try to kill me. A little peace in the middle of war.

Meanwhile, we Londoners, the same as everyone else in Europe, waited for Hitler to make his next move.

This was the bore war, the phony war, and people were getting used to this almost-peace. Adam warned me it wouldn't last. Sooner or later, Hitler would strike.

I hoped he would wait a long time.

I hope you've enjoyed Deadly Broadcast. If you have, please be sure to read the rest of Olivia's adventures in The Deadly Series. And go to my website www.KateParkerbooks.com and sign up for my newsletter. When you do, you'll receive links to my free Deadly Series short stories you can download from BookFunnel onto your ereader of choice. If you want to let others know if you found Deadly Broadcast to be a good read, leave a review at your favorite online retailer or tell your librarian.

Acknowledgements

While later in the war, it seemed there were Americans everywhere in Britain, earlier in the conflict, there were few. Many of the Americans in Europe went home when war was declared in September, 1939. One couple who had come over to work in broadcast journalism before the war and stayed were Edward R. Murrow and his wife, Janet.

Ed Murrow's life during World War II was well-documented and his broadcasts often quoted. Janet Murrow appears almost as a footnote to her husband's work. She interested me because she was bright, good-looking, well-educated, and she didn't have any children to occupy her time until the end of the war. Apparently, she was involved in writing many of his scripts. For instance, Murrow was afraid to go into the bomb shelters, so all his words about them were written by her from her experience. While I don't normally write about real historical figures, I decided Janet Murrow would make a good "sidekick" for Olivia in this story.

And since Murrow broadcast for CBS from Broadcasting House, which almost became another character in this story, I felt it was right to include them.

The information about the IRA, their terrorist campaign, the trial and subsequent hangings, and their desire to help Germany simply because they also were fighting Britain is well-documented. The idea of a double agent in the IRA was an interesting plot device, but someone who was in Frank Kennedy's position playing both sides certainly could have been true.

Finding information about BBC Broadcasting House in the early stages of the war wasn't difficult, the problem was conflicting information and timing. In the end, I just had to choose what seemed most logical. I also couldn't make sense of the technical aspects of the analog broadcasts sent out over shortwave signals across the Atlantic. In all of this I was aided by Ken Gates, a former AT&T communications technician who did lots of research for me and carefully explained his findings. All mistakes on this are mine.

I'd like to thank Eilis Flynn, Jen Parker, and Jennifer Brown for their editorial help, and Les Floyd for replacing my Americanisms with Britishisms. As always, any mistakes are my own.

I thank you, my readers, for coming along with Olivia on this journey. I hope you've enjoyed it.

About the Author

Kate Parker grew up reading her mother's collection of mystery books by Christie, Sayers, and others. Now she can't write a story without someone being murdered, and everyday items are studied for their lethal potential. It had taken her years to convince her husband she hadn't poisoned dinner; that funny taste is because she couldn't cook. Her children have grown up to be surprisingly normal, but two of them are developing their own love of literary mayhem, so the term "normal" may have to be revised.

For the time being, Kate has brought her imagination to the perilous times before and during World War II in the Deadly series. London society resembled today's lifestyle, but Victorian influences still abounded. Kate's sleuth is a young widow, now remarried to an army officer, who is earning her living as a society reporter for a large daily newspaper while secretly working as a counterespionage agent for Britain's spymaster and finding danger as she tries to unmask Nazi spies while helping refugees escape oppression.

As much as she loves stately architecture and vintage clothing, Kate has also developed an appreciation of central heating and air conditioning. She's discovered life in Carolina requires her to wear shorts and T-shirts while drinking hot tea and it takes a great deal of imagination to picture cool, misty weather when it's 90 degrees out and sunny.

Follow Kate and her deadly examination of history at www.kateparkerbooks.com

Also check out www.thedeadlyseries.com

and www.Facebook.com/Author.Kate.Parker/
and www.bookbub.com/authors/kate-parker

Made in the USA
Monee, IL
20 November 2022